Author/CLLinturn books by

Cheryle L. Linturn

White Lies Beyond

Author/CLLinturn

Series: Paranormal Soul

Book 1: Vanishing *Blue* (about spirits seen) published.

Book 2: White *Lies Beyond* (about orbs) published.

Book 3: Purple *Dreams* (about otherworldly language) late 2025.

Book 4: Golden *Voices* (about spiritual sounds) 2025

Author's notes:
I like to use a color in the title of this series, because they have their own energy that reflects our senses: smells, sounds, touch, sight, and emotions.

Acknowledgements: For the fabulous music of Korn, used only in the first chapter as reference to music being played by the character. All rights of said songs belong to Korn and all associates of Korn. I respect and appreciate their talent as musicians, singers, and lyricists. Thank you.

White Lies Beyond

978-1-935583-073
Paperback 2025

White Lies Beyond

Paranormal Soul Series
Book 2

By
CL Linturn

Dedications

To Brian for your patience and diligence in setting up our webpage when we started our business as writers. I thank you.

To Morgan for your love and aid in helping me bring this story to life. Your time and words supported and encouraged me as an author. Thank you.

To Cari for listening to me babble about supernatural experiences.

To Florence for your support and friendship. It never went unnoticed.

To Machu, thank you for being you it gets my creative thoughts flowing. And our journey together experiencing the supernatural world.

To Colleen, Brooke, Liz, Steve, and Mary, thanks for your support now and through the years in all my creative endeavors.

And always for Hailey, Madeline, Reece, and Cheyenne.

To my followers and readers! Thank you.

Note: White Lies Beyond captures paranormal experiences in my life. Ones that I have adapted into book two of the Paranormal Soul Series. Five orbs were seen in the trees by three of us on a warm summer evening. The wonderous nature of orbs aren't deniable, and are the main incident in this novel. I used other supernatural experiences that were slightly exaggerated to enhance the story. More notes on those incidents will be in the back of the book.

White Lies Beyond

Sweltering summer night
On the porch, no lights but the stars
Darkness cooled our skin from the burn of the sun.
The shadows of trees framed the land from the east.
Then they came...dancers that floated without wind
Orbs that glowed softly with flickering light,
A soul, a creature, intelligence bent upon purpose.
They rose and flitted about the trees weaving soft invisible
patterns that hugged the forest...it seemed.
Thoughts, or eyes, neither or both drew them towards us.
Above our head's orbs danced, curious of us.
Their voices lost, but their gentle beauty lingered inside our souls
to resonate and expand our thoughts beyond mortal existence.

Then it came, like all things...in time.

It rode in on the wind...evil. The orbs magical playfulness changed
to fear...and they fled.
We touched them that day, with vision, and emotion...

The next night two orbs came but watched us from a distance.
There was an evil last night. I hoped we were not the cause of their
fear, but we are 'human', and maybe our existence brought the
darkness.

Note: This novel is based on the experience related to this poem,
with the title the same as the book. Three of us shared this
encounter and I developed it into a fictional novel. Thank you for
reading.

Chapter 1

Boston, Massachusetts-March 11, 2001

The restless wind blew like a herd of wild horses undaunted by the woods it had to move through until it reached my small cabin. It neighed relentlessly and thumped repeatedly against the fragile window. The haunting sound awakened me from a deep, dreamless stupor.

I stood at the door and stared at the menacing and darkening sky that quietly changed the shapes of the trees into stone towers that blocked the stars from shedding light on my face.

I squashed my nose against the small window of the cabin door like I did as a young boy. My arms wrapped around my chest, and I sniffled like a child. I couldn't remember anything prior to now. What the hell was I doing standing here?

Loud music played in the background, and the scraping of the tree branches on the window drove the sound into an Edgar Allen Poe poem with its eerie and foreboding intonations.

"You know the one...tap, tap...tap, tap. Yes, the raven found me and brought madness. I hear you laughing-you think I was already mad, maybe so, but who are you to judge? You're nothing but darkness that controls the singular most important thing in my life...time. I don't appreciate that. I don't like losing time, there's just so little of it. Your silence doesn't bother me I know you're here-I sense your presence. You're always listening... I can almost hear you breathing, you never verbally speak with me, and I don't care. It's enough for me to know you're eavesdropping."

The provocative sound of the tapping branch lingered inside my foggy thoughts and for a moment prevented me from remembering the name of the song; then in exaggerated slow motion, I push through the heaviness that held my thoughts anchored on a ship lost at sea. The song came back to me; Coming Undone, by Korn, interesting how well the tapping played with the music.

The combination of the two sounds captivated me until I dug myself into a trench, while gunfire blasted against my skull that held my brain in place, attempting to force insanity out into the open; the involuntary reaction of my hands saved me from exposure by holding it in place. It didn't last. A savage hunger raged like a tiger from the pit of my stomach that forced my hands to loosen their hold. I tried to tighten their grip as they fought against me. I begged them to stop. My hands didn't comply and slowly released my insanity as they slid down the side of my face and clawed at my skin before they ripped the shirt from my body and slung it to the floor— I laughed.

I'm hideous. My god, I'd ripped the shirt from my body like an animalistic creature from a horror movie, but I knew only one thing controlled me, it was 'him' driving my mind deeper into his evil dark space, while he lived on my property without paying rent. I called it 'him', but I didn't really know if it was male or female or neither of the aforementioned. My urge to name 'him' John made it a man, in my opinion. The entity only spoke to me inside my head, I think. Maybe, his voice exploded around the room on a verbal level. I don't remember, but he made me do things that were despicable, shocking, and horrific. Those actions I'd forget about tomorrow. However, I knew it was criminal because I'd find bloody knives and pieces of clothing about the house and yard. The worst of it were the pools of blood that took me days to clean up. He wanted me to be aware that he had control over me. That was the way he played the game.

"Yes, it's possible that I imagined the entity to explain away my newly discovered insanity. I wasn't sure, was I? Don't ask me to explain how I know, I'll never remember this conversation tomorrow, or anything that's happened here today because I can't. You think the absence of my sanity plays a role in that? Really? I do understand things happen around here without my knowledge. You know, dirty dishes done, torn clothing, my clothes disappearing, and not sure of the last time I had eaten, except for the growling of my stomach that signaled hunger, oh, and loss of time. I hope that shows you, whoever you are, that I'm not completely without thought. However, being possessed by a demon breaks my rational thinking into irrational thought. Like a walnut after being crushed by a nutcracker. To sum up this conversation I'm possessed by a demon during what I call my blackout periods, or my own demon escaped the inadequately constructed and emotionally unstable prison of my soul, it's been known to happen...to others. I'm a normal person just like you, well...most of the time."

I clenched my teeth and drew my lips up into the Joker's smile out of the Batman comic books. I deliberately inhaled the darkness allowing it to chew out my guts, and through the pain the musty smell of its soul-filled my lungs, then, I exhaled sending out a whistle that sounded like an over-boiled tea kettle. That action allowed the pressure to release, and satisfied the sentient house with our combined toxic waste.

"Demon, I'm tired of you and the smaller shadows you bring with you, the ones without a spine that lurk around in the background of your presence, watching me and knowing my thoughts. You can't lie, I know. I've witnessed their exuberance and anticipation as they await the shattering of my soul. There are others here, I told them about you and your evil friends. The ones I call the others, are shadows, I think. They see everything and hear everything, but they never interfere but instead choose to hide from both of us, but I talk to them all the time."

"Did you hear a noise?" Others that question was for you if you ever choose to answer. I don't want confusion on your part about who I'm talking to.

"Who's there?" No one answered, it doesn't matter, it's part of the madness.

My nostrils expanded, I smiled and picked up the torn shirt, good God the stench was toxic. I slipped it on and tried with unsteady hands to button the two pearl-colored buttons that remained on the sticky, red, and nauseating shirt. Ketchup or tomato sauce was all over it. It took a while, but I got it done. My hands relaxed and I felt confident the entity could never beat me with my steady mind and powerhouse hands. The shirt hung from my body in tatters, like a zombie from the horror movies.

I wanted to scream, I'd already done that, but the darkness in my lungs demanded it; I controlled it and instead, I spewed out some sort of balderdash.

"It won't happen today, you foul shades of darkness. I will not allow you to take what's left of my humanity—and laugh as it's broken into remnants of uselessness upon the wooden floor to begin its journey towards the black void you hold open in contempt of my compassionate disposition." The bellowing of my agony hurt my ears, and tears burned my cheeks.

I saw nothing through blurry eyes, but something was there. There was a noise. Laughter? My hands trembled, because what voice I had left, and what little power I summoned to scream at them would never touch them, I couldn't reach their world. They might not even be here. But they quickly reminded me they were, because the quirky sensation of nausea kicked in spreading like a disease until the tingling fed me. . . they fed me, the wickedness wanted me.

Those damn spirits that lived in the darkest corners of the four walls of all the rooms in this possessed house. I hated how they laughed at my weakness and chanted obscenities. It had to be their fault; the reason numerous women have stood me up and left without dinner. My dates must have seen them lurking in the corners. Oh, couldn't the villains just leave me alone?

A layer of dust on the walnut cabinet annoyed me, and I grabbed a rag.

"You can't blame a guy for wanting company from time to time. You're a good listener, but I need to talk with someone who answers back. I don't mean the darker shadows they're cruel. The first time I heard them was the first time I realized I might be losing my mind. I brushed it off as being tired, but over the years it continued. I tried to explain away periods of lost time and confusing thoughts but didn't succeed. Nothing makes sense anymore. I can't see a doctor about the situation because I'd be committed to some institution or doped up on some hybrid test drug. What's that? You think I repeat myself? Maybe so, but that's part of the psychosis."

A horrible smell in the house filtered through my nostrils and seeped into my brain stimulating a headache. I collected some incense from an old cabinet that sat by a brown leather couch and lit it on a dragon head burner. Thank God it helped.

"Once when I was alone in the blackness of the evening hours the dark shadows spoke to one another, in some alien language that resembled hissing, oh yes, they made sure I didn't understand them. I was certain the sounds were real and not my imagination. I hear them now, don't you? One night I tried reasoning with the voices—a way to combat them by understanding what drove them, so I could conquer my presumed insanity, but nothing worked. They pretended like I didn't exist."

Candles would be a nice touch, opening a drawer in the kitchen I found two green ones and sat them on the counter.

"That's right they pretended I didn't exist, and their deliberate evil actions filled me with rage causing my shoulders to raise toward my ears. That always happens when I become tense. Then I would search for my marble sculpture of a black bull, and repeatedly turn it over in my hands rubbing its smooth surface until time became a fugitive and my anxiety dissipated.

What's that? You want to know where the bull came from? Well, I'd dug up the bull on a spring day when I first moved into my home and thought I needed a garden. The bull was quite small, and an interesting piece of art. The moment I touched it a name came to mind, but I can never remember it. I never named a piece of art before, but it suited it. Imagine that? I already told you its name, maybe not. I must finish dinner; I have a guest coming."

The house was tidy, but something was missing, and I needed to find it, now what was it? Oh, yes...

"Yes, I remember the name. Where's John? I know you think I'm obsessed with him, I'm not. Sometimes I misplace him, that's all. I don't need to find the bull at this moment, but I like to keep a close eye on it, because it's constantly moving from the top of my desk to the sink, the fireplace, and once I found it in the bathroom. *Don't blame me, I'm not the one that moves it, at least not that I remember."*

A chill, like the frost of the arctic drifting into warm waters formed icebergs where there were none and moved through my legs and into my spine, as sweat welled up across my forehead. I checked the thermostat; the temperature in the room was fine.

The tension built in my shoulders while I searched the room for my prized possession—John. I stopped and stood very still. The pressure of a drumstick was beating steadily against my skull and my eyes filled with tears. I momentarily grabbed the back of a chair for balance. I was getting headaches more often these days, no, not days, but in the evenings, and not every evening. I was crazy. The pain continued while I indulged in my favorite pastime of questioning my sanity. My feelings continually shifted, and I never held on to one image. Thoughts moved at a chaotic speed until answers bounced off my cranial wall, the pounding was like a tennis match with no winner because the game never ended, and the answers scared me. I quit listening. I couldn't judge my own sanity.

I slid onto the chair, closed my eyes, and gently massaged my temples to relieve the pressure. My skin felt feverish under my cool fingertips. I found the most painful pressure points around my face....deliverance. I didn't want to open my eyes, but I did. I should see a doctor, but it won't help.

The aroma of dinner filled the house and almost hid the awful smell that seemed to be lodged permanently in my nostrils. Dinner needed more garlic. I rose slowly and moved to the stove. A few stools sat around a small island in front of cabinets, sink, stove, and refrigerator marking the territory as a kitchen. Whoever designed this house had separated the dining room and closed it off to the main room. The layout was okay. I very seldom needed a dining room and preferred to eat by the island.

Dicing the garlic left a pungent smell on my fingers that was nice. There was another smell lingering behind the garlic that was unpleasant, and rather sickening, and I wasn't sure where it originated from. I glanced at my disgusting shirt and that was a clue. I lifted the lid and dropped in the garlic. The wonderful aroma from the sauce released the nasty smell. The aroma of my famous sauce was a better cure than incense.

I needed my clothes changed; my date would be here soon.

I put the dinner on low to shower and dress and danced towards the bathroom with a slightly giddy edge. I was excited about my date—I felt alive. But the expanding obscurities of the evening followed me.

My shirt was no longer recognizable as a shirt. It was filthy and smelled like a sewer. I threw shirt and pants into the hamper, until my guest left and then I would move them to the garbage. That red ketchup would never come out, and even if it did the shirt was torn. I turned on the faucet and stepped into the steamy shower.

The rhythmic pace of the water on my body was warm, the swirls were mesmerizing as the water changed from different shades of browns and reds before a nice clear liquid emptied down the drain, gross. I was dirty. It must've been from gardening. I got out, wiped down the shower walls and cleaned up the wet mat and towels.

While drying myself off I thought about living alone. Why had I lived alone all these years? I decided to. There was no particular reason other than the right person never came along, and a feeling in the back of my mind that felt it would be risky. I didn't know why I felt that way, but I did.

I put on deodorant and stared at my face. I wasn't sure who I was anymore, a lunatic, or a man breaking away from normal on his way to becoming a lunatic? Life was so confusing sometimes. I brushed my teeth, rinsed, and spit. There was something else I should have done, but I couldn't remember. I'd spent too long in the shower anyway, and dinner would burn.

I stood in front of the closet and sang to the music that was still playing in the background.

"Where's my red twill?" It was missing. Wait, I think I'd already worn it, oh that's right, I'd taken it off and thrown it in the hamper before I showered because it looked like I'd worn it at the Battle of Gettysburg. Oh, that irritated me. I wanted to wear it for my dinner guest, but my shirt looked like I'd lost the war, and it wouldn't be appropriate. I grabbed a black one, it matched my mood, and put it on, along with dark black jeans. I checked my look in the long mirror that hung over the back of my bedroom door. I placed my hands on both hips and smiled. "You are a handsome devil."

I reveled in my own good looks until a familiar nudge prodded at the back of my thoughts announcing something wrong, or different, a memory. I wasn't sure. It was one of those freaky déjà vu moments I've often had since I'd moved into this haunted house, at least that's what I presumed it was because things clawed at me all the time. The only peace I had was in the morning or when I wasn't home. I shook off the feeling of doom and waltzed toward the simmering dinner.

The kitchen was still cold. I will check for draughts later.

I lifted the popping lid from the boiling tomato sauce, grabbed a spoonful, and carefully blew on it— it tasted great. Spaghetti and biscuits were easy, and that extra garlic made a significant difference.

I sang to the music, until a noise outside drew my attention. It sounded like a car door. I glanced at the clock and my cheeks heated up in annoyance, she was over an hour late. I quickly checked my answering machine; no messages, of course, she hadn't bothered to let me know. I quickly released my irritation because I was behind schedule, as well.

The time seemed to be off. Had I been wrong about the hour we'd set for dinner? Obviously, these headaches were causing me some confusion, I'll call a doctor on Monday.

It didn't matter if she were late. I felt excited, she was here and hadn't stood me up. The anticipation felt good—almost too good, so much so, I wanted to run out to greet her, but that was an obvious schoolboy action, and I was far from being a boy. I needed something to do until she knocked on the door. . .plates. I'd set the table.

I took a deep breath; the oxygen filled my lungs and calmed me. I walked to the cabinet where I grabbed my best dishes from the shelf and headed towards the dining area. The room was dark. I flipped on the light and almost had a heart attack. I gasped, my hands trembled and released the plates from my grip. I watched in horror as the incident turned into a comedic relief of slow-motion that propelled the dishes towards the floor—I cursed. She was already here and sat at the table.

The music stopped as the plates crashed against the ceramic tiles shattering into odd-shaped pieces. I stood there speechless, distracted, interested, and intrigued by the various pieces: a heart, a dagger, and one piece of a jagged dish appeared in the shape of a large head, weird. A crack ran from one side to the other tilting up slightly giving it a lewd sneer. Although my hands shook from the shock of her presence, I laughed until it penetrated my ears. A laugh that resonated with a clown out of control, loud and loathsome in the silence of the room. My hideous laughter didn't provoke a response from the deadpan, 'queen of spades.' I knew then I didn't like her, no sense of humor.

She must've arrived when I showered and let herself in because here she was staring at me. Really? She didn't say she was sorry she shocked me, and not an, 'oh no, I made you break your good chinaware, how stupid of me not to say hello when you first came into the kitchen. I must be crazy.' Instead, her glazed over eyes looked as though she'd been drinking since she'd crawled out of bed.

I decided to stay calm. "When did you get here? You could've said something earlier." She looked angry. "What'd I do? Why do you look so mad?"

No answer. Great, the silent treatment. I suppose it was possible she didn't have the ability to manage more than one question at a time, but highly doubtful since she hadn't acknowledged either one of them. *Lunatic.*

"You startled me and now I broke my good dishes. I hope you're not mad because I was too busy with dinner to notice you. Sorry." There I went again, apologizing for something that wasn't my fault. Nobody would've noticed the shrinking violet in the chair, a zombie had more personality, and from the way her face looked, she didn't care one iota about my best dishes.

She never said a word, not one grunt.

I ignored her and tended to the broken dishes. The unusual, fragmented pieces that challenged my creativity were mesmerizing. The head shape had a hole in the middle of it and the dagger was just the right size and would fit into it nicely, curious, but more curious was why I wanted to see if it fit.

She watched as I picked up the dishes, but never offered to help.

This date wasn't going according to plan. She wasn't as caring as I originally thought, and now I regretted inviting her to dinner. I'd met her at the grocery store four days ago, and we'd hit it off in the fruit section, had a few laughs, and thought dinner would be nice to get to know each other better.

Well, let that be a lesson to me. Always meet my first-time dates at restaurants, never invite them home for dinner. I couldn't be sure if they were crazy, and she looked crazy. Being a guy, I thought it would be okay, but you just don't know.

Now infuriated, my voice quivered. "You're late."

She never apologized for being late. Her eyes were vacant like her thoughts were with someone else. . .not me. So, it started. I knew she didn't want to be here with me, it was the same old thing that I'd faced in the past. I should give up dating altogether. I never seemed to satisfy women, at least the women I brought home. After all I was incredibly good looking with an excellent job. It didn't matter, she wanted someone else, that was obvious. Her dreamy eyes were in bed with someone else. I wanted to vomit and smack that stupid grin off her face; it was too smug. I'd already made her mad and we'd only spoken on the phone twice since we met. It had to be her personality and nothing to do with me. What'd I ever see in her, anyway?

I couldn't look at her anymore, in fact, I wanted her to go home, and I didn't want to ever see her again. I walked to the door to see where she'd parked her car, and looked outside, it wasn't in view.

"I thought I'd heard your car pull up. I must've been wrong. It certainly sounded like a car."

No answer.

Weird. "Where'd you park your car," I asked?

She mumbled something that sounded like, 'she didn't,' but I really wasn't sure what she'd meant by that.

"Stupid."

Did she just call me that? I couldn't be sure, because sometimes there was that monstrous voice inside my head, the one that came out to play at the most inconvenient times, well whoever said it needed to be reprimanded.

"I've had enough of you, now quit calling me names." My voice boomed out like a trumpet, the force of it pierced my eardrums. There might be blood.

No comment. Of course not, that was obviously this woman's style; speak evil and then pretend it never happened. Well, I'd already cooked dinner and didn't want it to go to waste, but this would be our last date. I was sure of that. I put my anger aside and fixated on what dishes to use under the circumstances.

In my most cheerful voice, I said, "Well, I'm glad you're here." I wasn't. "Dinner will be ready in a moment."

It sounded like she said, okay, but I couldn't be sure because she mumbled.

The few conversations I had with her had led me to believe she was a shy woman and hadn't been keen on chit chat, but this was awkward.

I decided to let her stew in whatever her malfunction was and went back to the food, it was perfect, but we needed more music. What should I choose? I wasn't going to ask my dinner date, because I no longer cared what she wanted to hear. I chose Korn, 'Freak on a Leash,' it made me feel a little evil. I knew she'd hate it and that made me smile inside and caused little butterflies to go through my stomach. Excitement? Or was it a queasy feeling of dread? Dread? I no longer cared if she left. I would be fine on my own. She was a freak and should appreciate the song I selected.

Making sure I held a slow and deliberate pace as I moved back to the cabinet, I removed my old plates. Darn it, one of them had a chip on the edge. Ha. That one would be hers. I still had some fine chinaware, but I wasn't about to waste them on her. I couldn't even remember her name at this point, so it made no difference.

I covered my mouth to avoid laughing aloud.

When I placed the chipped dish in front of her, she never glanced at it, but just stared at me like I was an alien. I began to loathe her.

I turned away from her, composed myself, and served the spaghetti. I tried not to look at her vexing expression. Instead, I focused on the torn, dirty, and blue frumpy dress she wore. Who comes to dinner with torn clothes? Well, okay, torn clothes if it happened on the way, but the filth on her dress was obnoxious. I suppose it wasn't that puzzling. It was clear my feelings hadn't mattered. She pushed all my buttons, all the wrong buttons. My face grew hot, as if a willow switch repeatedly slapped my cheeks. What a pair we would've made if I 'd left on my filthy clothes.

A smoky, charred aroma floated throughout the house. Crap, I burnt the dinner rolls. It happened because of her; she distracted me with her detachment to our relationship. Well, that was a dumb thought, we had no relationship, she was detached.

I opened the oven and smoke filled the room. The pan was too hot and nearly scorched my fingertips, I forgot the mitt. Her fault.

Since she hadn't cared about her clothes, being late, or my broken dishes, I wasn't going to care about her feelings either. I put the crispy blackened rolls on a plate and sat them in front of her.

"I hope you enjoy these." I said it with genuine mockery, and wanted to scream out, 'freak', but I controlled the urge.

Still, I hadn't looked at her and she never commented. Oh, this whole evening was indisputably hellish. She could eat the rolls dry and without butter. I certainly wasn't going to offer her any sort of condiment. I'd wasted my evening on this so-called dinner date and refused to waste any more food on this mannequin. I needed a drink.

I poured us both a glass of red wine, a cheap red wine, and put the glasses on the table and sat down next to her but kept my eyes on my dinner. I ate ravenously. She never touched her plate or the cheap drink. I laughed inside. She was some piece of work.

"Why don't you eat? Sorry, if it's not good enough for you."
Averting my eyes while I'd spoken to her in a perfectly executed
sarcastic tone that would've gotten me a role on Broadway had a
director heard. I perceived the applause in the background, as I
chuckled, she mumbled. I didn't like that.

It'd been less than an hour since she'd caused me to break my good
plates, but as far as I was concerned this date was over. No, it never
started, it wasn't a date. I tried to be a nice guy even though an evil
'doppelganger' to the nice girl I met less than a week ago came in
her place. The evil side of her sat at my table while the 'real her'
gallivanted around with some handsome soap opera-type guy.

I almost coughed my brains out on the foul-tasting wine but
finished the bottle. It wasn't important because she wasn't worthy
of the cheapest wine, and only deserved one glass.

She smelled unpleasant. It nauseated me. What was that cologne?
Toilet water that's what it was, a shower would've been nice-freak,
or at least she should've avoided that cologne. I dare not say that to
her face. Don't want some crazy psycho reaction with all the 'poor
me tears', she was already in a mood.

I cleared up the plates; hers was just as I'd served it, untouched. She
might've eaten some of it, I couldn't tell, but a roll was missing. I
thought there'd been four, but now there were three. I certainly
hadn't eaten it. I picked up the charred buns. It stimulated my pulse,
and my eyes felt as though they popped out of my skull. I chuckled
and visualized my eyes popping out and rolling around on the table
in front of her; before they fell onto her lap, or better yet, stopped on
the table in front of her and watched her with intense contempt. She
might respond to that.

A noise from the porch got my attention. "Who's out there?"

The door flew open, and darkness crept into the room and slunk
along the floor, long gnarled fingers came for a visit and left their
body at home. The fingers belonging to the shadows slowly clawed
their way up the wall, until the gloom of the evening pressed down
on my shoulders and threatened to drive me through the floor and
into the earth beyond it. I struggled to move, but I managed to cross
the room and kicked the door shut. I spun around and cursed.

It was her; she brought the blackness. Carefully I placed the dishes
in the sink and scrutinized the overcooked buns.

The music blasted through the house like a rave party. It sounded
like she spoke, but I never understood the words. Why had she

waited to talk until after dinner and I faced away from her bridled mouth? What was wrong with her anyway?

"Get up you lunatic and help me with the dishes." There was no way she would've heard me with the background noise, but I said it anyway.

The charred buns looked creepy and matched her disposition. I held one in my hand, the urge to crush it overwhelmed my common sense. The substance pulverized easily between my fingers and turned into a grotesque flaky powder, which looked like it had chunks of burnt flesh in it. Possibly the skin from my fingertips. The crumbs fell from my hands to the floor, bringing a sense of exhilaration that welled up inside my gut, as simple as it seemed, and as crazy as it sounded, I enjoyed controlling the demise of the bun.

The powder settled in a mess on the red ceramic floor. "Ashes to ashes, dust to dust the devil will have you because he must." I honestly had no idea where that came from, but it made me chuckle. She must bring out the best in me. I laughed at my warped sense of humor and grabbed another bun and repeated their destruction until only one remained. I saved it for her, because she crawled into my skin and ripped it apart from the inside with her 'holier than thou attitude'.

My face burned as the flesh stretched tightly across my skull, dry as leather in a desert sun. The buzzing in my ears made me woozy. The black bun sat in my hand and encouraged me to set it free. I wanted to shove it down her throat.

My eyes blurred when something exploded inside my head. I tried to keep my balance. I managed with difficulty and staggered towards the woman I now loathed. Several times I almost crushed the one remaining bun that sat in my shaky hand.

My vision cleared. I wish it hadn't, because there she was with her mouth opened and her eyes accused me of being inadequate. Oh, I despised her ability to rile me. I was better than her, that was for sure. She held a butter knife in her hand, but it had ketchup on it instead of butter and I didn't put out either. Maybe, it was the sauce. It dripped all over the floor and the thick red substance had ruined her dress. Wait...there was something in her mouth. I leaned my head in to get a better look. There was an object lodged inside her mouth that created a ludicrous expression that held her mouth frozen in place. Sickened at the sight and smell of her, I finally saw what stretched her mouth into a clown's grin. Hell, it was the missing bun.

I stumbled in confusion, but just for an instant, until I realized she'd hogged down the burnt bun and must've choked on it.

"Do you see this? You didn't tell me, but the comical error on my part thinking she wasn't speaking to me because she didn't like me had been absurd. She hadn't talked during dinner because she'd been dead. I bet you had a good laugh watching my anger and listening to me talking to myself. Well, serves her right for trying to eat the entire bun at one time. Don't you think?"

Well, there you go, things happen from time to time. People choke on food. My head pounded. Something was wrong, but I didn't have time to think about it.

"Now, what am I going to do with you?" I giggled when I heard my question echoing off the walls. There was no one there to answer me, the shadows wouldn't, and she couldn't, that's for sure.

My body ached when I thought about how deep I was going to have to dig a hole to bury her; she was such a nuisance.

I grinned at her and pointed my finger. "Don't go anywhere. I'll be right back."

The illogical comment made me burst out laughing and I sat down until the tears stopped and my control returned. The song, 'Freak on a Leash' thrashed against my soul as it played repeatedly.

Numbed, I stood up and walked to the CD player and turned it off. I had it set to repeat, but now I needed quiet.

The house was silent. That scared me because I could hear the breathing. I mulled over the lyrics inside my warped mind; 'Sometimes I cannot take this place, sometimes it's my life I can't taste, sometimes I can't feel my face.'

I rubbed my stubbled chin with rough weathered hands. I'd forgotten to shave.

"I don't think that was ketchup on the knife, do you?" I mulled over that thought for just a moment.

There was a hollowness inside of me that grew into a chasm too deep to ever crawl out of. Before I could contemplate the possibility of some kind of logical conclusion to what went wrong on this day a loud noise knocked it out of my head. Instead, the crashing sound forced my feet to jump forward, and I listened intently. There it was again. Great, it sounded like thunder crackling off in the distance. I'd better hurry, I didn't want to be playing around in the mud.

My mood changed and I wasn't about to sing, but I did. He made me sing that stupid song.

"Only two lines, that's all I'm singing, and you can't make me sing any more than that." No response. "In eternity we touch, in eternity we breathe, but now, we break the rules." I moaned. "I'm tired, enough of that senseless song. Ha, I only sang one line."

"Now, where's my shovel?"

Chapter 2

Boston, Massachusetts–February 2018

"Hi mom. Yes, we just walked in the door."

Stan grinned at her as he bent down to pick up her suitcases. She mouthed to him, "I can do it." He ignored her and lugged them towards her room.

He bellowed from the hallway. "Tell your mom and Nana I missed my two favorite girls."

"Did you hear that, mother? I thought so, his voice does have a theatrical edge."

"I heard that. I have theatrical ears, as well." Stan yelled from her room.

Her mother's laughter rang through the cell phone like the delicate serenade of windchimes on a cool summer evening and lifted Claire's spirits higher than they already were.

Claire elevated her voice slightly. "Mother said she adores you, and Nana made some brownies with butterscotch chips, just for you."

"Tell them to come over for a chat and bring the brownies."

"Mother, do you guys want to stop by? I'll put on some coffee; besides, Stan can't wait to taste those brownies."

He returned to the kitchen and picked up his own bags and headed to the loft.

"I think he's drooling with the mere thought of them being shoved in his mouth at a steady pace. Although, as fast as Stan eats them, he must only taste the coffee he uses to wash them down with."

He shook his head as she watched him climb the stairs.

"Okay, mom, see you in a while. I can't wait to tell you all about the wedding."

Claire hung up and looked around the house. She shivered. It'd been a year since Gabe had gone, but the thought of him walking through the door and kissing her gently was fresh in her heart. There were days when she thought she heard his typewriter banging away with his passionate words. She dropped her cell on the table and went to unpack her clothes.

Her suitcases were on the bed, and again she wondered why she always took more clothes than she needed. She pulled out several sweaters and placed them in her drawer, and smiled. Gabe used to mix his sweaters with hers, insisting that he'd forgotten whose drawers were whose. The bedroom felt cold without him there. Stan did what he could to help, but the emptiness was too hard to bear at times.

Occasionally, she'd heard Stan whimpering at night. He missed his best friend, but was always strong for her, and that made her feel guilty. She was glad Stan agreed to move into the house with her and sell his, because the spirit world had become a little more challenging than it'd been in the past, and they both needed the extra support.

She and Stan got along famously, however, the memories of Gabe in this home drove her mad and at times she questioned why they'd kept the house. But even as she thought it, she knew it was to honor him and keep him close. It would get better over the years.

The furniture had a lovely, polished finish, and the house looked clean. She'd kept Gabe's housekeeper and was glad she had. Fran Polanski was Polish but could speak enough broken English to easily communicate with those around her. They got along quite well.

Fran was an elderly woman that never married nor had children but was content with her job. Claire had been meaning to talk to Stan about Fran moving into the extra room downstairs. It was a small guest room across from Gabe's study. Having the company of another woman in the house would be enjoyable for her, as well as Stan. They both worked so much, and Fran would have the house to herself most of the time, and it might be nice having someone there when they came home.

She finished putting away her clothing and went into the kitchen to make some coffee. Stan was still upstairs.

"Stan, you okay?"

"Yeah, coming."

She was glad when he appeared on the landing. Past events that'd involved Gabe still made her jumpy. She wondered if she'd ever get over it. Probably not, because they encountered the paranormal daily now, after opening their business. The other world had always played a role in her life, and she'd learned to manage it, but adding other people's experiences into her pool of supernatural events took a different type of concentration and added anxiety to her day. She smiled, knowingly, because it also carried with it some fascinating and unusual experiences, along with meeting interesting and strange people.

The doorbell rang.

Stan raced to the door as she poured out the coffee and set out plates, utensils, and a cutting knife.

Her mother was the first one through the door and hugged Claire with incredible energy. "Mother, I missed your hugs." As a child when her mother hugged her, the world was always better, and that feeling hadn't changed.

Dan followed behind her mom, she still had to suppress the urge to call him Father Logan, even though he'd lived with her mother for a year now. He gave Claire a big hug.

"So, good to see you, Dan. Have you been keeping mother out of trouble?"

"You must be joking? Hailey is incorrigible, and I must say, I wouldn't have her any other way." He smiled toward her mother, with a mischievous twinkle in his eyes. "Even with my background...well, we'll just leave it at that."

Stan came into the room with Nana on his arm. Dan pointed at Nana and said, "Now, that woman's an entirely different story. She'd argue with a signpost if it said one way only and she wanted to go the other."

"Ha, you just can't handle the challenge, Mr. Logan," Nana said.

Stan pulled Nana close. "There, that's what makes me love this woman so much. Dan, you need to appreciate the finer qualities of the Irish women, in this family. How many women do you know that'll carry on a conversation with a signpost and win?"

Everyone laughed.

"Even if it's in our own heads we still win." Nana grinned up at Stan and leaned her head against his arm and pointed up at him. "Dan, this man is incredibly observant, with an obvious talent for having good taste in women."

Hailey shook her head and moved to nana. "Oh, mother, give me the brownies, before you drop them while you and Stan get carried away patting each other on the back." Then she turned to Stan. "Stan, you're going to love these, and please stop encouraging her to be so ornery."

Stan raised his brows. "Like I've said in the past, you women need no encouragement. You are who you are, and I love it! Now, let me at those brownies."

***

She kept flipping her body, like a fish on dry land and tried to sleep. It wasn't working. She thought about the conversations the five of them shared over coffee and brownies. It was simple small talk that carried over into the early hours of today. Her mind wandered to the wedding and how beautiful and happy Felicia looked; she was happy for her.

Even though she was back in her own bed after being away from home for several weeks she continued to toss and turn.

She closed her eyes and stilled her mind. The constant ticking of the clock relaxed her, until the energy in the room shifted, and her eyes quickly opened. Wispy grey clouds pushed past the bright moon, as it peeked through the curtainless window. It brought and released Gabe's love with its brilliant light that manifested the warmth of his embrace around her. The mirror on the wall reflected the romance of his smile in her heart. His energy charged the room like a log was added to a dying fire and filled her soul. His breath gently brushed her hair and tickled her cheek, his lips touched hers; Gabe was here. She breathed him in deeply, held her breath, until she couldn't contain it and slowly exhaled him back to the moon allowing him to move with it across the atmosphere, as the clouds closed, once again, on the luminous orb.

Gabe had once told her that love was timeless yet wrapped inside time. He'd described it as a window on a speeding train that you could see into or out of, but only for the moment that belonged to the limited time of the window's view. However, the love found in that single moment moved through eternity, past your visual interpretation as the train moved out of view.

She missed Gabe and the ache would never go away. All she had left were those passing windows that were secret doorways inside her heart that she could open whenever she needed to.

A soft tap sounded at the door. "You asleep?" Stan's subdued voice held a tinge of urgency.

"No."

"I didn't think so; your thinking was keeping me awake. You want some tea? I'm going to make myself a cup."

"Sure. I'll be out in a minute." She sat up in bed. "Your impeccable hearing is one of your many superpowers, but really, hearing me think? I don't think so; I know what's keeping you up but it's not me thinking, you keep dreaming."

His voice rose several octaves. "I'd dream if I could sleep, and that's fine you be one of those non-believers, but you should really give that mind a rest. I don't like what I'm hearing-for the record, it's not the brownies!"

She jumped out of bed and grabbed her robe, tying the belt as she entered the kitchen.

"So, if not the brownies what's really keeping you from sleeping tonight? For the record, I do think it's too many brownies."

He sat the cups on the table. The light of the kitchen exposed his drawn face, taut mouth, and swollen eyes.

"Claire when your brain kicks into overload and begins over analyzing everything it crawls up the stairs disturbing my sleep, it was just too loud; and no, it wasn't the brownies. Never. It's too close to a full moon, I suppose. The light is quite bright in the loft with skylights."

"Are you sure that's all? It's never bothered you before, and the clouds are blocking it a good portion of the time."

He'd turned away from her to get the steeped tea water. His shoulders were rigid, but when he turned around to face her, his expression had changed. Those dark eyes were glittering, while a sweet smile caused his features to perk up.

"Yeah, fine, no worries. Just had trouble with the light, and all that noise, that's all."

She knew him, he covered up his emotions quicker than you could bat an eye. "I'm not buying that Stan," she said.

He sat down across from her, his eyes sparkling with hidden tears, and smiled. "No, I suppose you wouldn't. Sometimes, it's hard coming back into the house after I've been gone for a while. I know you understand. I still expect to see Gabe or hear him typing in the background. God, it's just so hard."

Her stomach trembled, and she had to keep swallowing to hold the tears at bay. She stirred honey into her tea and focused on the steam floating softly out of the cup. The distraction helped and after a moment she could speak. "I do understand." That was all she said, no words formed in her mind. Feeling shocked at her inability to comfort him, she lifted the cup to her mouth and sipped on the warm chamomile tea. Nothing inspirational came to mind.

He drank his tea and watched her without uttering a sound. Her own silence was deafening, but when the clock chimed 3am, warm tears gathered in her eyes and slowly slid down her cheeks. It belonged to Gabe; the clock, the sound, and the pleasure it brought to his heart. She'd heard it a hundred times before, but tonight it was haunting in the quiet of the house.

She was unable to help Stan and supply him with the solace he'd given her, as he grieved his friend. She felt ashamed.

"Gabe." She'd said his name aloud. Stan jerked his head up and quickly looked around the room. In the shadows of the kitchen, she saw Gabe standing by the sink and he held the hand of Vanishing Blue, but like the flutter of a hummingbird, they were gone.

"Did you see them," she asked Stan?

"No, but I felt them. Do you want another cup of tea?"

"Sure. Stan, I forgot to tell you, I listened to our messages for work." Changing the topic might bring a sense of peace to them both.

"Okay, good. Any freaky happenings we should be excited about? You know, I really do like the name we chose for the store, Nudges and Nuances has a ring to it, and it's appropriate."

She was glad they were out of the gloominess. The conversation picked up and it lightened her heart.

She said, "Yes, it is a good name. We have three interesting callers and situations. One that I think will appeal to your nature was a man named Marvin Schwartz who insisted that we check out dog faces that pop up at random in his trees."

"And how is that supposed to appeal to my nature?" He poured more tea and sat back down giving her his famous quizzical eyebrow thingy that he did, that made her suddenly erupt into uncontained laughter.

He stared at her with his poker face.

"You're killing me here," she said.

"You still haven't answered me; how does that creepy dog thing relate to me?"

"You like dogs."

"Okay, very funny, 'LOL,' I like dogs, but not freaky dogs in trees."

"Fair enough, but I thought you might enjoy that one. A woman called about smelling roses, not just in one room, but the smell follows her from room to room. I might like to take on that one, if you approve, of course."

"Fine, then, I'll do crazy dog trees, and you can do the nice rose smell."

"That's good, because the third one is on the way to the rose house, and I'll check on that one, as well."

"What's that one about?"

"Something about fish disappearing from a pond, not just one, but at least 400 or so," said Claire.

"Well, that one sounds really cool. Large ocean creatures' surface and stop for lunch at a local pond."

She ignored his last comment. "Okay, I'll go by the rose one first and you can meet me at the other house later in the day. We'll talk about it later, but right now, I need to speak with you about Fran."

"The housekeeper?"

"Yes. I'd like to ask her to move into the guest room across from Gabe's study. It'd be good to have someone in the house when we come home, and she wouldn't have to pay rent, just take care of the house. What do you think?"

"I think it's a marvelous idea. I wish I would've thought of it. Call her later today. Does she cook?"

"Oh, Stan, really?"

"Yes, really. While we're on the topic of getting help, I came up with a great idea, and yes, wow, I thought of it on my own. Let's get Morgan to help us with these investigations, she has a lot to offer this adventure. Friendly, intelligent and we could use another mind that believes in the paranormal world. What do you think?"

"I think it's brilliant. I'll call her at a more decent hour. By the way, we got a call from Charlie, and he has a new book we might be interested in. I really like him."

"Me too, but you're not thinking about dating him, are you?"

"No. Of course not, but I would like to set him up with someone special."

"Mind your own business, Claire."

Giggling, she headed to her room. "Goodnight, Stan."

"Goodnight and mind your own business."

She heard him go up the stairs, as she took off her robe and threw herself on the bed.

Well, why shouldn't she play matchmaker for Charlie Burns, he was a good catch. They'd met him about six years ago when he'd opened a quaint, and quite eccentric bookstore down the road from Gabe's studio. He had incredible books, some were hard to find, and others were old. She felt the history in the older books as they came to life when the pages turned, and the musty smell leaped up to take her back in time. She always got excited when Charlie informed her he'd found a book she'd be interested in looking at. Some of his books breathed heavily in magic with no published date and extraordinarily little info, but the pages offered mystical writings. She'd showed one to Nana who quickly confiscated it to examine its contents. She must remember to ask her what interesting information she found in that book; Nana had already sunk her inquisitive mind into it for over a month, surely something had unfolded.

The cover was intriguing, with a hand-stitched golden binding and a delicately painted phoenix that vibrantly decorated the soft black fabric that wrapped around the book. There was no published date, or author. Claire didn't recognize the language that was used to author the book, but more thought-provoking was that Nana hadn't recognized the dialect. A book like that was better off in Nana's hands than hers, that's for sure.

Over the past year, she'd carried on taking lessons with Nana and developing skills that increased her awareness of the physical world's connection with the spiritual world. It wasn't just the differences, but the similarities, as well. She compared it to driving a car. It was familiar, because it was part of her everyday routine, a habit, but if she advanced to speed car racing that change would naturally create an increased stamina and awareness of her surroundings. It offered a deeper comprehension of the vehicle's sensitive nature and how it adapted to changes in the road while she watched each vehicle and their influence on her own movements. Like the speed racer, she'd become one with all things that surrounded her, existing on several planes in as much mindfulness as humanly possible. It was similar to adapting to the paranormal world when moved into full-throttle and with more entities, as well.

It was the lessons of observation that made her take more notice of Fran, elderly and alone. They could help her out if she moved in with them. There was a bath in that guest bedroom, so her privacy wouldn't be an issue. She realized she didn't know much about Fran, but she'd like to.

Charlie was noticeable, as well. He lived alone and was kind. There must be someone out there for him. She was pleasantly surprised when he'd turned out to be an intelligent and highly interesting person. Charlie traveled a lot and was a scholar of books, geography, unusual facts, and cryptic writings. He didn't' recognized the dialect in the book of the phoenix but was interested in anyone who'd be able to decipher it. Over the past year, she and Stan had developed a great friendship with Charlie.

Now that she wasn't traveling as much as a designer, and spent more time focused on their new shop dealing with paranormal phenomena, it allowed her more time for closer bonds of friendship. It was a unique life, and she enjoyed the daily adventures that owning and running the paranormal business brought into her world.

Dailey encounters with random ghosts that the business provided had kept the one demon at bay. Nana had been right about the entity from the airport. It hadn't visited her once since she'd played around in the paranormal lives of strangers. Occasionally, she'd think about the demon that had followed her from Paris and chased her through the airport on her return to Boston, and wondered exactly what it was planning? She closed her eyes, and hoped sleep would give a peaceful, but temporary retreat.

***

The morning was cold, and both of them were running late. They grabbed protein shakes on the way out of the house, and soon stood in front of Nudges and Nuances. She loved this store and its location. Stan unlocked the door just as a car pulled up in front of their building.

The car door opened and a short, stocky man with thick glasses leaped out. He was running towards them while waving his arms over his head.

"I'm so glad it's you. You must be Claire and Stan. I couldn't wait; I'm driven to madness. Those dogs in the trees are growling at me, and their red demon eyes are evil and threatening. You won't see them in the day. They only find pleasure in torturing me at night." His thick greying mustache twitched as he spoke, and his boisterous nature matched his appearance.

She looked at Stan, they both grinned before she pushed open the door and went inside.

"Come on in Marvin Schwartz. That's your name, right?"

"Yes. Yes, it is." What little hair he had left from his receding hairline was long and blew about in the wind, as his hands tried repeatedly to tame it, but to no avail.

Claire said, "Marvin, I thought we would meet you at your house; you did leave me your address and number."

"Yes, I know, Claire, but I couldn't wait. I need someone out there today, well not today, but tonight." Marvin continued to flatten his hair to his head as he moved towards one of their leather chairs. Their rich shades of espresso, and high tufted back appealed to clients that wanted comfort without needing help to get up. He planted himself down giving them the message he would wait until they guaranteed him immediate help.

"Well, it's nice to meet you, Marvin." She pointed to the chairs that sat around an old oak table. "I'd offer you a seat, but you've already found one to your liking. We'll be with you in a moment."

"That's fine. I'll wait," Marvin said.

"Okay." She had no doubt that he meant what he said.

She and Stan headed to the back office.

She would never get bored with the old-worldly look of their shop. There were antique style tables and chairs that sat around the room. Her favorites were overstuffed wingback chairs and ottomans. The warmth of the colors had jumped out at her when she first saw them; one-inch stripes of deep gold, reds, and greens gave the furniture a vertical motion, while two-inch red stripes moved in a horizontal direction. The legs of the chairs reminded her of three chocolate donuts on top of each other, prompting her to buy three of them, along with three wingback chairs that had a cinnamon-colored paisley design on top of a golden linen fabric. What caught her eye was the shape of a medallion that decorated the back of each wingback, it reminded her of something, but she wasn't sure what. Their shop quickly became a home away from home.

Bookshelves decorated the length of the wall that backed up to the shop next door. Some of the books were magical in nature, while others were based on runes, candles, magical scripts, paranormal events, and various other educational books revolving around their business. Scattered around the room were small unique tables that held unusual artifacts. All of it belonged in their world.

Once in the back office, she removed her coat and hung it on a rack. Stan moved in close to her and hung up his coat.

His sarcastic tone didn't go unnoticed. "Thanks, Claire. That mad scientist is my dog man?"

She slapped him on the arm. "Oh, Stan, don't be such a spoilsport. It could prove interesting. Please keep an open mind."

"Easy for you to say. You won't have to worry about being stalked by mad Marvin, who acts like he's a paranormal event himself."

Before she could answer he turned and left the room, heading to the front of the store. She followed him out, watched as Stan sat down next to Marvin and tried not to giggle from his last comment.

"So, Marvin, what exactly is going on and when did it start?" Stan began questioning him, while she sat down on her favorite chair, and threw her feet on the ottoman.

"It began last fall, October 25th to be exact, I remember, because my wife and I had a barbeque on one of the last nice days of the season. We lit a bonfire and enjoyed the night with a few friends and a bottle of champagne. Our friend Irene noticed the faces first and pointed them out. My wife and Irene's husband had a tough time seeing them, but I didn't. I saw four pairs of red eyes, and the longer I stared at them an outline of a dog face appeared. We freaked out a little, but because of the champagne we blew it off. I don't believe in apparitions, but it gnawed at my mind because two of us saw them. I kept checking the trees just to put my mind at rest."

The narrowed eyes and pursed mouth of Stan resembled a stern professor about to reprimand his student. "Marvin, if that happened in October, why'd you wait until February to come and see us about the situation?"

"I thought I was going mad, and my obsession with the dog faces drove my wife insane. She's never seen them; not like I had. She thought it was shadows and lighting making it appear on occasion to look like dogs. I quit looking for them for a month or so, you know, trying to retrieve what little dignity I had left. Then one night in January, my wife wanted ribs grilled outside. I went out back and wiped the snow from the cover and fired up the grill. It was around six in the evening and as I barbequed, I stared at the trees. God only knows why. There they were, but this time clear as my hand in front of my face, evil looking dogs with red eyes. There was blackness behind them, blacker than the night, almost as though they were sitting in a black hole."

Marvin's voice had risen in pitch, his body twitched from the stress, and his eyes wildly bulged from their sockets. Stan leaned towards him and placed his hand on Marvin's arm.

She quickly came to Stan's rescue. "It's okay, Marvin. Stan and I are here to help you. Just relax and continue."

Just then the bell sounded, as Morgan entered the shop. Her hair was bouncy, and her beautiful wide smile complemented her rosy cheeks from the cold February morning.

Claire jumped up and greeted her at the door with a warm hug. "Oh, Morgan, I've missed you. I'm so glad you've decided to join us."

"Ditto, Claire, and I can't wait to be a part of your company. I hope I'll be able to help."

Morgan waved at Stan, as he looked up from his chair. He stood up and ran to her, lifted her into the air, and gave her one of his famous bear hugs.

"I'm excited, too, Morgan. I think you'll bring a lot of intelligent thoughts into our paranormal world." Stan gave Claire a look that clearly said, 'thanks for letting me know you called her.'

Twisting her lips and raising her eyebrows into a distorted imprint of, 'I'm sorry,' Claire turned to Morgan and said, "Well, let's get your coat off, and you can listen in on our conversation with our new client, Marvin Schwartz."

She introduced the two of them, as Morgan removed her coat and followed Claire to the back.

"So, what's his story?"

"Dog faces in trees."

"Seriously?"

"Yep. He's very sincere and waited for months before approaching us. I think this might prove to be an intriguing, yet scary case. We might bite off more than we can chew on this one. Demons, and other realms, that sort of thing."

"Interesting. Do you think I could join whoever is investigating that one?"

She smiled and locked arms with Morgan, as they went back into the room to join the conversation.

"Stan, when you go to Marvin's this evening, Morgan would like to go with you, if that's okay?"

Stan raised his eyebrows at Claire, then slowly turned his head towards Morgan and nodded. "I'd love for you to join me. I'll pick you up around eight, if that'll work for you?"

"Sure," said Morgan. Her face glowed with the excitement of a child lighting a Christmas tree for the first time.

"I'm glad you're both willing to check on my trees," said Marvin.

Stan nodded. "We'll talk-price later if you want, Marvin. We initially evaluate the situation for a small upfront fee of thirty dollars."

"Oh, sure, Stan. I can give you that now." He took out his wallet and handed over the cash. "I need no receipt. I'll see you tonight at eight." Marvin stood up, shook hands with the three of them and walked toward the door.

The bell sounded as he left and in walked Charlie Burns, smiling at Marvin as they passed in the doorway, Marvin acknowledged him with a wave of his hand.

"What do you have there, Charlie?" Stan shouted across the room. "I hope it's what I think it is?"

Charlie wore a long gray wool coat, and a bright blue scarf hung around his neck. His neatly combed, long grayish hair and his nicely trimmed mustache and beard gave him a look of sophistication.

"Yes, it's exactly what you think, Stan," Charlie said, as he walked towards them with a couple of steaming cappuccinos held up in the air. "I thought you could use these, and it's kind of a welcome back celebration."

He waved Claire back down in her seat. "Claire don't get up; I'll bring it to you. Good morning, Morgan. I'm sorry, I didn't know you'd be here."

"No worries, Charlie. I had my share of coffee this morning, you know, a caffeine transfusion before the kids got up."

"Right," said Charlie.

Claire sipped her drink. "Oh, this hits the spot, thanks."

"You're welcome, but more importantly, what type of crazy are we talking about today?"

"Dog faces in trees," said Stan. "And before you ask, I get the pleasure of checking them out. Although Morgan will join me, and that my friend, will make even the dog trees much more enjoyable."

Charlie threw his head back and his laughter rang through the room. "Stan, I think it sounds intriguing."

"You would think that Charlie, you're not the one going." Stan made a growling sound.

"He's been cranky ever since I told him about it, and now he's sounding like the dogs he's investigating," said Claire.

"Have not and am not."

"Yes, you have, but can we focus on other topics?"

Morgan grinned. "What would you like me to do today, Claire?"

She was glad Morgan changed the subject. "I have a couple of phone numbers for several other clients that we should set up interviews for today or tomorrow. I'm taking the one with Connie and her roses. Can you call her and see when she's available and get her address and all of her information?"

Morgan took the sheet of paper with the names on it and nodded. "This one's bizarre. Fish disappearing? Strange, whoever called left no name, or time available, but we have an address and phone number."

"Yes, I thought that was peculiar, as well. You can use the back office. We have tea and coffee back there, too."

"Morgan, just so you know, you're welcome to pick up any of the books from our dark paranormal library and study on your own," said Stan.

"Oh, thanks so much. The perfect excuse to read historical and mystical books. I'll be doing that. I can't wait." Morgan flashed them both a smile before heading to the office.

Charlie sat in a chair and relaxed.

Stan said, "Charlie, are you staying for a while?"

"No, not really. Just thought I'd join you for a moment. How was your trip, Stan?"

"It was fabulous. The wedding was incredible and those two are so happy. Claire and I did some sightseeing while in New Zealand. It's a picturesque adventure over there, but I'm glad to be back home."

Charlie's face was expressionless, as he reached into the deep pockets of his coat and pulled out a book. He'd only been making small talk, but Claire saw what really held his thoughts, and it wasn't the wedding of their two friends; it was the book his hands gently stroked.

She grinned. "Yeah, yeah, I had a good time, too. Charlie, my curiosity is about to explode, what's that book you have in your hands? So, you stopped by to bring us a gift?"

There would only be one reason Charlie brought it here; to show them it was magical. He usually waited for them to stop by his shop if it was just another interesting book.

Claire sat on the edge of the ottoman to get a better look and controlled the urge to grab it out of his hands and surrender her mind to whatever mysteries the book held. After all, she saw the white glow that circled the book and moved about it like wispy clouds hiding the top of mountain peaks that could only be discovered by the struggle of the climb. The essence of the book whispered; the climb would require will and endurance giving way to everything else just to feel the accomplishment of success and knowing at the end there was a view spreading beyond incredible and passing into the realm of heavenly.

Charlie glanced at the object in his hands and looked in her direction with raised eyebrows. "Yes, the book. Another one of my unbelievable finds. While you were gone, I took a trip to the northern Catskills in Green County, New York. On my second day there I was having coffee and a bagel when out of the blue I felt the urge to take a hike through the hilly terrain even though the weather was overcast and chilly, I couldn't stop the urge to wander out into the wild, wearing only a light jacket, hiking boots and a wool cap. Something drove me in one direction until I came across a small cave, and of course, I had to investigate it. I'd gone in about twenty feet when an old man stood up from a pink glowing rock he'd been sitting on and said, 'I've been waiting for you.'

"No way," said Stan. His voice a whisper.

Charlie stood up and in a theatrical way moved about them and drew them deeper into his story. "I began stuttering incoherent words, and my mind had no clue what my mouth was trying to say. I backed up and stumbled over a rock, falling and landing on a smooth white boulder. I looked at the old man again and noticed his ashen skin looked paper thin in the blue glowing shadows of the cave allowing blue vessels underneath to protrude like a road map across his face. His sunken eyes steadily burned into mine, his lips appeared painted on his face with a finely pointed pen, almost completely gone. I wasn't sure how he grinned without them, but he did. Three huge teeth hung from his gums, he looked undead, alive past the normal time of human life, but he moved and acted like he was in his forties. I know that because he jumped over rocks and helped me to my feet."

"No way," said Stan, again.

"Did he have a bed in there?" Claire asked him behind a huge toothy smile, she'd once dreamed of living in a cave before she'd met Gabe. It would've been an adventure.

Charlie sat back down, looked them both in their eyes as he leaned in towards them until his chin extended past his knees. "He had a grass mat that looked quite comfortable. He sat on rocks and had a wooden table with books all over it, not to mention the many that were piled up at least ten feet all around the cave. According to the caveman, he moved into the cave about twenty years prior to my visit. He took only the simple things he loved, had no more family, and wanted to escape."

"Escape from what?" Stan's eyes were the size of quarters.

"Taxes, maybe." Claire spoke as she reached for the book. "May I?"

"Sure." Charlie handed her the book. "Claire, you would've loved his place. He had a stone shelf loaded with all sorts of hardback books that were finely bound. He'd brought them with him for reading and used some of them to study about living off the land. The one you have in your hand has a picture of The Golden Dawn Rose of 22 Petals. It's exquisite. I don't know a lot about it, but I recognized the rose."

A tingle moved through her fingertips, as she ran her hand across the leather-bound cover with the rose of 22 petals burnt into it with fine artistry. Hints of faded red, blue, and yellow were the only colors left of the three petals at the center. The colors of the 7 petals in the second circle, and the 12 in the outer circle were completely gone, except for a few spots that she knew held the proper color during the book's creation.

Stan got up and moved behind her, to get a better look at the book. "Incredible. Was this before the Hermetic Order? It has no cross behind it, although the small one in the center is there. Surely this couldn't go back to the Egyptians?"

"I'm not sure, but the rose was related to the pentagram, and I think the number 5," said Claire.

She grinned, the energy in her hands was pure power. "I hold the flower of Venus and the sign of secrecy. There's so much related to the rose of 22 petals, where it originated from and what the design represents. It even has a mark on history with the Freemasons. I wonder what an old man living in the mountains would have to do with The Rose of 22 Petals?"

Charlie shrugged. "He didn't say how he came by the selection of books he had. I asked him, but he never answered me. I never knew his name; he never shared it. He told me I would find that book interesting and handed it to me without uttering another word. I do know the letters are in Hebrew and the three petals represent air, fire, water, and earth, it shows the seven planets, and the 12 zodiac signs."

Stan reached for the book, and she allowed him to take it. "Wow. You were meant to find this Charlie. It's odd that the old man said he waited for you to come. The Hermetic Order further developed the symbolism of the rose of 22 petals, by developing a deeper and richer meaning of it. Although the society of The Hermetic Order wasn't so secretive, they embraced the light, not the dark and even allowed women into their order, and it's the 22 paths of the tree of life," said Stan. He gently handed the book back to her with the care of holding a baby.

Charlie frowned. "It was odd that he said he was waiting for me. I never found out why, or exactly what he meant."

"The whole experience was peculiar and mystical. That is one book Nana will have to let me read first," said Claire. She allowed the power of the rose to warm her hands, as the energy of the ancient and symbolic book stimulated her senses. The artifact around her neck heated slightly.

Stan said, "Charlie, are you sure you want us to have the book? The caveman said he waited for you."

"It's a loan, and it's what you people do. Figure things out. I have a sixth sense that it was meant for me to bring it to Claire." He winked at her and smiled.

Morgan came back into the room. "I have your schedule, at least for the rose smell. Connie will be waiting for you around 2:30 this afternoon. I left a message at the disappearing fish location, there was no answer and no mention of who I was calling. Do you think I could join you at Connie's this afternoon, Claire? I'd have to drive and leave from there to be home for the kids."

"Sure, Morgan, I'd love your company. Let's try that number again later, if the man doesn't call back within a couple of hours. Stan and I'll check it out today, if possible."

"Okay," said Morgan.

"Morgan, I'll pick you up tonight? No sense in both of us driving, you're on the way, anyway," said Stan.

"That'll be great," said Morgan and noticed the book. "Hey, that book with the rose is beautiful. Any ancient mystery to it?"

"You could say that, Morgan." Claire nodded and stared lovingly at the book while running her hand over the spine.

Charlie stood. "I need to get going and open the shop. I leave you three to your thoughts. Claire and Stan, good to have you back, it was lonely without having someone to pester." Charlie bent down and kissed her on the cheek, shook Stan's hand, gave Morgan a hug and buttoned his coat before heading out the door.

Chapter 3

Roses, water, and darkness

The penetrating fragrance of roses matched that of a florist shop the minute Connie opened the door. A vaporous cloud moved about her head, a sign that someone belonging to the other world had taken up residence.

"Connie Downs?"

"Yes, and you must be Claire."

She nodded her head, and said, "It's nice to meet you. This is one of my associates, Morgan Spencer."

Morgan shook Connie's hand. Claire couldn't tell whether Morgan saw the haze or smelled the roses, because she'd asked Morgan earlier not to say anything, until they'd completed checking out the situation. Their goal was to observe her first and let Connie do the talking.

Connie Downs was tall and slender, with thick hair that hung in a straight sweep to her shoulders. The color of her hair was eye-catching, a sort of autumn auburn colored fantasy with streaks of gray running through it, adding a touch of winter's frost. She had a rose tattoo on her left cheek and wore no make-up except for a soft lavender lipstick. One word that came to mind when she first saw her in the door, eccentric.

"Come in, and thanks so much, I appreciate it. Would you like some coffee, or a drink?"

"No, thank you. We'd like to work first and then have a chat about what we experienced. Now, why don't you tell us your story."

"Well, I called because the smell of roses follows me around the house."

"You're not wearing any fragrances of any sort that might have roses in it?" Before Connie could answer, Claire continued, "Morgan, you stay next to Connie and I'll move into the kitchen, if that's alright with you, Connie?"

"No... no fragrance of rose, and that's fine. The kitchen's through the dining room and to the left."

Claire could see the dining room from the entrance and as she moved into position, she couldn't help but notice that the vibe of the house offered a lot of style and flair that painted a picture of Connie's personality, with unusual art gracing vibrantly colored walls.

She raised her voice slightly from the other room. "The smell is gone in the kitchen. Morgan, you stay there, and Connie move towards me."

A flower shop of roses filled the area the closer Connie came towards her. "Wow, it's attached to you, that's for sure," said Claire.

"The smell is gone in here," piped Morgan from the other room.

"Join us, Morgan. I see what you mean, Connie. I'm assuming you smell the roses when you leave the house, as well?"

"No, actually, I don't."

"Interesting. If you don't mind, I'll take that cup of coffee, now."

"Sure, I could use one myself. Have a seat. I'm curious as to what you have to say about it," said Connie.

Connie moved about the kitchen in a long purple skirt that flowed just above a pair of green army boots. She wore a white tee shirt, and an open green jacket that had a velvety texture and purple satin cuffs and lapel. A pink scarf hung around her neck. Claire studied Connie. The woman could've put on a load of rose cologne to gain attention, or hidden rose petals in her bra, but she didn't seem the type.

Connie placed the cups on the table and sat down.

Morgan sat across from her and smiled. "Connie, I love the rose on your cheek. Does it have a personal meaning?"

"Yes, it does. I love roses. They're my favorite flower. I enjoy their representation of timelessness, peace, love, wisdom, and honor, to name a few."

Claire said, "Through centuries roses were labeled with powerful significance. Do you live alone?" Her mind raced back to the beautiful book of roses; she'd held in her hand's only hours earlier. Obviously, today was to be the day of the rose.

"Yes, I live alone. My husband died a year ago, he was quite young."

"I'm so sorry to hear that. When did you start smelling the roses?"

"About a month ago, in fact it was on my birthday. January 10th to be exact."

"Did your husband always buy you roses for your birthday?" Morgan asked.

"No, never. I have a severe allergic reaction to them and could never grow them or have them around me for extended periods of time. My eyes and nose run, and itch like mad. It devastated me that I couldn't enjoy them. That's another reason I got the tattoo."

"Connie, when you first opened the door, I saw something. Did you, Morgan?"

Morgan said, "Well, there was the overpowering fragrance of roses, but now that you mention it, I did see a slight fog when the door first opened. It was there for only a moment and then vanished. I thought it was my eyes playing tricks. I guess I didn't really understand what I was seeing. Claire, are you saying it was a spirit?"

"Exactly. I don't feel any negative energy. I'd say it's gentle and loving." Claire reached out and touched Connie's hand. "Connie, it's possible your husband wants you to enjoy the one thing you couldn't. Your body can't physically respond to pollen from the other world, so you can enjoy roses without the effects of an allergic reaction. I'd say that's fascinating, and a good thing for you."

"That's awesome. My first day and I learned something remarkable about the paranormal world," said Morgan.

"It's possible for my husband to do something for me he couldn't do when he was alive; buy me roses. I was never afraid of the smell or the feelings I'd get periodically throughout the day, if I'm honest, I kind of knew it was him, but needed verification, I suppose," said Connie. Her face lit up, as she glanced at them. "Actually, I feel blessed that my husband loved me enough to hang out with me after he passed over. Since he's been gone, I've never felt empty, I suppose that was because he's been with me the whole time. Kind of spooky but nice."

"Yes, it's nice," Morgan said. "I think I'd find it nice if Derry hung out with me when he travels to the other realm. I don't want to use the word dead, because that's so final, and I can't think of him that way. I think you're blessed, Connie, that's for sure."

Connie tilted her head allowing her girlish charm to surface and glanced around the room, as though searching for something that she'd lost. "I do feel special. Thanks Jack," she said softly."

The warm air cooled slightly bringing with it a garden of roses. They all giggled, and the intensity of their deep breaths continued for the next five minutes, lifting their spirits.

"Wow. Connie, you're one lucky lady," said Claire.

"I certainly am. That was stronger than normal. He must be glad I'm enjoying it."

"I have one last question for you. I know the rose smell doesn't go with you when you leave the house, but does he go with you when you leave the house? I mean do you feel his presence, or are his visits limited to your home?"

"It's exclusive to the house, or at least the smell is, but as for him coming with me, I'm not sure. I didn't think about that because it was the smell that drew my attention. I just know when I'm out, it never happens. When I first smelled the roses, I thought I'd imagined it, and just blew it off, until it didn't go away. I work a lot of hours and am often preoccupied with other things when I leave the house. A week ago, I realized the smell didn't follow me outside, at least I didn't feel Jack accompanying me, but that doesn't mean he didn't."

"Some paranormal events occur in a vicinity, others move about. I never could figure out why that happens. There have been many discussions about certain entities that become attached to a person, or a place and clues we find in our physical world are the only way we can relate to the paranormal, and even then, it's hard for some people to wrap their thoughts around it.

Is it a choice of the entity, or has some external influence beyond our understanding caused the attachment? Can they leave when they want? What gives them staying power, the person they're attached to or the place? That's something I want to investigate further. In situations like this, if the smell extended past the house, it would be nice, but at the same time, overwhelming if you didn't want the attention," Claire said as she took a deep breath.

Morgan said, "I see what you mean. What if Jack understands that, so only limits it to their home? How much control does the spirit have on each situation? Are they limited by their power? Does power increase with the length of time the spirit is freed? Or, does the power have something to do with their physical life? Why do some spirits seem to leave and never return, while others are more attached? Okay, that's enough. I'm driving myself crazy with the non-stop questions and believe me, I'm just getting started, that's why I said non-stop."

"Great questions. I love that about you, that's why I wanted you on board. We can't feel, see, or approach anything beyond our visual if we don't first ask questions. You have an open mind, and without that scientists wouldn't have discovered anything past the hand in front of their faces, if you know what I mean. I'm a firm believer that one should believe in things that are out of reach, otherwise, a person would become stagnant."

Connie said, "You're right. I've never thought of things in that perspective before now. There are so many mysteries, our world is so small."

Connie's brows came together, and her eyes drifted as though searching for a place where she could look into that small world, find her Jack, and bring him back over the physical and spiritual crossroads. She liked Connie.

"I hope we helped you today."

"You did and I really appreciate your time, and now, I'll embrace the wonderful gift. I'll just have to be careful using perfume, and not overdo it. Although, I do have one more question. How long do you think this will continue?" Connie gently laughed.

"I honestly don't know. But, it's possible until he feels you're able to move on, or until he decides he's given you enough of the romance he couldn't share with you in this life, and because we know so little about the why's of the spiritual world, it's something we can't say for sure."

Stan would kill her, but Claire didn't care. She decided to find out if Connie had a boyfriend.

"Connie, I hope this doesn't sound too forward, and if I'm out of line, just say so. But, I do have some unhealthy habits that tend to get me in trouble from time to time, like setting people up on dates. I think I might have the perfect guy for you if you're interested."

Connie's eyes widened, and she sucked in her lower lip. "Well, I have to say that you surprised me. I think it's a kind offer, but I'll need to give it some thought."

Morgan said, "One thing you'll learn about Claire is her uninhibited nature."

Connie chuckled. "I noticed that when I first met her."

"Okay, you two, have your fun. But, Charlie is one of the nicest people you'd ever want to meet. He's intelligent, well-read, and handsome on top of all that."

"I'm sure he is, Claire. I appreciate the good intentions, but I'm not ready to date yet. Give me a little time and I'll give you a call. I promise."

Morgan shook her head pulling her shoulders up and in towards her body. "She won't stop," said Morgan.

"I will too. Okay, I will after you join us for dinner. We'll make it a small dinner party and you can see for yourself. How about sometime in March?"

"Okay, Claire, an informal dinner with more people sounds like a fair proposal. March, it is, just give me a week's notice."

"Perfect. Well, we better get out of here, and if you don't mind following us to our cars because I just have to make sure no perfume smells past the door, not that I don't trust you, but it's for science, you see, then I'm off to check on an alien abduction." Connie and Morgan quickly looked her way slightly making a gasping sound. "Kidding," said Claire.

The women made their ways to their cars, and Morgan waved to Claire, as she closed her door and drove away to get her kids from school. No smell followed Connie outside of her home.

The drive took about twenty minutes and soon she pulled up in front of the house that had the mysterious fishpond. The man had never called back, so they had no name and no more information, except the address. He must've allowed Stan in without an appointment because Stan's car was parked in the driveway, and he wasn't anywhere in sight.

A well-tended yard matched the cleared and empty flower beds that lined the walk towards the house. It was a 2-story red brick cape cod with white awnings hung over the windows that in the summer would shade the interior from a hot burning sun. The white door expressed an organized and no-nonsensical person who lived in this almost cold home, if not for the flower beds.

As she walked towards the house her thoughts shifted to spirits, and how they moved through the physical world. She would love to have more answers. She used to think it was simpler, such as a spirit attached to a person, building, or place, but it wasn't that simple at all. What caused it and what allowed it was more complicated. She pulled her coat around her and knocked on the door.

When no one answered she rang the bell. There were no sounds of conversation or anyone walking around inside, so she walked around the house to where she believed the pond existed.

A fenced back yard blocked her way, but she was able to open an unlocked gate and continued down a stone path that led through a small forest of pines, the smell reminded her of Christmas when she was a child. She heard Stan's voice before she saw him.

When he came into view, he was talking with a young man who was slightly shorter than her partner in crime. His blonde hair was neatly combed, and brown rimmed glasses nicely framed his features. Both stood facing her from the other side of an extremely large pond. Stan waved.

She waved back and hurried towards them. "I hope it's okay we just showed up, but you never called back and all we had was your address." She held out her hand. "Hi, I'm Claire and I see you've already met Stan."

"Sorry, yeah, I should've given you more information. I was hoping you'd just come out when you had a chance, but I didn't expect you so quickly. My name is Tom, and lately I'm preoccupied with a work project and a deadline that detaches my mind from everything else."

"No worries. It's nice to meet you." She considered the gray and still pond. "I see what you mean. It feels dead. No energy. Nothing, yet you have plants on the bottom. How many fish did you say you had in there?"

Tom said, "Quite possibly 400, and some of them were quite large koi. You tell me where they went. It's about 6 feet deep, and I went in there and walked around stirring up the water with a net. I found nothing."

Obviously, Stan came prepared. He was wearing wading boots above his knees and scuba dive gear, including wet suit. She grinned.

"You going in there, big guy?"

"You bet, I am. I want to check it out. It's heated, and for that I'm thankful." With that comment he waded into the large pond.

Stan wasn't afraid of the unknown, even after what they'd been through.

"I'm not sure about that Stan. Aren't you worried about a black hole that could open up and suck you in with the fishies?"

"Not even close. I'm looking for more of a Loch ness. You know, a baby Nessie."

Tom said, "I don't find that funny. If you people aren't taking me seriously, please leave."

He didn't know them and had a right to feel indignant.

"I'm sorry, Tom. We joke. It helps us get through the day. We've seen things that are unexplainable and dangerous, so please forgive us when we appear to make light of your situation, because we're not doing that. We take this very seriously."

"I appreciate that. I live alone and jog the perimeter of the pond several times a week when I don't have time for the gym. I'd just ran around the pond this past Friday; the pond was full of color. Saturday my girlfriend was visiting, but I was busy on a job. She came out to jog and loved watching the fish, but noticed they were gone. It's enjoyable to watch the colors move slowly through the water. We have schools of fish, because of how many are in there, well how many used to be in there. So, their disappearance was noticeable. They've been gone for at least two days."

"I can imagine that it would be noticeable, and two days is a long time." She watched Stan continue through the water, but nothing appeared. Not one tiny brush of color.

Stan looked up, after 45 minutes of probing and wading in the pond. "I found nothing. Did you two see any movement?"

"No nothing," said Claire looking at Tom, his jaw had dropped. "Tom, I would say racoons, but considering how many fish you had, I think it would be impossible that they were eaten."

"Once in a while we get a few Blue Herons, but seriously that's a lot of fast eating," said Tom.

"I do feel a strangeness... no, the words I'm looking for are 'absence of energy'," said Claire.

Tom nodded and in a zombie-like tone agreed with Claire. "Yes, lacking energy, because there are no bodies."

Tom held out his hands to help Stan out of the pond.

"Sorry, I didn't find your fish, Tom," said Stan.

"That's okay. Thanks for trying. I guess I didn't expect you to find any of them, considering I looked on Saturday and Sunday, but also produced nothing tangible."

Stan took off his boots and wet suit and put on his warm shoes, and clothes, and Claire handed him his coat and scarf. "Let's go, Claire. I need a break before tonight."

She grinned at him, and they both tried not to laugh, remembering how Stan felt about the dog trees and knowing tonight he'd have to face his nemesis.

Instead, Claire focused on her client, and said, "Tom, I'm sorry that we couldn't help you any further. The only thing we can do is check some books and ask a few colleagues to see if we can find any mention of similar incidents. We'll get back to you in a few days, in the meantime, please let me know if there's any change."

Tom nodded his head and shook their hands.

"I'll walk back with you," said Stan.

She delighted in the smell of the pine trees, as they followed the path back to their cars.

"Are you going back to the shop, Stan?"

"Yeah, it's still early and I thought about researching our books to see if there's any similarities with Tom's fish disappearing. It's incredible. I can't imagine this type of thing happening."

She opened her car door and got in. "I know what you mean. Tom doesn't seem like the type of guy that would remove them all and then call a paranormal crew to check out how they disappeared."

Stan shut her door for her and nodded. "I agree. He's absolutely a no-nonsense guy, with no time to play weird games."

"Right. See you back at the shop."

His head seemed lower into his shoulders as he slowly walked back to his car. She worried for him, because Stan bottled up his thoughts when he couldn't explain things away with a simple explanation. The fish incident was mysterious, and he would put every effort he could muster up into finding out what happened.

***

She'd spent the better part of the late afternoon looking over The Rose of the 22 Petals book that Charlie had brought her earlier, it was captivating.

The mystics of the rose cross were children of light and were opposed to darkness, people after her own heart. The twenty-two paths on the Tree of Life and the twenty-two letters of the Hebrew alphabet stood for the petals of the rose, and to explore such a book gave her a grand sense of satisfaction. The history of it sank into her spirit and mind taking her back in time feeling the presence of those who honored such a way of life. Their ghostly hands reached across eternity to help in the fight against darkness; such a beautifully crafted book had to hold magical secrets.

It was getting late, and Stan hadn't returned to the shop. She yawned and checked her phone. No new messages. Claire headed to the bathroom to freshen up and then made another pot of coffee, because she still needed to research anything she might find on the disappearance of the fish. Although Stan was working on it as well, they both approached things differently and that could prove to be beneficial.

It started to snow. She opened the door and went outside for some air.

"Claire."

She waved. "Hi, Charlie, just out for some air, are you working late?"

"Me too. Out for air that is. Yeah, I'm working late just trying to reorganize some of my older books, which hasn't been done in years. However, I was just thinking of stopping for the day and heading home."

"Heading home so soon? Isn't that shameful?"

"Well, yes, it is. When you put it that way, I shall stay open and suffer the next two hours in an empty shop. On another note, are E-books really that popular?"

"I can't say that I approve. I'm hands on, give me a nice book to read. I have to feel it to be in it."

"I hear you. I'm having a book signing this weekend, for Eleanor Daybring. You know, the author of "The Journal of Your Dreams. That should bring in a group of readers."

"I hope so. I think I'll come around and liven up the place," said Claire, giggling.

"Great, hope to see you then. I'm going back inside, too cold."

"Yeah, have a good night, Charlie."

He disappeared behind the door. "You too."

Her shoulders shivered and she was heading inside when a car she recognized pulled up in front of her store. She went into the building, brushed the snow from her clothing, and grabbed two coffees.

The door chimed and in came the cool air along with Detective Brandon Stone.

She smiled. "Brandon, how are you doing? I've missed your grumbling attitude around here."

"Me grumble? You've got me mistaken with your partner in crime, Stan. I should take him in, lock him up, and throw away the key."

She laughed. "On what charges detective?"

"Annoying the crap out of me." He took off his long black trench coat, shook the snow off, and hung it on the coat rack.

"Well, if that was a crime, three quarters of Boston would be behind bars," said Claire, laughing, and handed him a coffee.

"Ha, that's true, most people do annoy me. Thanks for the coffee."

Claire offered him a seat. She wasn't surprised to see black jeans and a black shirt covering his dark-skinned body. He thought it made him more secretive, more undercover, and that's why he always wore black. Sweaters, turtlenecks, jackets, and not to mention black socks were part of the MO of the man her and Stan grew to love, even though they'd met him during the unfortunate incident when he'd investigated Gabe's death.

Of course, there had to be an investigation, they found Gabe dead at the bottom of the stairs in their own home, and Detective Stone had no other choice but to interview all of them in the death of her boyfriend. They were lucky that Stone was an open-minded individual who knew when something beyond everyone's control had occurred. Although, it'd taken him five months of interrogation to finally give in. He'd closed the case and listed the death as accidental. Claire imagined a lot of closed cases were accidental, instead of murder, because no one would believe that the paranormal would be involved, and you certainly couldn't bring a spirit to trial. That's one reason she and Stan did what they did, to prevent innocent people from going to prison. It was rare that someone would go to jail over a paranormal incident, but not unheard of.

Stone was clean-cut with a practical attitude, somewhere in his late forties, he'd never married, but was a handsome man, resembling Denzel Washington, with large hands, broad nose, beautiful skin, and deep black eyes that pierced into the soul. In fact, there were several times she almost fell apart in interrogation, because of his stare. If someone were guilty, he'd get them to confess. And she had felt guilty about Gabe's death, she hadn't saved him, and the guilt back then was heavy on her heart, it still was a daily quilt trip.

"So, girl, how've you been?" He sat down and sipped on his coffee. "Oh, that's good stuff."

"Really busy, Brandon. I hope you don't mind me asking but were you always graying by the temples, or did that just happen?" She grinned.

He kicked back in his chair, rocking it on the edge of the legs. "Nope. You and your group gave me all these gray hairs, with all that paranormal stuff-it was inevitable. What'd you expect? I walked into a crime scene with pentagrams, incense, and strange words written on the walls. Oh, and then there was the matter of the dead boyfriend at the bottom of the stairs, you screaming, and a big bear looking guilty as hell, where is that big guy anyway?"

"I was wondering that myself. I thought he was coming back to the shop, but he must've decided against it. I suppose we were a lot to take in, but you'll be happy to know we've added a partner in paranormal, Morgan, just to make your job more interesting and fun." Claire narrowed her brows and leaned towards the detective. "Just wondering which of those gray hairs are mine and what brings you out on this snowy day?"

"Oh, you brought that sweet lady in on your criminal activities, tell her my condolences." Brandon leaned closer to Claire and pointed at the left side of his head. "See those right there? That side is yours and the top and right side belong strictly to Stan."

Claire smiled. "I'm glad that Stan has more than me, he should, that's all I'm saying."

The detective sipped his coffee, closed his eyes, and smiled. "That's good stuff and helps my thought process, but this isn't just a social call Claire. The reason I ventured out into the weather was to talk to you about a case. My department head moved me to cold case files, in case you didn't know, and that's why I'm here. I like it and it keeps me busy but some of these cases are making me lose sleep. I went from a street beat-cop to detective and now, it seems, I'm chasing ghosts, and thought that'd be right up your ally."

She chuckled. "Only if ghosts are involved."

"Well, that's the thing; after working on your case, it opened my eyes to other possibilities, and I have one that seems unsolvable. So, I thought of you and Stan. Pick your brains. It's the women that disappeared that bothers me, no bodies were ever found and if I'm seeing this correctly...I think it could be a serial killer that might go back decades." He scratched his head. "That's the thing, isn't it, I'm not really sure when it started."

"Why else do you think it's related to the paranormal and not just another homicidal nut?"

"Because it makes no sense, no logical sense. Like your case, the kind that'll drive you mad, because the clues don't mesh, yet these crimes appear to be the same MO going back further than I'd like to imagine."

She gazed out the window at some shoppers fighting the windy snow, two steps forward, one back. "Yes, Brandon, I know what you mean. What do you have so far?"

"Well, between 1962 through 1968 there were 28 women who disappeared without a trace in the Boston area. I guess you could say it was a serial killer at large, but it's more mysterious than that. My father was a detective at the time and still talks about it to this day. He and a detective named Joe Sheen muddled through it for over ten years, and like most cops, could never let it go."

"How so," Claire asked?

"They were all single women, well educated, involved in their community, and healthy. Their clothes were hanging in their closets, and suitcases unused, and cars still parked at their residences. Bank accounts untouched. Never heard from or seen again. My father found similar incidents that traced back further, but I found a link even further back than he did. He still has trouble sleeping." He paused and looked deep into her eyes. " Claire, it's hard for detectives to let go of a crime that hasn't freed the lost souls; cold-case files get in our heads, haunting them and demanding restitution."

"That could be a serial killer on a mission. I'm sure it's happened. Think of Gacy, horrible, yet guys disappeared for years before the police arrested him and put him away."

"I know, but they caught him, and bodies were found. So, back to our killer; after 1968 they began again in 91, the disappearance of 35 women started again, all single, all educated and independent. Then it abruptly stopped in 2011. The killings were so sporadic that we can't find a connection. Some were on singles websites, others weren't. The only thing they had in common was intelligence and attractiveness. Not a hair-color type, eyes, race, or size."

"Detective, it's mysterious and horrific, but not unusual for serial killers, is it? There are killers that start up, stop and something sets them off again, right? Some are even copycats, which could explain the period."

"Sure, possible, but something didn't feel right to me, Claire. I dug further. In 1895 through 1910 forty single women disappeared, again the same M.O.-educated and most of them were over 30. Where did they all go, Claire? For the life of me, I can't put a finger on it. There was one significant difference, during the 1991-2011 killing spree, the age group got older over the years."

"It is weird. What else did you find?"

"Well, I keep seeing it from a detective's point of view, I thought maybe you might be able to go over the files of information with me and offer a fresh point of view. You know, from your perspective."

"Sure, I can do that. How about this weekend? Bring over the files around 5 pm on Saturday evening and we can have dinner, as well. Make a night of it."

"We might have to make several days of it. Extensive information. I just find it strange that no investigator found a killer, not one, even though they did interview family, friends, and known male dates. None of the men on the lists of dates were associated with any other victim on the list but one. No repeats."

"Well, it's interesting, that's for sure. I think Stan would love helping on that as well. I could invite Derry and Morgan to give us more people that have an eye for the unusual and they are part of this paranormal investigation team."

"That's marvelous. Thanks for your time. I got to run." He got up and placed his cup on the table, squinted his eyes and rubbed the middle of his forehead. "Darn headache. This case is causing me anxiety. I want it solved for my own peace of mind and my father's."

She followed him to the door and helped him put on his coat. He looked tired after their conversation; the discussion appeared to have drained his energy.

"Are you going to be alright, Brandon?"

He took her hand, smiled, and held her gaze. She saw something troubling in his sad eyes but couldn't put her finger on it. "I'm good, Claire. See you Saturday."

"Okay."

His steps were lively as he walked to the car, but a darkness hung over him.

Chapter 4

The night of the trees

It was freezing and flurries of soft snow formed a blanket over his wool coat as he pulled the ends together and buttoned it up. The night wind cried and rode on the back of nightmares that hammered against the trees to awaken them from winter's slumber, but instead they stayed in their comfortable hibernation allowing the blustery night to awaken something else.

An indecipherable, ear-shattering scream escaped into the darkness that surrounded them and caused them to move closer together. Stan knew the sound was nearer than it seemed. The trees slightly yawned-the demons were coming.

Morgan shivered next to him; her warm smoky breath blew out from between chattering teeth and into the frosty air. "Did you hear that, Stan?"

"Yes, but I haven't seen anything, have you?"

"No."

Marvin's hair blew away from his face, and under the moon's shadow he looked like a Neapolitan mastiff with glasses. The dim light focused on his wrinkles and accentuated them into deep crevices. The stress he'd been through had drawn his skin down on his face, his jowl sagged and shrunk his darting eyes. Stan shook his head to get rid of the image and focused on the trees.

"Do you hear them panting? I hear the beasts panting. Patience...patience. Stay alert. They will come," Marvin said. His voice shook on the verge of hysteria.

"Marvin didn't you tell us that they don't always show up?" Morgan shifted and looked at the dark forest in front of her. "We could be here for days," she said.

"I think they're already here." Stan's words quivered uncontrollably. It could've been caused by the cold, but he knew better; it was fear. The negative energy moved through his head and down his body reaching into his toes. It was malevolent. He tightly curled his toes in an effort to plant his feet to the ground to keep from falling over.

Morgan gasped and stepped back. "I feel them. I feel their evil."

Marvin shrieked. "I don't see them. Why can't I see them? I hear them breathing, panting like wild creatures." He backed up, pulled at his hair, and almost tripped over a tree branch before he caught himself. His eyes bulged. "They're collecting souls. They want mine; I can hear them begging for it, it gives them strength."

"Marvin shut up before I have to slap you. We didn't say we saw them. We feel their presence," said Stan, as he tried to steady his voice. The thought of the beasts collecting souls made him want to run from this place and never return.

"What does that mean? How can you feel something that you can't see? I hear them, I hear them breathing."

"They're watching us and will choose when to be seen, stay calm Marvin." He heard Morgan breathing heavily, but her silence strengthened his determination to see this through.

Marvin stepped further back. "That's not very comforting. It freaks me out to know that they're watching me without showing themselves. If my wife knew, she'd move out at once."

Morgan pointed towards a large willow. "Over there."

Stan moved closer to the willow. At first, he saw nothing, then a misty circle gradually formed on the tree at eye level and gracefully encircled the entire trunk. It drew him in, like a calling of the wild that he had to answer. The mist shifted colors, from shades of grey to royal blue. He leaned his head in for a closer look, and wished he hadn't.

The mist filled vortex extended past his vision, but there was a dark tunnel down the center where demonic creatures flew in and out of view and never noticed him watching. Dogs with two heads, bats with tiny human skulls, cockroaches the size of cats, dark floating deformed shadows flew in and out of the clearing. A demonic dog with two heads that defied the laws of nature noticed the uninvited guest. One of its heads had fangs that dripped blood with eyes that shot flames of fire within its giant orbs. The other head had ice blue eyes and a mouth that produced saliva that oozed from its fangs and became frozen after it left its host and turned into deadly spears of ice. It screeched and came at him pulling the other head with it; his eyes never blinked, he couldn't move but stood like he was already a corpse.

Suddenly Morgan appeared beside him, grabbed his arm, which released the spell he seemed to be under that freed him enough to regain his sanity. "Thanks. I got it."

Marvin panted heavily, in rhythm with the dogs.

Stan glanced back at the mist, the deformed dog looked out and then back at the creatures in the portal. The creature became interested in another beast that drew it back into the hole. The blue fog deepened in intensity and flames the size of two matches flickered towards him, it summoned his soul. He couldn't resist and once again leaned his head forward. The flickers moved closer and grew in power until they danced inside circular black eyes, and exposed a twisted inferno mixed with screaming faces of its victims. The dog sneered out from the mist and protruded past the bark of the tree. He fell forward; Morgan pulled him back. He caught his footing and looked back at the hound. Its teeth were huge and dripped blood. Stan's eyes followed the trail of blood to the ground. The blood scorched the earth with blackness; nothing would grow there again.

He felt confused. Run and it could chase them but stand there and they could die. If the head jutted out of the hole so could the body. The beast looked around, almost surprised that it had moved past the hellish hole. Then its high-pitched yelp curdled his blood. Marvin screamed and ran. Morgan was steadfast and held on to his arm, as though their bond protected them from anything that came out of the tree.

The tree moaned as several creatures inside the mist fought and snarled, forcing the demon dog to retreat inside the portal to face its attackers.

He and Morgan stood frozen for several minutes, afraid to move and risk the dogs running into their world, pouncing on the two of them, killing them or dragging them back into the portal, but that never happened. The brawl occurred inside the tree and had the full attention of the demon.

Nausea welled up inside his stomach, as both of them stood side by side clutched together so they stayed grounded to their world and supplied strength to each other to take on all that the demons would throw at them. The mist finally evaporated into the cold February wind, then the air stilled and the silence on the land was a graveyard that offered no whisper. His ears hurt from the land's deathlike struggle for life, but a voice warmed his heart, even if her words were raw.

"The tree is in pain. If we don't figure out a way to close off that portal, it'll die." Morgan's voice was fierce, but her teeth still chattered.

"I agree," said Stan.

The winter wind picked up again, and stung his cheeks, bringing the evening back to a normal winter's night. It awakened his soul and reminded him that he still owned one. His nostrils stuck together, as he inhaled the fresh pine-saturated air.

Morgan clung tightly onto his arm. "Stan, I was just wondering how many trees have a fiendish portal. Can there be more, or is it only one? Surely, someone had to place it there. Do you think there's more to Marvin or his wife than meets the eye?"

His face tightened. "You could be right. I think it's something we need to consider, even with Marvin's theatrics. One thing I do know is we have to close this portal. The creature was surprised it could move past the veil. We don't have much time before they're running around in our world."

"What would that mean to us?"

"Death and destruction would follow."

Morgan's grip tightened on his arm, but she was silent. The snow fell, as they both stood motionless and stared at the tree in front of them.

He wished he were still in the warm water of the fishpond, instead of there in the cold night. The heater now warmed a lifeless pond. Where did all the fish go? He needed to leave this place, but his thoughts left without his body, hiding from what he'd just witnessed.

"Stan, what if other things come out of the portal? Worse things."

The sound of her intense fear brought him back to her side. He nodded. "It's quite possible."

Keeping their arms interlocked he walked with her back towards Marvin's house. His body was stiff, and his muscles ached as though he'd worked out for 24 hours non-stop.

When they approached the house, the door opened for them. Marvin waited inside the entryway. He anxiously pulled at his hair. "What was that? I didn't know it could come out of the tree. That's unwelcome news. What happens when my wife goes for her nightly walks and the yard is full of demonic dogs? What can I do?" Marvin's raised eyebrows and wild hair added an amusing note to a not so funny situation.

"I'm not sure you can do anything," said Stan. "You might have to let us worry about this, but there's nothing I can do tonight. I'll consult Claire and see what we can do if anything. Someone opened this portal, and the trick is how to get around their magic. Have you or your wife noticed any strangers lurking about your yard?"

Marvin paced around the kitchen, chewing on his nail. "No, not all. That's great. What'll I do in the meantime? Feed them?"

Stan nodded. He had no solution. "If it helps, but just make sure it's not you."

"That's good. That's real professional. I came to you two for help and all you can do is tell me to feed them?"

"You suggested it. Listen, Marvin, we make no guarantees to our customers that we have an answer, each experience is different than the next. We do what we can with what knowledge we have. It's possible we'll need to consult someone else, but we do need time to do that. This isn't like fixing a fence."

He was tired of neurotic people who wanted immediate fixes to everything in their lives. It didn't matter that he was a supposed professional, the day had been long, and professionalism no longer applied.

Morgan spoke up. "Marvin, I suggest you avoid going out into the back yard and stay away from the trees. Don't encourage them to want to visit this world. Keep your curtains closed, as well, especially the ones that face the forest and we'll get back to you as soon as we can if anything changes let us know right away."

"Okay. Sure. Fair enough."

Stan was impressed with Morgan. She kept her cool like Claire and saved him from more sarcastic replies to their customer. He wasn't known for his patience with people, and for him sarcasm worked quite well.

"Let's get out of here, Morgan."

They said their goodbyes and walked to the car. He turned and saw Marvin watching them from his window. That jumpy little guy is a strange man.

"Thanks for saving me, Morgan. I don't understand what people expect us to do about some things. Wave a magic wand and it's fixed. Annoying. Marvin gives me the creeps. There's something strange about him, you know abnormal. Why would someone watch us leave?"

"People don't understand what they can't wrap their head around. We're taught that the paranormal doesn't exist from the time we're young, but people are changing. Science, right? That's what they say, but science is the paranormal. We know so little about what we can't explain away with our small tools and even smaller minds. I always believed a person should believe in everything first, then go from there. No surprises. If you don't believe, you can't find out what made it happen without the ability to first acknowledge it. That's it, all I got. Let's go," said Morgan.

It was pitch black as they drove through the country. The stars were dim under the veil of snow.

"I can't stop thinking about that weird little man. He stood in the window watching us." He looked at Morgan and grinned. "Alternative motive? He put them there. Do you think he's the beast father of the demons?"

"Have you lost your own mind? I'm sure he was just glad we were gone. What a beautiful night," said Morgan.

"Yep. Nice night, now don't change the subject. What about him being the father of the demons? Any thoughts?"

"None."

Okay, maybe Clarie would bite. He wasn't going to get a response from Morgan, he drove her nuts, and she was still shivering. He turned up the heat in the car.

 "There's something you made me think of though when you said we're taught to ignore the paranormal. When I was scared as a child and thought something was in my closet my parents never told me I had imagined it. My mom just came in the room and looked around and told me whatever was there was now gone. I didn't really appreciate that until now. It showed she believed in me and for kids that's important. Parents dismiss what children have to say about things parents can't explain. Children are perceptive about paranormal happenings, until it's beat into their heads that those things don't exist, and then they get all grown up and forget that it happened to them."

Morgan smiled. "Glad I could stimulate those grey cells. Maybe it's smart not to have children deal with another world, ours is crazy enough sometimes. I don't know."

Stan looked at her. "Did you notice Marvin watching us from his window until we were gone?"

Morgan stared straight ahead and said, "You won't stop until I answer, will you?" He grinned and shook his head. "Of course, I saw him. What of it? More importantly, where did that come from? Your mind just keeps getting stuck on one thought, and you refuse to let go."

"Pretty much. He is a weird man. I feel like he isn't telling us something."

"Like what?"

"I'm not sure. Any thoughts?"

"I get what you're thinking, but I think he's just paranoid, and so he watches."

"Yeah, that does lead to staring." He chuckled and stared at Morgan.

"Cut it out you freak. Thank God, I'm home. Let me out."

He watched her walk up the stairs to her front door where Derry met her and gave her a hug. Once she was safe inside, he drove home with his dark thoughts bouncing all over the place.

When he arrived, the house was dark. He needed to talk about what he'd seen and felt, but he didn't want to disturb Claire.

It would be more fun if he went to bed and wallowed in the demon dogs, imagining every worst-case scenario after they escaped through the portal, and then dreamed about them taking over his brain.

Instead, he put his coat back on and went for a walk. He would check the trees in the area, just to make sure Marvin's house wasn't the only entrance into Boston using trees as portals.

***

Claire looked out at the grey morning; it looked like more snow. She poured herself another cup of coffee. Stan walked into the kitchen rubbing his eyes.

She was the first to speak. "Morning."

"Morning. Did you sleep well?" He poured a cup of coffee and leaned against the sink, closed his eyes, and sipped. "Good stuff."

"Yep. I started reading the rose book but fell asleep around eleven and woke up at seven with it still in my hands. You look tired though. I didn't hear you come in. I closed the shop and came home early, when did you get in?"

"Somewhere around one. I wandered the streets for a while, just thinking about what we do for a living. Those demon dogs messed with my brain cells." He downed his coffee and started frying a couple of eggs. "Want any?'

"No thanks. I already ate. Why do you think they messed with your mind? Literally or figuratively?"

"Probably both. They reached past the barrier."

"Did any get out?"

"Nope, not that we saw." Stan threw his eggs on a plate and sat down. "You should have seen them, Claire. Morgan held her own, but I can still feel her nails in my arm. When one of them reached its head past the barrier, the dog was surprised. It had to be the first time, and if other hounds didn't come knocking, that demon dog might have led them all out into our world." He put a bite of egg in his mouth and washed it down with coffee.

"So, you believe they can escape? When it returns do you think it'll remember that it bypassed the portal?" She warmed her coffee and filled Stan's cup. They drank it down quickly today.

Stan grunted and finished his eggs. "I don't know if it even knows that it's behind a portal. I'm sure that if anyone approaches those trees before we figure out who opened those portals and how to get them closed the risk of demon dogs escaping and running all over Boston is inevitable."

"That's horrible. I might have a book at the shop that could help with closing portals. Is Morgan coming in this morning?"

"As far as I know, unless the hounds chased her away."

"Oh, I doubt that, Stan. I have more news. Detective Stone came into the shop and wanted us to go over some cold-case files with him, so I invited him to dinner Saturday evening, with the files."

"Why, Claire? What are we doing looking at cold-case files? That's just homicidal maniacs, not paranormal, and I'm sorry, but don't you think that hearing voices is just a criminal's way of seeking an insanity plea instead of facing their own demons?"

"Maybe so, but this is different. It's a file that might extend past a criminal's expiration date. And what if the detective arrested one of us for murdering Gabe? He didn't because it made no sense, so I think he gets the paranormal."

His head jerked up and his mouth opened. "Wonderful, just what we need; a cold-case file that might come with the hot fires of hell. What are we getting ourselves into with this one, Claire?"

"I'm not sure, but Detective Stone needs our help, or at least our input. I already offered to look at the files. If you don't want to be a part of it, I could do it by myself. No worries, besides, I'm inviting Derry and Morgan for dinner, as well."

With a lopsided grin he nodded his head. "Well, that doesn't surprise me. You're clever, aren't you? You pull in the whole support team without their knowledge, how can I say no? I'm in."

"Shame on you for thinking of me in that way. I would always ask Morgan and let her know what's going on, but I'm sure she'd say yes."

"Of course, she would. She has the O'Leary curiosity."

"And you don't?"

"Nope. I'm not crazy, well not totally, but I can't resist the charm of said curiosity. Is that the "Tubular Bells" I'm hearing from the Exorcist?"

"Yeah, sorry, just a minute." She pulled her cell out of her purse and answered the call.

"Okay. That's great, weird, but great. We'd like to come out and look anyway if that's okay with you? Sure, and thanks for calling us back with the news." She hung up and threw the cell in her purse.

"Back to the music, Claire. Did you reprogram your cell with "Tubular Bells?"

"Yes, I did. Don't you approve? I like it and you're not going to believe what happened. They're back, the pond is teemed with fish."

"What? I want to go see that. Same car, or separate?"

"Let's join up today. One vehicle, and stop by the pond on our way to work?"

"Sounds great. Let's go."

They both grabbed their coats and ran out the door towards Stan's waiting car and left the dirty dishes still sitting on the table.

He backed out of the drive and looked over at Claire. "We're not done with the music or dinner on Saturday."

"Oh, Stan don't be such a grump. I couldn't find out anything about the disappearing fish in our books, maybe a portal, or alien. That's all I got. I'm glad they're back, but it's got me flabbergasted."

"There you go changing the subject. The Bells? Don't you think it might prompt an attack? Just the sound of it gives me the creeps." He stretched his mouth, exposed his teeth, and shivered.

The snow had stopped, but the roads were still slick with icy patches.

"A little over exaggerated on the face expression. You make me laugh. The detective thinks he should lock you up and throw away the key. I might help him if you don't leave me alone about the tubular bells, fair enough?"

"Really? That's nice, and it's not fair enough until I make you both laugh so hard you both bust a gut."

She shook her head and wondered what was going on in his head. "You're prompting an attack on our guts? Do you hear yourself? The demon dogs got to you last night. I find the music appropriate, and I like it."

"Oh, that's nice for you, but I find it disturbing. Look at these crazy drivers. Get out of my way you lunatic, haven't you ever seen snow? It's not like they don't live in the north where snow comes every winter."

"Some drivers are more cautious," said Claire.

"Caution is one thing, but this is madness." Just when she thought she'd seen everything Stan rolled down his window, his face pinkish, he clearly had road rage, and screamed, scaring the elderly couple in the car next to them. "Move to the south you lunatics. Better yet, invest in a snowmobile!"

She couldn't duck down low enough in her seat to hide from the angry looks. One guy walking down the sidewalk made the crazy sign circling around his ear with one finger. Stan just got back from vacation, so he shouldn't be so anxious. What happened to him last night? She was worried.

"Stan, please roll up your window, it's cold out there, and you might give them a heart attack. Are you okay? Did you tell me everything from last night?"

He rolled up the window. "Hey, just for the record, I'm not the one driving like a sixteen-year-old who just got their license and trying to handle my first snow experience."

"Really screaming out the window? I hate to tell you, but that's a little lunatical."

"That's not even a word." The pink on his cheeks eased up. He looked over at her with a sweet smile that showed the dimple in his left cheek and there was a slight twinkle in one eye. "But, I have to say, I like the word-it suits me quite well."

"It is your favorite word; you use it all the time anymore. Everyone is a lunatic in your book," she said, smiling.

"Well, it fits."

They both chuckled, as the car worked its snail-paced way toward the fishpond.

She glanced at him and wished he wouldn't avoid certain topics that made him uncomfortable. He hadn't finished telling her exactly how he felt about the dogs, but she tried to avoid his attacks about the dinner party and her choice of music. She loved him and was sad he hurt so much in silence. She let it drop for now.

The house looked empty when they arrived, so she and Stan followed the path directly to the pond. Before they were within twenty feet, she could already see the white and gold of fish moving about in a now healthy pond.

Standing on the side and looking into the water left her speechless, but not Stan.

"What the hell? There's something wrong with this, Claire. Do you see all those fish? Do you see them? I do, and it blows my mind into the stratosphere, and I don't think it's coming back anytime soon. It's impossible, just impossible. This is above my pay grade, no, there's no pay grade for this. How? That's not even an answerable question, so why'd I even ask it? What are we supposed to do with this one, Claire? You're going to have to tell me because I've got nothing. Mind-blowing that's what this is. Surely, they must have had the pond stocked yesterday after we left. There's no other explanation. Claire, it's beyond paranormal...it's alien, yep that's what it is, alien."

She didn't know what to say, so they both stood there for at least ten minutes and watched the fish in silence. After telling Connie and Morgan yesterday, in jest, that she was going to see about an alien abduction, today, as she looked into the pond, that comment didn't seem so far from the truth.

Tom must've seen them; he walked towards them and soon joined them at the edge of the pond. Stan was all over him.

"Okay buddy, I get the joke, very funny, but a little bit of a waste of our time. You didn't have fish before, and you thought you'd pull a fast one on those of us that believe in the paranormal. We came out here and saw an empty pond the day before you planned on stocking it up. Thanks for the good time."

Stan started walking back to his car. "Stan, wait a minute, if he'd done that he would've given us a day to come out, instead he was surprised we came out so early." said Claire.

Tom yelled in the direction of Stan. "What? Do you think I'm crazy? I don't have time for that type of nonsense. I don't care what you think or believe in, I don't even know you, and don't forget you showed up on your own. I had no idea when you would be coming. Besides, I don't need to explain myself to you. Your business is the paranormal and I thought 'you' might supply me with an explanation."

The emphasis on 'you' didn't go unnoticed by Stan. He turned and came back.

"Maybe you are crazy Tom and do have time for nonsense. There are some things we can't explain and for you to think that this alien abduction, for lack of a better explanation, is one of them leaves me astounded at your ignorance--that all things are explainable. Really? And we can't supply you with an explanation for a pond full of disappearing fish. Well, all I got buddy is, like I said alien abduction, or would you prefer a portal to another dimension? You can pick your own damn choice of what you think it is and don't call us next time."

"You two knock it off. It's okay. It happened, and Stan you and I don't for a minute believe that Tom would do that." She turned to look directly at Tom. "Tom, you're a logical man and certainly you must understand how Stan and I feel. This would appear to most people to be a hoax, but given the circumstances I believe it's not. Now, although we have no sensible explanation for this one--it'll go in our books as a cold-casefile, until we run across it again, or you call us with some additional information."

"I understand, Claire. Sorry, Stan, no hard feelings."

Stan held out his hand to shake Tom's. "No, sorry on my part, as well. It just blows my mind. That's all. The more we see the more confused I become about what we consider normal. I question normal every day, you just now found one abnormal reflection in a supposed normal world, but I see that reflection all the time."

Tom said, "It must be hard. I couldn't do it. Thanks for your help in this and I hope I won't need to call on you again, but I had nowhere else to go. I need to get back to work, please show yourselves out." Tom walked across the land, up a hill and into his house, leaving her and Stan stood there feeling dumbfounded.

"Claire let's go. I remember seeing a book on demons, maybe there's something about portal openings."

"I know you're upset, but Tom really isn't the type that has time to play games, he couldn't even stay and chat for a while. I need to look into this more, and did you like the idea I'm calling some of our cases cold- case files? I got that idea after my visit with the detective. It's only Tuesday and already crazy happenings are begging us to start the weekend tomorrow and move past the rest of the week."

"You're right, he's not the type and that freaks me out more. Why don't we start the weekend tomorrow?" He looked serious, but grinned as he put his arm in hers and they started up the hill together. "I need to get a grip. I think I'm losing it."

"No, you're not losing it."

"I'll let you do the paperwork on this one, I don't want to think about it."

"Of course." She was concerned, but agreeable.

Traffic was lighter as they drove to Nudges and Nuances.

Chapter 5

Facts, or fiction

"Good morning, Morgan," said Claire.

Their new paranormal agent had gotten there earlier than they did and already had the shop opened and coffee made.

"Morning," said Morgan, handing them a cup of warm coffee.

"Smells like cinnamon," said Stan.

"That's because I added just a pinch. Do you like it?"

He pushed his nose into the cup and sniffed deeply. "As a matter of fact, I do."

"Yummy, so do I. I'm glad I hired you." She gave Morgan a quick hug and hung up her coat.

"What happened to you two this morning? Long night?"

"No, stopped by the now stocked pond of disappearing fish." Stan threw his body on a chair, kicked up his legs, closed his eyes and sipped.

"What? You've got to be kidding me?" Morgan's voice had gone up an octave.

"No, he's not joking. We had a call that the fish were back. We went to the pond to check for ourselves and it was teeming with fish. Tom, our client, is so far from the attention-seeking type that we have no choice but to believe him and will document the case. And for an answer right now we have none. You're welcome to investigate the incident within the books of our library and feel free to go outside of that, currently a cold-case file."

"Wow, that's fascinating but also insane. Loving them listed as cold case files, nice touch." Morgan looked at Stan with all her teeth beaming, and said, "That had to be hard for you Stan? You must've gone wild." She giggled and knuckled his arm before she sat in one of the overstuffed chairs and kicked her shoes off, pulling her legs under her.

"I didn't go wild."

"You did, Stan. You went a little wild," said Claire, as she pointed a finger his way. "He was wild before we got there."

He grinned. "Okay, so I was a wild man this morning. Did we get any messages, Morgan?"

"No, nothing new. I can help document, or check out information on the rose book, or the demon dogs."

"Great idea, Morgan. You can help me document Connie's roses first and then help Stan with the dogs. Since you were there for both. I'll document the fish." She sat down and held the coffee in both hands bringing warmth. "Afterwards, you and I can check on the rose book, I'm so excited over that one. Also, see if you can find out any information about the guy who retired to a cave. Stan, do you want to hit the demon books?"

"That's fine. Since I get the dog trees, I think I'll check out portals and hell hounds. Those red eyes were demonic. I'm going next door wanna see if Charlie has any books I could borrow."

He stood up with his coat still on, finished his coffee, set down the cup, and left without another word.

She needed to speak with Morgan without Stan being a part of the conversation, and now was the perfect opportunity.

"Morgan are you okay after last night's encounter. I was concerned. Stan was clearly stressed this morning, and I believe he's faced worse. He didn't think you'd show up again. I was really worried about his mental state. He wouldn't tell me anything. What happened out there?"

"To be honest, Claire, there were times last night when I wanted to bolt and never come back here again, but I knew Stan needed me. Last night I almost fell apart, but we were stronger together, somehow, I understood that. So, thanks for asking, and it was a fear like I've never felt in my life. I couldn't sleep all night, and if I didn't have Derry holding my hand, well, I honestly don't know what I would've done. Stan became lost inside the portal, as the dogs pulled at his psyche. I had to dig him out."

Claire nodded and gave Morgan a hug. "Oh, my God. No wonder he didn't want to talk about it. He would see that as a weakness towards me, that one day he may not be able to help me when I needed him most. I'm sorry I wasn't there. Marvin was so out there; I wasn't sure what to expect. I should've come with you both, it won't happen again. You're new to this and I need to be more sensitive. Sometimes I forget. We've just seen so much, I forget that even I feel the fear of the paranormal more than I care to admit, and now I have to support the newbies."

Morgan grinned. "I am a newbie. I get it but having you there would have been good. Stan was almost pulled into the tree. It looked like the beast called him. I had to ground him more than once. I'm glad I was there, if I wasn't I don't know what would've happened to him."

"He won't talk about it with me. He's too tough and doesn't want to disappoint me. I think after Gabe he believes he needs to look after me, to save me, keep me safe."

Morgan said, "Of course, he feels the need to protect you from harm. He needs to open up, but he'll only do that with you, I'm sure. I did speak with Derry about last night when I got home. He was waiting by the door. He's worried for me, I for him, but we know this needs to be done." Her eyes drifted far away and looked back at her before speaking. "The lady in grey could come back for Derry and I won't let her get him. I need to learn in these situations to strengthen myself for him. I want to know everything I can." Morgan's misty eyes looked deeply into hers. "Give me everything, hold nothing back, and teach me."

Claire nodded and placed her hand on Morgan's knee. "You got it, and I understand. I'll start with Detective Brandon, who stopped by last night and informed me he's been assigned to the cold-case division. He has a file that could be related to the paranormal and was wondering if we'd look and see if we spotted something out of the ordinary. You and Derry want to join us around five on Saturday night? Dinner will be served." She smiled at Morgan.

"Sounds good to me, I'll see if Derry's available. He's been working late. If he can't make it, I'll still come over, but I'll come after dinner. I'd want to make the children's dinner and eat with them."

"Let me know about dinner if you and Derry are both coming. Brandon thinks it'll be several days of work. It might get late before we're done. Cheyenne or my mom could babysit for the evening if you want them to. You can check if one of them would take them for the night and part of Sunday if you've nothing planned. Just a heads up--it's entirely up to both of you how long you stay."

"Sure. The kids love both of those ladies."

She and Morgan got busy and made quick work of the rose file, and then they all started on the other two cases, after Stan returned.

She watched Morgan and Stan as they began putting together the dog files. Morgan was strong and if I were the woman in grey I wouldn't mess with her. However, she was still concerned that the incident of the dogs freaked out a seasoned veteran like Stan, which meant Morgan could be holding fear behind a locked door. That could prove harmful and dangerous. She'd talk to her later. Stan's frown was a sign of all business and Morgan's smile was a woman on a mission. What a pair.

She labeled the fish disappearing under 'Vanishing'. It was an easy write, but also a difficult one. Easy because there wasn't much to tell, and difficult because there wasn't much to tell. She chuckled and got the attention of Stan. Their eyes caught, and she saw his concern. She smiled at him to let him know she was okay. Stan believed she might go over the edge, so he kept a close eye on her actions. She was doing fine but worried for him. He was more stressed than she'd ever known the laid-back Stan to be. She missed the old Stan.

She finished the document and filed it. At least they had something on file if it ever happened again, not that it would, sometimes things only happened once. A flux in the dimensional code. Well, the three cases they had were almost closed, except for the demon dogs. She had an idea.

"Hey, you two, I'm done with this file. I thought I'd look up Marvin's address and see who's lived there in the past. See if the house had a history of strange incidents or crazy residents."

Stan looked up. "I think that's a great idea. I'll check into the backgrounds of the residents and see if I can turn over demon worshipers that liked to scratch the belly of demon dogs. Morgan can check on spells relating directly to portals."

"Sure, I can do that," said Morgan.

The wind whistled outside and picked up momentum. The energy of its power reminded Claire of the two paintings of Gabe's that they'd covered and locked away in a black chest in the back of the shop. She'd put a sealing spell on the lock hoping to keep out curious intruders that might come across it. Only the three of them went to the back, but she wasn't taking any chances. But who would protect her from looking?

Maureen was a powerful entity, and Claire wasn't sure that her evil was gone for good. The fact that the painting had changed and showed Derry in it kept her on edge. She didn't understand the paranormal world enough to know if Maureen needed to recharge her power to utilize it again on a physical playing field, or if she couldn't get back. Time would tell. There were some days when she wanted to look at the paintings to see if they'd changed. It might prove beneficial if they knew in advance what to expect, but the consequences on Derry could mean his death and she couldn't take that chance. Sometimes her curiosity overwhelmed her sensibilities, and she would argue with herself whether to look at the paintings or not look at the paintings. Stan had no idea she was fighting her own internal battle. If he knew she was wanting to check out those paintings he'd have them moved to a vault where she wouldn't have access to them or worse, burn them.

She'd spent over an hour looking up information on strange events over the years at the dog address and got nowhere. She threw up her arms and said, "Okay, does anyone want to go to the hall of records with me? The internet is useless sometimes. I can't access enough information on who lived at Marvin's address over the years. I may have to research back before they built a house on that property. That's what I'm betting on."

"I'll go with you, Claire," said Stan.

"I'm happy to watch the shop and continue my research."

Claire smiled. "Great, just lock up before you go. Oh, one more thing, Morgan, if you could do me a favor and call Marvin to see if he has any idea who lived there before him, or if he has any history on the house or neighborhood?"

"Glad to."

Stan grabbed their coats and helped her on with hers. The wind almost pulled the door from his hands as they stepped out into the blustery day.

She checked her cell and no messages. "Well, nothing new, Stan. I suppose that gives us more time on your dogs."

"Oh, thanks, Claire, now they're my dogs? Truthfully, I've never been so scared. Not even Maureen could do that to me. I was close to having my soul sucked out of my brain, leaving me a zombie. Look at that idiot. Get a license. Boy, a little snow, and the lunatics come out."

"And the saga continues... some people feel safer driving slower, it's all okay." She smiled. "That's a heck of a way to describe your experience with the demon dogs. Did it come that close for you? I'm going with you when you go back."

"Yeah, it came that close. If you need more detail, how's this, I felt my soul moving to my head pushing on my skull to escape." He glanced at her, and his sad eyes pierced her heart. "I almost lost it and compromised Morgan." His hand lifted to his eyes and wiped his face. "She saved me."

"I'm sorry, Stan." She didn't know what else to say. His words were raw and honest. Her soul ached to see him hurting.

"Yeah, me too."

Neither of them spoke during the rest of their ride.

It took a while to get to the records building, the silence made it seem longer. Luckily, it wasn't busy.

The information at the records department was quite helpful, and by the time they'd finished, the building was closing.

"Are you ready to go, Stan? I think they're kicking us out. I printed off copies of what might be some interesting material."

"Yeah, I'm ready." He looked at the printed copies. "Really, you paid for that?" He took the papers from her hand, until she buttoned her coat. "Do you want to stop at that new restaurant on the way home and try it out?"

"We could do that." The wind smacked her face the moment they left the building. "The wind hasn't given up," Claire said, and tightened her grip on the papers.

Stan watched her struggle with them while he opened her car door. "Why didn't you take a picture of that information with your phone?"

She looked at him, stuck out her tongue and tilted her head to one side. "Really, Stan? Too aggravating and too small. I want to read it all at once, not enlarged. If I'm holding it, then it feels like I did something today."

He laughed as they both got into the car and shook his head. "You need to come into this century. You could've uploaded it to your computer for a larger picture."

"Really? We're going there? Paper, I got papers in my hands if the electricity goes out, Stan...I got paper."

He held up his hands and started the car. "Okay, I get the message. You got paper."

"Yes, thank you."

"Poor trees," he said.

"Stan. Did you ever hear of recycling?"

"Okay, but we know how that is really working out. Luckily for me the restaurant isn't far. It's a new organic vegan cuisine. Might be nice."

"I'm sure it will be," she said.

The blowing snow made it harder and harder to see, but they finally arrived.

Stan managed to get a parking place in front of the building. Claire put the papers in her bag, and they headed inside.

A young man took them to a quiet corner of the modern and clean-line room. The lighting was romantic, and each table had a small chandelier hanging over it. Stan sat down and looked around the place like he was investigating the building for criminals or ghosts. She couldn't be sure which one. Then he mentioned an old topic.

"Has that spirit from the airport been back?"

"Not for the past year. I'm not sure why, maybe because I'm involved with the paranormal every day. Can we talk about something else please unless you're feeling a presence?"

"No. Look at this menu. I think I'm going to try the curried coconut quinoa with greens and roasted cauliflower. This could be heaven."

"I know what you mean. I'm going for the butternut squash linguine and fried sage. Sounds interesting."

The young man came back and took their orders but quickly returned with glasses and poured them some red wine.

Claire took that opportunity to get the papers out of her bag and placed them on the table.

"Look at this, Stan. There was a group of occultists that lived in the area by Marvin's house, and their specialty...got a guess?"

He shrugged his shoulders. "I suppose I could venture a guess, but I'd rather guess how soon my food will be placed in front of me. More importantly do you think you could guess how long it'll take for me to devour it?"

She ignored his wicked sense of humor. "Black magic." If she wanted a reaction, she was barking up the wrong tree. The play on words made her laugh.

"What's so funny?"

She shook her head. "Nothing, Stan, nothing at all, just my own inner thoughts at supposed humor."

He frowned. "Okay, be that way then. When you do that, I think you're taking a mental jab at me, but don't let my hurt feelings stop you." He put his hands into fists and rubbed his eyes, sticking his lip out so far, she could have sat on it.

She laughed harder "Sorry little boy, but seriously, this was in the early 1900's. It seems they were arrested for some of their actions. I won't go into detail. I'm sure that caused what's happening now."

He took a sip of wine and sat back. "If that's true, Claire, why would the dogs appear now and not sooner?"

"Magic is strange that way, isn't it? It's possible the dogs were there but had never found the portal. A portal can sit forever, unused, until something or someone comes upon it. I don't think the mages created the dogs, just the portal, and someone forgot to close it."

"True. What if we can't close it, Claire?"

She frowned. "There is that."

The waiter came back with their food and placed it in front of them.

"Nice," said Stan.

The last time she saw him that pleased was when they just got back from New Zealand and her mother brought over the brownies.

"By the way, Fran returned my call about moving into the house. She thought it was a promising idea, but didn't want to give up her freedom. She's going to check on renting her place on a six-month lease, as a furnished home. In case it doesn't work out for her or us."

Stan nodded.

The atmosphere was relaxed, and the dinner was delicious. It reminded her of the old days when her, Gabe, and Stan would just chat and hang out with only their jobs and a few local ghosts as gossip. Things had changed dramatically. Although she loved her new job, and life with Stan was quite entertaining, but her heart ached for Gabe. She glanced at the engagement ring that she always wore on the ring finger on her right hand. If she'd been home alone in her room the tears would have flowed down her cheeks wetting her pillowcase, but Stan always sensed her melancholy and made her laugh.

"Claire, there's a live performance next weekend at the Grand Round and I thought we should go, it's your favorite, Fiddler on the Roof."

The Grand Round was dinner and theatre in the round. The theatrical group that performed there was incredibly talented. She hadn't been there in years.

"That's a great idea. We could use a nice distraction. Should I call and get tickets?"

"Already done, 7 o'clock next Saturday night. I'll pick you up at 5- we can do dinner. Oh, I forgot we live together." He smiled up at her as he took the last bite of food on his plate and leaned back, chewing slowly making sure he enjoyed the last morsel to its fullest.

Stan always enjoyed the simpler things in life. She felt quite full but decided to be Stan and took one last bite, chewed slowly, sat back, and concentrated on the flavor and smell. Decidedly, it was an enriching experience, one she would learn to do more often.

The young man came back to check on them bringing a to-go-box, he smiled knowingly at her, and she nodded, prompting him to put her food in the container for her to take home.

Stan looked deep into her eyes, and she fell into his dark orbs that danced in mischief. "What if something happens to you on the way home and you miss your chance to enjoy the food in that container. Incredibly sad, Claire, incredibly sad."

He was a challenge. "Okay, Stan I have something for you. Suppose I eat the whole thing giving myself a sick stomach and I throw up in your car all the way home. You wouldn't be happy, and I might never eat at this restaurant again just because I became ill after eating here. It's not always something to do with the food, sometimes it's the experience that keeps you away from a place." She paused, looked at the waiter, and took the box. "Sorry, you won't need to do that. Stan if you just wait while I finish this we can be on our way. I'll keep the box for vomit on the way home."

"You've made your point. Not to worry, anyway, if something happens to you, I get to finish your meal."

"Ha, ha, very funny." He did think of crazy things to make her laugh, but he would finish it without a second thought of her dead body.

They tipped the waiter and left the nice experience behind.

Her cell phone had been off while they were eating, so she checked for messages when they got back in the car.

"Well, Stan, Morgan called and no surprise there; Marvin had no idea who owned his land or what happened on his property, at least we have a handle on it. Thank goodness for the paper trail."

He chuckled, but then his face turned serious. "Claire, you mentioned the portal might've been opened in 1900, but what if the occultists never opened it and stumbled across it, and the portal exists as part of discrepancy in space and time? What if that's how ghosts get here? It's possible they happened across the portal. What if it isn't a portal created by personal magic, but a discrepancy in space then how can we close it?"

She felt a chill. "Thanks."

"By the way I went for a walk last night, you know, just checking out the neighborhood and you'll be glad to know I didn't find any portals in trees."

She shook her head. "What would I do without you?"

***

On Saturday morning they decided to close the shop, if anyone wanted them, they could call and leave a message.

She was excited for Charlie and hoped the book signing with Elanor Daybring would bring him more business, at least for the afternoon.

The signing started at 3pm so she had to juggle dinner by moving it to 6pm instead of 4:30. She'd hoped to have dinner earlier since the detective said there was a lot to go over, but she didn't want to miss attending Charlie's event.

She sat on the porch overlooking the dark grey ocean as crashing waves beat the stones and promised more beach-side property in the future. Indigo clouds formed a line across a never-ending horizon, intimidating and purposeful. It was breathtaking and captivated her heart. She sighed and returned to flipping through her books on portals that she'd picked up from the shop yesterday. Stan was finally up; she heard him as he moved about in the kitchen.

The door opened and he stood on the patio in his jams, heavy robe and with a knit hat pulled down over his ears. "Morning," he said. "I thought you'd be here."

"Morning yourself, and that would explain your hat, you came prepared."

Coffee in hand he brushed the snow from the lounger, sat across from her and smiled. "Yes, I came prepared, can't be without my hat it's my life. At least it's not snowing," he said.

He hadn't questioned the fact she was sitting in the cold February morning on the snowy deck, drinking coffee and reading books. She'd done that quite often on her days off and he'd started joining her about two weeks earlier.

"Stan, you'll be glad to know I heard from Morgan this morning, and they're sending the kids to moms for the night, and she's excited about having the children around. So, her and Derry will both join us this evening."

"It'll be good to see Derry, haven't seen him in a while, and the evening should prove to be interesting."

"I'm glad you think so. I wasn't sure whether you were happy about it or not."

"Oh, come on Claire. I love helping and jumping into a mysterious project. I just have a reputation to uphold, like being a grouchy colleague."

She wasn't sure what made her smile, what he said or the way his brows came together before they raised high on his forehead and turned him into a comedian waiting for applause. However, his words struck a chord within her heart. She wondered if Stan enjoyed being known for owning a rather testy disposition when most of the time he was a teddy bear. She knew it was a front to protect his heart.

"I know, and you're doing a good job of upholding that reputation." She smiled at the gentle eyes of her long-time friend.

He nodded and produced a sideways grin. "I see you're looking at books on portals. Any interesting thoughts about it?"

"Not yet."

"Okay then. What happened to your rose book? Give up on that, or did you already discover its hidden secrets."

"There's too much to uncover, just from the cover itself. The combination of the cross and the pentagram holds many symbolisms. The pentagram represents fire, water, air, and earth, which in turn relate to the zodiac signs. The cross and the rose together emphasize the dawn of eternal life. Because the representation of it is defined by individual emphasis on society, religion, universal guides, life, and death, it can become complicated. The Order of the Golden Rose brought more into the original meaning by adding their own touch to what already existed. I've only begun to tap into its powerful symbolic indications."

"A deep mystery of ancient wisdom combined into one book. That has me intrigued," said Stan.

"And it should, my friend. There's power in words and symbols. Sometimes people don't respect and understand them."

"Oh, I agree. Understanding them creates respect. I think that applies in most things. Don't you?"

"Yep." Claire said.

"I've never asked you why you sit out here in the cold. So why do you sit out here in the cold?"

She chuckled. "You're finally asking me then?"

"Of course, I am. What do you think I meant when I asked why you sit out here in the cold?"

"Very funny, Stan. I enjoy the brisk air on my face; it helps me think and tends to make me think harder."

Stan frowned. "Makes sense. You think harder, so you can arrive at a conclusion quicker, so you can hurry inside to warm up. Job done faster. I like it."

Her robust laugh made Stan's eyes light up. It penetrated her soul and the cold no longer touched her." Yes, I guess that's a sound theory. Now, you answer a question for me. Why do you join me out in the cold?"

"I was trying to discover your reasoning behind it, and really couldn't find one, but now that you've enlightened me, I approve. So, if it's not a blizzard tomorrow I think I'll bring out something I've been studying to see if it works for me in the same way."

"What have you been studying, if you don't mind me asking?"

"Not at all. How to understand the O'Leary women. The books are a complete set of captivating encyclopedias from the days of yore."

She laughed, and Stan chuckled.

"Oh, foolish man. You'll never be able to unleash the power of understanding women in a book, much less the O'Leary clan."

His smile faded, and his head lifted slightly, as his eyes drifted off into the distance. "I was afraid of that."

He stood up abruptly and went in. She sat in the cold alone.

Hum, wonder what brought that on? His sensitivity had her baffled.

"Look at the time, I have to get ready for the book signing at Charlie's shop." It annoyed her when she spoke to herself out loud. It was becoming a bad habit and a frequent one.

The wind blew wildly, and the sun went behind some dark clouds as she headed inside.

***

Claire had parked three blocks away from Charlie's bookstore and hurried towards the warmth of the store's sanctuary. She wasn't able to convince Stan to join her, and Cheyenne had other plans, so she came alone.

The store was crammed full of potential clients as she fought her way through the door. She was happy to see such a great turn out, Charlie deserved it.

A petite woman brushed past her weaving in and out of people trying to get to the front where the author was signing books. It reminded her of the small cars that weaved in and out of larger ones on the expressways in the same careless fashion. As if on cue an elderly woman had her book signed by Eleanor Daybring, turned, and moved aside for the next customer and in doing so accidentally knocked the small, pushy woman into a gentleman waiting in line.

"Watch where you're going. You could've hurt someone," the small woman yelled embarrassing the woman who accidentally ran into her royal highness.

"It wasn't her fault. You should be at the end of the line," said the tall man into whom she was pushed.

The aggressive woman ignored him and squeezed in line between two women just as small as her. Both of whom looked annoyed but were too polite to say anything. Maybe, they knew it'd be a waste of energy.

Sharon was a young college student who worked for Charlie part time and could be seen at the register ringing up book after signed book. Her red curls bounced as she looked up, smiled, waved, and pointed Claire towards the back of the store. Mouthing a thank you and giving Sharon a thumbs up, Claire headed back to locate Charlie.

She spotted him piling books up by the author as he directed clients towards the check out and answered questions.

The author was pleasant looking, and Claire knew she was fifty, after reading about her and her book before joining them at Charlie's store. Eleanor Daybring had long brown hair pulled back into a braid with a slightly greying temple. Her dark eyes danced as she spoke with customers waiting for her to sign their book. The brown tweed jacket went well with her complexion, and her smile was genuine and not forced.

Charlie could date her, attractive and accomplished. Her thoughts of match making were disrupted when she felt a nudge against her back. The nudge was something she knew as a disruption in the continuum. Something not in the current playing field of vision. It was that familiar experience that alerted her to a wrongness.

Charlie looked up and smiled. His smile slowly faded into a scrunched forehead and his eyes questioned her expression. Her head darted back and forth around the shop searching for the disturbance. It wasn't always an entity, sometimes it was just a feeling that something could be off with an individual, but that could mean a number of things; an illness, worried, upset, or possessed. Possessed was the worst-case scenario.

She couldn't tell where it came from and looked back in Charlie's direction and waved. He motioned her towards him and placed more books on the table by the author.

The nudge left as quickly as it had arrived. Gone. Nothing left to think about. It was possible someone brushed her and left the store. She hadn't noticed any off energy moving about on its own or surrounding a patron.

She hugged Charlie. "Claire are you okay?"

"Yeah, I thought I felt something off, that's all."

"Oh, one of your feelings, or nudges?" He looked around his shop.

"Yes, it's gone now. I'm so glad you have a great turn out, Charlie."

"So am I. Eleanor, this is Claire who owns the store next to mine. Claire-Eleanor."

Both women smiled and simultaneously said how nice it was to meet the other.

The author immediately returned her attention to signing books and chatting with fans.

"Claire, I'm so glad you've come. In a half hour Eleanor is going to give a chat in the back of the store, you might like that."

"Sure, but in the meantime can I help do anything?"

"Thanks. Could you go to the back and maybe assist Don who is making sure there are enough chairs, and everything is set up."

"Okay, but who's Don?"

"Don's Eleanor's agent."

Giving Charlie two thumbs up, she said, "I'm good to go." She quickly turned and headed to the back of the bookstore where she located a man in his late thirties that could only be Don the agent.

He wore a dark blue sweater and blue jeans that fit nicely. He placed chairs around the room and when he bent over it exposed a small balding spot on top of his head that would otherwise go unnoticed because of his thick dark brown waves.

"Hello Don, I'm Claire. Charlie sent me back here to see if I can help with anything." She walked up to him and shook his hand.

"Thanks Claire. You could fill that pitcher on the front table with cold water. Waters in the back. Eleanor likes cold water, but doesn't use ice, it makes too much of a clunking noise when she's speaking."

"Okay." She grabbed the pitcher by the podium and went to the back of the store and filled it with water from the refrigerator.

The agent already had posters up around the podium and more books on the table in case fans hadn't had a chance to buy the book yet.

She placed the pitcher with a glass on the table next to the podium, grabbed some chairs, and helped set up the rest of them. She never realized what a large backroom Charlie had at his store, he could easily get 50 chairs in or more. Maybe she should author a book about her experiences with the paranormal. It might prove interesting, although the publicity was unwanted. She and Stan had enough jobs that dealt with freaky occurrences.

She needed a cup of coffee and thought Eleanor might enjoy some as well. "Hey, Don. Charlie has a coffee pot in the back do you think Eleanor might want some?"

"She might like that. Thanks."

"Don't mention it. It's my pleasure."

Eleanor might need a-pick-me-up before the chat. She just had enough time to stay for the chat unless it lasted too long. Her guests were scheduled within the next two hours. Hopefully, Stan would've started dinner. She had better text him. '*Stan, sorry going to be a little late. Did you start dinner?*'

After a few minutes he replied. '*Of course, enjoy. Cul.*'

Stan's message lifted her spirits as the aroma of the coffee slowly changed the essence of the room. She poured a cup; it was good. She heard the door open, and Charlie, Eleanor, and Don's enthusiastic voices reached her, but she couldn't make out what they were saying. Claire peeked out into the chat room. "Eleanor your water is on the table, but would you like a cup of coffee?"

"Oh, I would love one. Black please."

Claire brought her a cup and sat it down next to the water. Eleanor finished speaking with Don and immediately grabbed it with her long-manicured fingers that were covered in a kaleidoscope of unique rings. The author sat and sipped her coffee slowly.

"That's nice, Claire. Thanks, I needed it."

"You're welcome. I thought I would stay for the chat, although I must be honest-I've never read your book."

Eleanor stood up and took her hands. "Claire, I've heard so much about you from Charlie, I would be honored if you stayed. Not everyone here today has read my new book, in fact it just hit the market and I'm doing a three-week tour promoting it. I've acquired fans from my previous books." Eleanor winked at Charlie who stood next to them. "This could be a horrible book and not what they expected, but their purchase today is based on my past accomplishments. Let's hope I stand up to their expectations."

Claire liked this straightforward woman who clearly had a fetish for rings. "I'm sure you will."

"It can be exhausting, but well worth it. I meet fascinating people. I've known Charlie for years." The author now took Charlie's hands in hers and smiled. "He's one of my most admired distant friends. I live on a beach in Bar Harbor, Maine. I absolutely love it and have begged Charlie for years to visit, but he's a busy man."

Charlie smiled at her, followed by a slight pinkish color on his cheeks.

Claire said, "Yes, he's a busy man."

Eleanor turned towards her and said, "Forgive me, Claire, I must get my mind ready for the introduction to my new book. I have another signing this evening and tomorrow morning but would love to have dinner with you and Charlie Sunday night, my treat. Could that be arranged?"

Claire thought about her dinner guests for the evening and decided she wouldn't allow herself to get tangled into Brandon's investigation, and wouldn't allow it to run into Sunday night. She had a bad habit of permitting projects to overtake her life. She might enjoy an evening away from the supernatural. "I would love that. What time is good for both of you."

Eleanor said, "It would have to be 7. Charlie does that work for you?"

"I'm there."

Claire enjoyed Elanor's discussion on her book but left quickly afterwards.

Chapter 6

Saturday evening with Detective Brandon Stone.

Stan enjoyed cooking for his friends and was impressed with himself after he made such a great tasting meal. He carried glasses and a bottle of wine into the great room where they'd all retired after dinner, but he couldn't remove the stupid grin plastered to his face, a grin that said, 'I'm awesome.' He poured the wine and glanced at Claire, she smiled at him, and her eyes reflected his ego shining like a new penny, of course he had an ego and of course she thought he was amusing. Stan knew her and that grin meant she would hit him with a sarcastic remark.

He deflected it before she had a chance, and he said, "So detective, what's with the tie? Is it one of those mood ties for murder? You know the closer you get to solving the crime the blood slowly goes away?" He couldn't resist the urge to taunt the detective, and was a little worried about the looks of it; who would wear that kind of tie, anyway?

The black tie was not unusual for Brandon, but the grey skull with a knife embedded in it that dripped tiny droplets of blood on the front of it was quite the sight.

Stone laughed off Stan's comments. "You're quite the funny man. I know it's a little morbid, but it was a gift from one of my partners. Dead bodies have always been attracted to me and popped up with regularity when Fred and I were on the beat. Then there was my obsessive behavior in trying to figure out why someone would kill. I couldn't let it go. Still can't." His voice conveyed a liking for murder. "It wasn't surprising when I moved to homicide. A box of clues was candy... laced with cyanide," said the detective with eyes that exploded with fireworks and lit his face with a sinister edge.

The detective's dark personality gave Stan the chills. There was something about his behavior that wasn't quite right, something Claire had noticed when Brandon showed up at their store and approached her about helping him with these cases. She had mentioned it to him and voiced her concern about the detective's behavior, and because of her previous comments the skull on the detective's tie was like a fluorescent beacon that persuaded Stan's eyes to drown in the blood that dripped into blackness. If he wanted to be a part of these possible paranormal killings and work with Claire, he needed to concentrate on what was being said and remove his thoughts from the provocative image that screamed murderer.

"So, detective, give us your thoughts," Claire said.

Derry piped in. "Yes, detective please do."

Stone went to the front door where he'd left three boxes when he'd arrived for dinner and now placed the drab brown containers on the table in front of them. They were all marked cold-case files, but each had a name written across the top in bold black marker. One had the name Sally Dodger, another Margaret Trend, and the last one was marked Incident 305, Dates: 1825-1835 box 1 of 30.

Stan cringed and felt a twinge of sadness. The names made it personal and brought the women to life.

Derry was eager and pulled the Margaret Trend box towards him and said, "I thought I'd leave the 1 of 30 box for those of you that do this type of thing for a living. Too much for my head to understand." He removed the lid and broke the seal that locked away the mystery of the life and death of Margaret Trend.

The air cooled and Stan heard the sound of leaves as they swirled around on the floor until they lifted the spirit out of the box and freed her soul to share the secrets that took her life prematurely. It was a tomb, of sorts, paper was all that bound the victim to life. Claire bit her bottom lip and shuddered, Stan knew she felt the spirit, he did too.

Morgan frowned and felt her neck and glanced at Claire with a little fear in her eyes. "It feels as though there are fingers wrapped tightly around my neck. Derry, we could wait for the detective to lead us forward."

Stan reached for his neck. "Morgan, are you feeling a tingling on the neck hairs? I got it too. When Derry lifted that lid, a door opened into the depths of a crypt, freeing the long-forgotten person, that was Margaret."

"Yes, I feel it, not just Margaret, but other souls left inside the box for too long. I can feel their restlessness and hear their lonely whispers escape into the air begging to be heard, and a hand around their throats...choking.," said Morgan.

Claire pulled out a file and scratched her ear. "Very intuitive. Some deaths we may never know about. It's hard to conclude how many souls might've gone unnoticed and missed getting on the list of possible victims because they were runaways or had no family. I think serial killers rarely remember all their kills, although some sick ones remember it all."

Morgan shivered and hugged herself as her hands moved up and down her arms to warm her body. "So, you think I might be feeling other spirits that were killed by the same killer, with no name, or a box of their own?"

"Yes, it's possible." Claire looked into her eyes when she answered her, and Stan knew that look. She was checking to see if Morgan was ok.

Stan said, "You hear the stories of how they keep trophies from their kills, like jewelry, fingernails, eyes, whatever they associate with, but at the end of the day, I agree with Claire, they lose track of the number of kills. The number of objects you find after they're captured might be a clue, but some serial killers work up to taking different things from their victims as reminders. Sometimes they might've gotten interrupted during the murder and were not able to retrieve a particular item that had meaning to the killer." He lifted his hands in one fluid motion and knocked over his wine glass.

The red liquid dripped off the table onto the floor and brought his attention back to the detective's tie.

Claire rose. "I'll get it." She left the room and returned with a cleaner and a rag.

"We may not always find their trophies, but other killers take nothing except life. They also may keep things in various locations, making it more difficult. We can only identify with the number of bodies we uncover. It's a sick game of hide and seek, and sometimes they forget where they hid the prize, if you get my drift. Too much time can pass, and the kills run together, and the only thing that matters is the next victim to satisfy their needs," said the detective as his hand played with his tie.

Derry carefully removed information about 31-year-old Margaret Trend and placed it on the table. "Well, no gory pictures in this one, thank goodness. Just a photo of Margaret with her age and the year she went missing written on the back. Wow, 1925. I can't believe they kept this information all this time."

Stan stared at the worn out black and white photo of Margaret's angelic face with mysterious, sad eyes, no smile, and her face unveiled a delicate jawbone with her dark hair hanging freely to her shoulders. No one ever smiled in those old photos, he wondered why.

Brandon stood up and peered over his shoulder. "The detective that worked her case was only 20 when it happened and assisted the head detective, but he wouldn't give up and by the time he was ready to retire my dad joined the force and continued his battle to find the body and the murderer. Here I am decades later still obsessed with Margaret. She went missing and they never found her body. Her boyfriend died in a fire that burnt down the cabin he'd built, never knowing what happened to his fiancé, at least that's what he told the police a day before the fire. Back then they didn't have DNA kits and all the modern tools of our time, so I'm hoping for luck. Sorry to disappoint Derry, but no gory pictures when no bodies are found."

"Right," said Derry as he pulled more things out of the box and nodded his head.

Claire watched Derry as he played with the pictures. Her head tilted slightly, and her eyes shifted to the detective. "Brandon, your interest in this case is because you believe all these cases are related, right? What makes you think so? That's a huge time frame."

"Yes, it's huge." The detective's eyebrows creased, and he looked into her eyes. "That's why I brought you in. I think it's related to the paranormal somehow. I don't know why, but something doesn't make sense. All those women disappearing doesn't make sense." His head moved side to side and took in the room. Then he took a deep breath. "All disappeared in the same area and in groups, I don't mean they disappeared together, but one right after another. As for my interest in this case I had no choice, cold files are assigned to me, but I remembered my dad being obsessed with this one, so I started there. I'm working on other cases that I believe are normal murders and not related to the paranormal."

Stan leaned towards the frustrated detective and inquired. "What about a father and son team, they could carry the killings out for decades? Don't you think that's possible?"

"You're right, but again, no clues left and not even a body. That's a lot of women with no bodies being found and no information leading in one good direction, I just feel they're paranormal, call it a detective's gut feeling. How can we find no clues to a killer that for unknown, but obvious reasons stayed within a certain radius without fear of being caught? I'm beginning to question what I'm seeing, maybe I've missed important information. What scares me the most is what if the killings go back further than our records show?"

The detective stood up, walked slowly to the window, and stopped. He stood in silence with his back to the room, his shoulders slumped forward, not in his usual self-confident stature. He never moved, moments passed, and the tick of the clock sounded louder than normal in the stillness of the room.

A rainy day at a graveyard materialized around them and invited the spirits out of their boxes. They came with their sadness and begged everyone who listened to release them from purgatory.

The clock ticked and penetrated Stan's ears, moved into his head, too close, too loud, it felt like a time bomb was duct taped to his body and ready to explode, bringing the whole building down with him. He would be at the center of the fireworks. He shook his head to clear the image and glanced over at Claire; she watched the detective.

Her blank expression and distant eyes haunted him, he shuddered. What was going on in that mind of hers that made her unavailable? He dared not speak because her moment could be ruined and if she sensed something paranormal, she'd be madder than hell at him for the interruption. The temperature plummeted and something touched his arm as it brushed past him, but circled back around and hovered nearby.

No, he didn't want to feel anything weird, that's why Claire was there. He had enough of his own encounters with the unknown, and her paranormal intuitions that spilled over into his space were too much. The entity touched his mind, her thoughts overloaded with grief. He choked out his next words. "Get the hell away from me, whatever you are, I'm not interested."

His words didn't send the entity running to Claire. The cold stung him in the middle of his chest and for one second, he was frozen. His insides were located in the arctic and he stood on a snowy bank naked and felt driven to jump into the icy waters of a lake. He wore a polar bear hat, and he belonged to one of those 'crazy' fraternities of insane brotherhoods that enjoyed freezing their butts off in the middle of winter.

Claire quickly shifted her gaze to him, she felt it. He was vulnerable.

The clock struck the hour with its relentless bongs, the sound hurt his head, and he thought his ears oozed a red blood-like goo.

The bomb strapped to his chest went off and he wondered why he was still alive. What happened to all the flying debris, body parts turned to mush, shattered glass and people that screamed and ran around frantically? How could he still have thoughts? It meant one thing; his imagination was out of control.

He heard a word, just one tiny word that made absolutely no sense whatsoever: bull. He wasn't sure he'd heard it, but the spirit repeated the word over and over. She refused to relent, and her weapon of choice was a sledgehammer that drove the word deep into his brain. It would remain there forever.

He understood and wanted her to stop. Claire couldn't help him, he tried to communicate, but his voice went on vacation and left him sitting there trapped and speechless with a ghost.

Tears were running from his eyes, and he wasn't sure if it was normal tear liquid, or something freaky like blood, or maybe a creepy greasy substance, but judging by the way Claire opened her eyes and raised her brows so high her bangs levitated–it was creepy grease.

The air in the room warmed and his voice returned from its trip and for obvious reasons was bored without him, after all he gave it a voice, and the voice was lost without, 'The Stan.'

"Bull. Just stop I hear you already. Bull, bull, bull." Humiliation. His voice escaped his mouth on its own and screamed with a girly scream that clearly wasn't his choice of reactions to the whole ghost thing, but nevertheless, it got heads turned and made him the center of the discussion for possibly the next day or two, could he be any happier?

Claire's calmness hadn't done a great job of being connected with her facial expression, and the detective turned with a stone-dead stare. Stan considered it a little weird that the two of them hadn't reacted, however, Morgan and Derry got up and flew over to his side, the ever-faithful players in this game of supernatural madness.

"Are you alright, Stan?" The concerned look on Morgan's face was consoling.

"Ah, sorry, never saw that coming," Stan grinned sheepishly.

Claire hadn't settled for his cheesy comeback, not one bit. She hunkered down, and gritted her teeth as she pulled in all the reserves she could muster up to get him to confess to what happened.

"Stan?" It was only his name, but a paragraph was attached that she didn't need to say, and he knew it.

He said the only thing he could and, of course, that wouldn't sound insane. "Bull."

Morgan and Derry both sat down at the same time and grabbed the nearest chairs, while the detective headed back to his seat, but Claire cocked her head to the left then the right, twisted her lips in some sort of demonic possession pose, narrowed her eyes, and sighed.

"Bull? That's all you keep saying. Is that directed at me, or does it actually mean something tangible?"

He cleared his cowardly voice, as all eyes were now on him and awaited the outcome. "I don't know if it means anything at all." Usually he was a talker, not shy, and clearly not afraid to speak up, but he couldn't explain his lack of communicational skills in that moment, maybe it had something to do with his voice when it evacuated him in his time of need, whatever, it wasn't important.

"What? Then why would you say it? Just, bull, that really makes a lot of sense." Claire's face turned pink, and she appeared to be having trouble breathing, because she grabbed at her throat, like she wanted to cut her head off, that paired with her bulged out eyes, should've told him to run, but he couldn't, she would've found him anyway.

"Sorry Claire, I think the wrong voice must've come back." She seemed more annoyed with him than normal.

She shook her head, as if denying she even knew him.

Derry laughed and Claire glared at him and cut his laughter off mid-stream.

"Never mind." He gulped and gathered his adulthood. "I felt something." Claire's stare passed annoyed and moved to kill mode. He looked away and continued. "I suppose it was a ghost, a woman, she froze me. Why are you so mad anyway, Claire? It is the paranormal. Are you forgetting the dog trees?"

Stan thought maybe if he shared he was frozen, and reminded her about the dogs Claire might've shown a little compassion, it didn't work.

"She froze you?" Morgan spoke up and looked just as confused as Claire, but not as mad.

"Yes, that's what I said. She kept repeating one word, *bull*. Don't ask me, I don't know what it means, all I know is it was beaten into my brain with a sledgehammer."

Claire looked at the detective. "Brandon, does that mean anything to you?"

That cut into his heart. Why was she angry with him? He'd faced demons before, but not dead people wanting help. It was different, the emotions were different.

The detective frowned. "No, nothing, but it's interesting, maybe if we look through the boxes, we might come across something like that. A bull wasn't looked for in the past, but anything different is better than nothing."

Derry never took his eyes off Stan, like he was waiting for 'The Stan' to go mad. But Derry listened to the conversation at the same time because he nodded and patted Stan on the back and said, "Well, that's something then. Okay, bull it is."

He still felt a little strange, like leftover residue moved around in his head from the ghostly plasma, or whatever energy gave them their power of expression. He placed his fingertips on his face and was surprised to find no black substance. "Claire, we need to do something about that clock."

Claire's head spun around like a rehearsal for the exorcist. "Okay Stan, you had an encounter. I'm not sure what you're talking about, so I'm just going to ignore that comment about the clock for now, and hope you get your mojo back soon. You're going to need that magical bag filled with charm to charm me for the next month."

He wasn't sure why he said that about the clock, except that it drove him mad when the ghost was communicating with him. He knew Claire was sensitive about it because it had meant so much to Gabe. He missed Gabe and remembered the day Gabe shared the good memories with him, explaining that as a child the sound of the chimes comforted and warmed his good friend's heart.

"Sorry." What else could he say, he was a jerk, and no leftover ghost juice should cause him to react that way, it wasn't cool.

"That's fine." She spoke under her breath and avoided eye contact.

Okay, that hurt, but not as much as Derry still staring at him, he squirmed. "Derry, I'm not going mad, or changing into anything, so you can quit with the eyes, you're not at an observation deck, and I'm not a plane about to take off. I got some extra information, so let's get back to work."

Derry nodded. "Sure pal, just concerned, that's all."

"Yeah, I'm good, nothing to see here." His voice was playful as he tried to keep up with his fun nature, but inside he was scared as hell. He needed a distraction and grabbed a different box but wondered if the boxes should be left alone. He didn't want to be in the middle of another ghostly encounter.

Claire took away any worries he had when she said, "Stan why don't you and Derry go through that box you have and see if you find any mention of a bull, or if anything else pops out at you, just holler." She looked at him and grinned. "Just try not to use that girly scream of yours, it's scary."

"I was offended by it too. I'll be sure to contain it."

Claire was hot and cold these days. He needed to speak with her about how confused she made him feel.

Derry patted him on the back. "I'll be thankful if you do, Claire's right, scared the life out of me." Derry sat next to him and waited for him to get the box opened. "Well, let's see what's inside box number two."

Stan had chosen Sally Dodger because there was no way he wanted to open the tomb from 1825, there'd be no photos, but possible notes that he didn't want to get involved with, so he lifted the coffin of Sally Dodger and waited for something to come out.

The only thing that came out was a whoosh of breath that had the smell of a strong disinfectant that reminded him of a hospital room.

A chilly apprehension entered his lungs and summoned a slight breeze. He heard his heart; it was in what he called his freaked-out mode. Relax. He allowed a forced smile. He was good.

The air swirled around the box and picked up a picture of two women with their arms around each other, one was in a nurse's uniform, the other one in jeans and a tee-shirt, behind them was a happy birthday banner and a cake was clearly seen off to the side on top of a counter. The picture floated in front of him, and paused for him to view it before it glided to the table, like a parachute holding the two women in safety, it landed gently. His neck hairs tickled, and his eyes felt like balloons as they bulged from their sockets at the black bull in the picture that sat on a shelf behind the girls' heads.

"Okay, that floating picture...a little weird," said Derry.

"There it is." His voice almost went girly again. "The bull is in the picture, and it has a red glow around it. What's with the bull anyway, and is it the same bull that Margaret was referring to? It's just an object and doesn't look expensive."

Derry leaned over and looked at the picture. "Well, I don't see a red glow around the bull, but I do see the nurse and smell the antiseptic from the box. I'm assuming the nurse is Sally, our victim?"

"Yes." He turned over the picture. "It appears it was Sally's surprise thirtieth birthday party; she was a beautiful lady; the other one is her sister Meg. I got the impression from their faces they were close. This is a sad business," said Stan.

Sally looked tall and her elegantly chiseled face was wrinkled from her smile. Stan hadn't known why, but he saw her as a piano player with those long fingers that held onto her sister with love and joy.

She had a nice face, with sparkling eyes that held a gentleness, and quality of being a caregiver. Her blonde hair held a shine from the sun coming in through a window. He probably would've gotten along with Sally Dodger.

Claire and Brandon's interest in the picture piqued when they heard the talk of the bull and moved behind the boys to get a better look.

Claire's eyebrows raised as Stan handed her the picture. "You're right Stan, what's with the bull? What would it have to do with a serial killer? It looks plain enough, but I suppose we should look it up and see if we find anything. I'll ask Nana as well, she's kicked down a lot of doors in her time, she might know something we don't."

"Yes, she has, and if anyone knows anything about bulls it would be her. Maybe the statue has nothing to do with the murders, but possibly a name of someone, or a nickname. I'll check into that in the surrounding area." He grabbed the picture as Claire passed it back to him and looked again. "Hum, it does look quite old, but maybe the reddish glow is making it look older for some reason."

"What glow?"

Stan glared at her; his voice quivered. "What? You're joking, right? You don't see the red glow around the bull, either? I thought you might because of your gift."

"No." Claire took the picture again and looked at it. "No, I don't Stan."

Derry said, "I didn't either, I don't know what he's talking about." Claire handed the picture to Derry. "I still don't see it." Derry scratched his chin. "It did fly through the air. That was scary. Did you see that, Claire?"

Morgan leaned over him to get a better look. "Nope, don't see a glow."

"Detective?"

"No, Claire, no glow."

Claire nodded. "I did see it lift out of the box and move to Stan."

Okay, he officially considered himself an alien, not because he saw the glow, but because the four of them looked at him like he was one, it had to be a dead giveaway. He looked back at the picture trying not to see the obvious glow that separated him from those in front of him, some of whom had an extensive background in the paranormal, not to mention those that suffered at the hands of demons, and paranormal paraphernalia on a daily basis since childhood. He closed his eyes and looked again. It was still there, that diabolic torture of having seen things others didn't. The luminosity seemed to grow larger the more he stared at it. He wasn't going to hell, he was in hell, and his friends knew it.

"Alright, would you guys quit looking at me like I have horns protruding from my skull. I know you might think it's far-fetched when I was the one who heard the spirit and that the bull is glowing only for me, but keep in mind, I had no idea we'd find a picture of a bull. Really, how many bull statues are there?"

Claire studied his face, and her blank eyes masked her thoughts. "I've known Stan for a long time, and one thing he isn't-is a liar, although it's possible he's worked something into his mind to help the investigation, but I don't think so." Claire released him from her sea green eyes that trapped the soulless inside the waves of ocean drowning them forever, and instead glanced at the detective. "Stan's been tapping into his own spiritual connections with the other world, and the more he works in this field the better he gets at seeing things others can't, it's part of the game."

Claire stood up and walked to the kitchen without saying another word. Large chunks of ice clanked against a glass and the noise of the cubes settled down before splashes of water hit them, causing the ice to shift slightly. Her hair was pulled up behind her and Stan watched her pentagram earrings move back and forth as she walked back into the room sipping on a glass of water. All eyes were on her slow movements. She'd fallen back onto the chair she'd left moments before and pulled her legs under her body. She released a deep and slightly spooky breath that blew the chill left from her icy drink into the air. It lingered around her face before her lips closed and allowed the explosion of cold to be trapped inside her mouth.

The detective spoke first and broke the ice. "Claire, you're saying that this must be true, about the bull, and I have to agree. It's something that had never been considered, who would've guessed that a simple object could be important to a murder investigation. It's not like it had the blood of the victim on it. I suggest we check out any other photos that might have the same bull statue in it. In the meantime, someone should research any historical events relating to a bull, or anything that would consider the bull a significant paranormal object."

The detective's head bobbed up and down while he spoke, a gesture that reassured him that the bull mattered, and it could be the connection needed to bring this mystery to a conclusion. The man knew his job, but Stan still watched Brandon's tie, the knife appeared to move in and out of the skull and hypnotized him to believe whatever the detective wanted him to believe. A slight tingle rose in the frontal lobe of his brain, an answer to the killings was working to the surface...

"Stan, what's wrong?"

Gone. So close, something was so close, it might've been an answer, but he didn't discover the answer before his thoughts were interrupted.

"Nothing Claire, nothing at all. I guess we should check out the other boxes."

Morgan sat next to Derry on the couch and put her hand on his knee. "I'll help check out Sally's box with Derry, looking for bulls or anything important."

"Okay, but Stan because you seem to be in tune with the paranormal or ghosts involved in this case, I want you with me focusing on the giant tomb, the boxes of many. Your perception could prove valuable in this case. I'm not sure why, but for some reason these spirits are reaching out to you and wanting you to help them." She winked his way. "Maybe they felt your gentle nature, or they're attracted to the big bear of a guy, but it's possible they just want to freak you out."

"I'm sure it's the latter, but okay, I'll help you. I'm not sure why the glow would be red, do you have any ideas on that?"

"No, not really, but it may be demonic, that's all I can think of right now," said Claire.

Stan grabbed the first box. "I don't think I'm going to like this. It feels dangerous and toxic, that's the only way I can describe what we're doing. These women have been missing for a long time, if their spirits are still here, it's possible they're angry, it's as though the world forgot about them, and if it's paranormal with a twist of the demonic that's just not a plus on our side."

Claire's face looked worried, not for the job, but for him, and he knew why. She couldn't lose two guys to the paranormal. She looked fragile for just a moment and that scared him in ways he couldn't explain, but then her tough as nails chin pushed out, she sipped her water, looked at him and smiled. He couldn't believe she just smiled. She never said a word, but opened the box Stan had pulled in front of him seconds before...he held his breath.

Chapter 7

Boston, Massachusetts, November 1981

Mabel looked up at the autumn sunset and inhaled the colors, she was sure it had a taste. A whipped dessert, creamy with strawberries and blueberries, like sorbet, but not as sweet. She licked her lips enjoying the subtle flavors of the night.

Amy stood next to her, took her hand, laughed, shook her head in disagreement, and said, "Well, I know what you're thinking and you're wrong, you know, about the taste. Wrong time of year my love. Look over there at the dark orange, pumpkin pie, I can almost taste it, and over there, homemade blackberry jam to put on toast for our morning breakfast with a nice hot cup of coffee, delish."

Mabel nodded. "I have to say your taste is really nice, but what do you think of the house?" She was anxious to know if Amy was pleased with the house, it had taken her two months to find one that was reasonably priced, secluded, and just the right style for the two of them.

Amy Day's joyful personality had been one of the main things that had attracted Mabel to the short and playful soul who only wanted to find the light in the world. It was tough on them, the life they chose, but Mabel wouldn't have any harmful rays bouncing off of Amy's happiness, so they packed it up, moved out of the suburban life, and went for seclusion.

Amy threw her arms out and turned a circle, then pinched her arm in disbelieve. "I love the cabin, but how did you get such a good price?" Before she could answer, Amy turned, pointed to a beautiful hill that faced the morning sun, and did a dance. "Oh, Mabel we could have a vegetable garden over there and flowers drinking in the sunrise, this is heaven."

She stared at Amy's tattoos across each finger spelling out soul on her right hand and love on the left, with a tiny heart tattoo on each thumb. Amy had gotten the tattoos before she met Mabel, because she believed their was a perfect love for one soul. When she would meet hers, Amy intended to put their initials on the thumb hearts. She had an appointment next week to have theirs added. Mabel wasn't sure if heaven could be found on earth, but with Amy, anything was possible.

"I agree, Amy, it's perfect for a garden. There's a lake just through the woods on the west side of the property. Maybe we could explore that in the morning, but let's get some dinner and blow up the bed, the truck won't be here until tomorrow afternoon."

"I suppose you're right, as always. I am hungry, what do we have to eat?"

"Before your flight arrived, I made some spaghetti and put it on ice in the cooler, you want to grab it out of the trunk while I unlock the door? Nothing like cold spaghetti."

Amy said, "That's true, wanna unlock it?"

She pressed the trunk button on the key chain she still held in her hands. The gentle clunk of the trunk being released was a reassuring sound, they were home.

Mabel had only seen the house during the day; it seemed more foreboding in the darkening evening sky. She walked up the steps and onto the front porch as a heaviness crept into her legs, and goosebumps quickly tiptoed across her skin to vanish behind hair follicles, like they were afraid of being noticed. The pressure on her feet lifted and she searched for Amy and found her still entranced with the notion of a garden. The key was a tight fit and just when she thought it wouldn't go in, it did. She peered through the glass window on the door and for a moment she thought someone moved quickly out of sight.

She looked around the porch and saw a stick to carry into the house, just in case someone had gotten in, she knew she would use it. The piece of wood held firmly in her hands was security leverage, at least in her mind. She didn't want to frighten Amy. It'd been a long week, and her eyes were tired. She might be a little paranoid, after putting up with some of the things they had to endure as partners.

Amy jumped onto the porch carrying the cooler. "Mabel, what are you doing with that stick? Shephard, druid, or wizard?"

The darkness seemed to run away from the gentle and childlike nature of amazing Amy. It was possible her own soul had been darkened these days, and if it weren't for Amy she'd be in a secluded prison inside her own heart and void of happiness.

She couldn't help but laugh. "None of the aforementioned, just a stick I found on the porch. I thought I saw something move in the cabin."

"Do you mean something or someone? Probably just shadows of the evening enjoying our new home."

"You're probably right, but just in case."

Amy nodded and followed Mabel inside.

The home was gloomy and chilly; she wondered if she'd gotten it so cheap because it was haunted. It felt haunted. She wasn't afraid of spirits, she'd seen some over the years, mostly of dead relatives, but she believed they couldn't harm her, and it was just an apparition.

She walked through the house with her stick checking for intruders, none were found. She believed in hauntings and was certain she'd seen a figure, but before she could think about it further Amy jumped in front of her and giggled.

"Okay, what are you still doing with that stick, Mabel, looking for a bogeyman? You retired your wizard, 'Stark' years ago. Our last D&D adventure, I recall." Amy's eyes were shining. "I love this place, it has potential. It may be a little drab at the moment, but we can add color. I think it's fabulous." Amy danced back into the front room. "We can use the extra bedroom as an office."

Mabel smiled. "I do miss D&D. The bogeyman? That's funny." She held out her hands like a zombie and walked towards Amy. "Don't you believe in the bogeyman little girl?" The topic of spirits was one they'd never discussed together, but she would leave that for their dinner conversation.

Amy laughed and backed away. "Yes, but not zombies. You're a nut."

She put down her arms and giggled. "Yes, I am." She looked around the house. "I think utilizing the extra room for something other than sleeping is a great idea. You should use it as a place to make your jewelry. I think I'll put my desk in the front room by the large window it's a better place for writing."

Amy bounced towards her with black curls that flew about her dark glowing skin, threw her arms around her, and grinned showing off her perfectly large white teeth. Amy was only five feet tall and had to jump into the air to reach her six-foot-tall lean frame.

"Thanks so much, Mabel. You're awesome. Tomorrow I'm going to draw up a plan for that room, and possibly come up with a name for it. A fun name that catches the attention of everyone. I might call on your brother, Tom, to see if he has any thoughts on names. He's good at that."

Amy had no siblings and loved chatting with her kindhearted brother. Mabel nodded her head and pictured her desk at the window and was already getting ideas on how to make her own space more creative. Her publisher was on her to finish her latest children's book. She'd completed the story but was behind in the artwork, and the window offered perfect lighting.

It was a little chilly, so she checked the thermostat. It was November and 30 degrees outside, with snow expected later in the evening. She was upset that the temperature wasn't checked and adjusted before they were scheduled to arrive.

"Sorry, Amy the temp wasn't on, but I've pushed it to 72 just to get it warmer in here a little faster. The realtor should've checked it."

The ever-positive Amy said, "At least they left us wood for the fireplace, I'll get it started, maybe we might heat up that cold spaghetti after all."

"I'm on it. Once I get it started, I'll bring in our overnight bags and the bed." She leaned the stick against the log cabin wall and picked up the cooler Amy left by the door.

The kitchen was open to the living quarters, but Mabel thought they needed an island, there wasn't enough counter space. She placed the red cooler on the available countertop and looked inside to find; a pan, utensils, two plates, spaghetti, and a now chilled bottle of champagne just for a little celebration of their new home. Mabel smiled; she'd placed it there earlier. She almost always remembered everything. Amy, however, lived in the moment and would persevere anything that came her way. That ability was enhanced by her rough childhood, her mother was African American, and her Scottish father died when she was only five, and people could be unkind.

She'd had a different childhood. Her parents were born in America and came from humble ancestors. Her dad had more Italian than anything else in him, but both her parents were mutts. That's what her mom called them, and she would laugh and say they had no room to be prejudice because they had a little of everyone in them. She had a wonderful childhood with her loving parents and her only sibling, Tom. Her parents lived in Florida now, and her brother was a city dweller deep in the heart of Boston.

At least the water ran clean, and the hot water tank worked fine. She rinsed out a pan, spooned the spaghetti into it, and placed it on the stove. She carefully adjusted the heat on the electric stove because she was used to a gas one, but knew electric stoves heated quickly.

"Okay, that's done, I'm off to collect our bags, how's the fire coming?"

Amy looked up and grinned. "Almost ready to start. You know the more I see your new bob haircut against your sculpted cheekbones the more I love it." Amy lit a match and threw it on her wooden masterpiece, a stack of wood that resembled a pyramid, the dried-out wood caught immediately making the room more friendly.

This was their second place together. They'd shared an apartment in Manhattan, but the atmosphere was too crowded for them, quite costly, and no fireplace. The warm glow of a fireplace was something they'd wanted.

"See you in a minute." Mabel closed the door behind her and left the warming cabin.

She walked down the steps of the front porch and stood by the car. It felt chillier than it had moments ago when they'd first arrived. She paused and lifted her face to the wind and allowed the fresh feeling to compliment the exuberance of her emotions that the night brought. To the west of the property, the dark looming forest became the main attraction and blocked the colors of the vibrant sky, only hints of pumpkin pie peeked through small windows, momentarily left open by the arms of giant trees. The wind moved the branches about, before dropping the shades and leaving the land in darkness. Something about the blanket of black bothered her more than usual.

A noise to the east startled her into quickly twisting around. Instead of fear she stared at the hill and forgot the blackness that engulfed the woods, and for one fleeting moment, she felt alive with thoughts of vegetables and flowers that Amy would eventually rejoice in planting. They were vegetarians, so growing vegetables of their own to eat and then can for the winter would be great for their lifestyle.

A branch broke in the woods to her right and returned her attention to the chilly night, something was there. She grabbed the blow-up bed and a suitcase, shut the trunk of her car, locked it, and walked slowly up the five steps that led to the cabin's railed front porch but turned one more time facing the black woods.

A healing breath of joy lifted the trees out of the suppressed darkness of the night. It was a song of love that awakened them. Bluish-white lights brought the trees to life as they frolicked about their trunks and branches that made the orbs appear as stewards of the trees. That's something she'd never seen in her 30 years. She put the bags down and leaned on the rail and tried to decipher what they were, they were too large for fireflies, and the color was wrong. Their dance captivated her, as they moved independently of each other with gentle, graceful flirtations of tiny ballerinas. Their wild movement added an energetic appeal of erratic jazz to their dance and made it hard to see exactly what the glowing orbs were, or what they were made of...without warning the dancers disappeared like a black curtain closed on the show, and there would be no applause.

Mabel froze, something evil drove them away. She felt the life drained from the orbs, as their lights were snuffed out. The smell of fear lingered on the breeze of something unnatural. A whiff of cold rotten breath blew across her face plastering her short red hair to her skull. The overnight bags were slammed against the door; the bed lifted from the bag and blew up in front of her. The window formed three sheets of ice one right after another covering the entire glass. Sweat dripped down her face and neck and soaked her shirt. The sharpness of a skater's blade dug deep into the icy window, the noise was so loud she held her ears and watched helplessly as a word was etched across the glass...leave.

A loud crack broke the window into tiny shards that turned to sparkling powder and scattered everywhere, the night was hushed, and her head felt as though she were underwater.

She hadn't hesitated and reached down and picked up their bags and bolted inside. She slammed the door and locked it. Her heart pounded as she tried to catch her breath. Her hands shook and she dropped the luggage to the floor.

Amy stood by the stove, stirred the spaghetti, and piled it on the plates.

Confused by Amy's reaction, or rather her non-reaction, Mabel said, "Aimmm...ee."

"Yeah?" Amy turned around quickly. Her dark curls covered her rosy cheekbones and small pug nose. "You ready to eat? It does smell good; you make great spaghetti."

"Didn't you hear the window break?"

Amy frowned, and her nose wrinkled. "No. What window? Where's our bed?"

Mabel swiftly turned and faced the door. No broken window. She shook her head and moved her hands down the unfractured windowpane. She backed up slowly and found the stone hearth to slide her weakened body down onto, but there was little comfort on the cold surface of the grey slabs, as the newly started fire hadn't had time to warm the flagstone.

"Mabel are you alright?" Amy rushed to her side with dinner in tow and placed the plates on the floor in front of them. "What's this?" Amy picked up a small statue of a black bull that looked out of place on the hearth, she moved it to the mantel and then sat down next to her and took her hand. "That's an odd item, I don't remember seeing it earlier, do you?"

She glanced at the bull, but her eyes revisited the door. No broken glass. The presence of Amy's energy spiraled around her own.

She shivered. The room spun like a roller coaster ride gone bad. Her stomach lifted into her throat, and her fragile body almost broke...She gasped, and her breath left her lungs in spurts.

A whisper brushed against her ear.

"Get out."

The deep, harsh, and rasping voice transported her to a dark closet inside her own mind. She clutched her chest and searched for Amy's eyes; a familiar kindness to bring her back from hell.

The warm hand of Amy took hers, but the fear in her partner's voice rose like an ocean wave that crashed against a rocky cliffside forcing her against a jagged edge piercing her soul. "Mabel, what's happened to your hair?"

Her wound bled into the darkness of her thoughts, and she cowered in the corner of the closet inside her mind. Her eyes were now locked on the bull that sat on the mantel. She twisted her hair around her fingers and smiled.

The closet door closed and left her in dark silence.

Chapter 8

Current–First Thursday after the dinner party with Detective Stone.

The flurries had her transfixed as they quickly accumulated on the trees and gave them a blanket of white, a godlike shelter against the bitter cold.

"Claire, where are you? Hello? Earth to Claire."

Her head fell back and forced her eyes to the ceiling. The laughter that followed seeped into each corner of the quiet room. "Stan, that's so cliché, but it works. The words 'earth to Claire' fit my life like a glove."

"Like a glove? Now who's being cliché?"

He quickly found words to throw at her and attacked without batting an eye. He was a poltergeist in a man's physical form using words instead of objects. She nodded in agreement.

She took off her boots, touched her cold feet, put on a pair of thick socks, threw her legs on an ottoman, and relaxed with a sigh. He sat across from her, sipped on his coffee, and reviewed pages from a crime scene; the boxes on the table in front of him were part of the detective's serial killer investigation. Stan was always strong, she counted on it, but his eyes had been saddened by the loss of his best friend. There were times she noticed dampness in the corners of his eyes, though tears never escaped. Fear replaced sensitivity.

They needed lighter moments. "Hum, remarkably interesting, I didn't know men could do two things at once: drinking coffee and reading. You're ticking all the boxes for the perfect male specimen. I think I might be a little turned on." She could play the poltergeist game just as well as he.

His brow creased, and he looked up. "How cool am I then?" He threw the papers he held in his hand on top of one of the boxes and shook his head. "I can't believe what goes on in the world. How can this be remotely related to the paranormal when it seems too much like an ugly and violent crime, inhumane, yet very human behavior? If that made sense, we both should be committed to a fine institution and be put under a microscope for observation."

"I agree, it's hard to believe what heinous crimes are committed in the world, but we have to balance that with the beauty. There are more wonderful things than bad, but sometimes we forget to breathe it in. Humans are morbid beasts, otherwise, the beauty would override the horrendous. Maybe, some things we can't let go of because they are too unbelievable to be real, and in our weak minds we try to find a place in there to explain it in order to dismiss it."

Stan looked into her eyes, held them for a moment, and nodded, but quietly changed the subject. "The detective called and said he'd be by later today to see what we've discovered. He certainly has a world of hope after only four days. I still feel a little freaked out after that dinner party. I was glad nothing came out of the last box you opened."

"So am I. I'm glad we ended the dinner early. Looking through things slowly and in our comfort zone away from the house makes me feel better. I can't help but feel the lady in grey is waiting for us to mess up." They never spoke her name. She leaned over and touched his knee. "The detective does expect something out of us. Morgan should be here soon to give us a hand. She took Margaret Trend home to do some research, hopefully she was successful and discovered something useful."

Stan threw his hands up in the air and waved them around in front of his face, pushed his hair back from his forehead and rubbed the top of his head. "I'm frustrated Claire. What do we consider useful? I'm glad she took that one, I think it was one that spooked me out. No, I didn't like that at all."

"I'm sorry Stan, frustration is part of this business. A spirit tried to communicate with you, that's all. They found you a sensitive person they could relate to and that's complimentary."

She had been too hard on him at the dinner party. He had faced worse things in the past, so his actions surprised her and made her concerned. Maybe having priests around helped him, or maybe he had expired his spirit allowance before going mad. Her own actions were brought on by the fact she hadn't looked at the paintings. It made her edgy and needed to speak with Stan about it before their partnership, or worse, their friendship was ruined. He would be mad.

"Okay, maybe you can let the spirits know that I'm a terrible communicator, sometimes I can't even hear well, you know, not a good listener. I'm a one-way communicator, listen to myself only, and almost always deliver a sarcastic remark, just tell them that."

She sucked in her lips and released them, which created a loud popping sound. "Really, Stan? That's ridiculous. Do you hear yourself?"

He pointed a finger at her and made a growling sound. "You need to focus on your communication skills, you asked me if I heard myself, of course I did, I just told you I only listen to me."

She sipped her coffee, shook her head, and closed her eyes. "You're impossible, Stan Bradley. I think we can agree that you can't manage spirits communicating through you, to you, or with you."

"Yep. That about sums it up."

"Well, what the hell are you doing in this business then?"

He closed his eyes. "I don't know."

She wanted to indulge him, neither of them asked for this life and her heart ached for him, but time refused to slow down for unnecessary hand holding. She changed the subject least they spend the entire day in contemplation. "Did you find anything important in those boxes that caught your attention, other than the obvious unforgiving behavior of the spirit world that defiled you?"

His eyes twinkled and his brows lifted as he grabbed his coffee and guzzled it down before he spoke. "Funny Claire. I found something interesting, but it goes back to 1895. That time frame still doesn't jive with me."

"Why not? We know it could be paranormal events, so the dates won't matter, unless you think he's fishing in a dead pond?" Claire enjoyed her touch of humor.

His skin wrinkled in the corners of his eyes when his smile deepened. "I like that term, and yes, he could be fishing. Ten women disappeared from 1895 through 1910, with no clues to their whereabouts, but that's not the half of it. The women were between the ages of 21 and 38 with no prior history of depression, all were happy with their lives, none of them married, but three of them were single with small children. They wouldn't get up and leave their kids. Being single with kids was unusual for that time frame, maybe that's why he snuffed them?"

"Nice, Stan. Snuffed them? Really?" She knew he used words to add humor, but it was more for him than anyone listening.

"Well, you know what I mean. He might've had a problem with single mothers."

"Interesting, were they connected in any other way to each other?"

"Not that I could find. There was a man named Todd Griffin. He was a carpenter who'd purchased over 30 acres from a lady named Rose Cliff in 1917. It appeared that the previous house had burnt down. He spent the next seven years cleaning up the land and building a home during the evening hours after he worked all day at his regular job. He never lived on the property during that time frame, but in town close to his fiancé. He moved in in 1924, but in 1925 the cabin caught fire, and he died in the home he built. His girlfriend disappeared two days prior to the fire. I don't think that was a coincidence. Also, weird, two fires on the same property."

"It makes sense if the killings stopped for a while after his death. Weird, and the bull? Was it in any pictures? Do you know if the police interviewed him about her death?"

"Oh, sure they wanted to, but they only had one conversation with him at his home, and then again when he was in the hospital. A relative was worried about her and informed the police. The police found him bleeding and messed up. He told them his girlfriend was taken by several men that had beaten him up and had left him for dead. He had no idea who they were or what they wanted. He assumed they'd taken his girlfriend. Then his house burnt down with him in it before they could interview him again. His girlfriend had told family members before she disappeared that Todd had changed during the year he'd moved into their house. Family members told police he was more mysterious, violent, withdrawn, and began talking out loud, like he was carrying on a conversation with someone not there. Spooky."

"Well, no wonder our friend thinks it's related to the paranormal." She leaned forward and placed her cup on the table and chewed on her bottom lip.

Stan grimaced. "It's possible. But I find it hard to believe that all those women could be the focus of the paranormal, but more likely a killer gone wild. It's not the first time a killer has taken a vacation and started up years later, you know chipping away at the brick wall inside his head until he crashes through after a trigger puts a massive sledgehammer in his hands."

She stared at him and shook her head. "Well, Stan, I didn't know there was a wall that held back a serial killer?" She nodded and continued staring at him. "A vacation? Nice terminology, except it doesn't work, he died in the fire." She shifted her eyes to the gentle snowfall.

"Oh, yeah, there is a wall, sorry you didn't know that. Thanks, I thought vacation seemed appropriate. Maybe he didn't die in the fire. Another interesting fact his girlfriend told her family he found a black bull on the property and was obsessed with it, but no pics."

Her head jerked around to face him. She couldn't control her shaky voice. "A black bull. What's with the bull? I forgot to speak to Nana about it. Knowing that makes it incredibly significant."

Stan frowned. "I think you might be right. It was something attached to the property, you know, an item no one wanted, or it could be that the spirit of Margaret whispered bull to me because it was the killer's weapon. They still could've been murdered by a serial killer, and nothing paranormal."

"That might be possible, but we need to find out what the meaning of the bull is about."

Stan said, "Sure, then we should keep looking for that type of reference and sitting the bull in its own file. There might be other paranormal experiences with a bull, and we'll want it noted."

The door opened and Morgan strolled in and brought with her a little frosty air that raced around the room and landed on the two warmest spots there. Claire shivered.

Morgan asked, "What should have its own file?"

Stan said, "Good morning, Morgan. Claire and I either have big mouths or you hear like a bat. We found a reference to the bull back in the 1800's. I'm thinking there's possibly some connection to that and the murders, or it's just a meaningless statue that made its rounds; never got sold or trashed, as far as I can tell."

"Oh, wow that's interesting." Morgan removed her coat and set a box on the table marked Margret Trend. "And for the record, Stan, bat-like hearing." His brows rose with a tilt of his head. She hadn't resisted an evil grin. "Don't look so surprised it runs in our family."

Claire laughed and Stan stood, picked Morgan up, swung her around, kissed her on the cheek, and stood her on the floor.

"Morgan, you'll be more careful next time. He does that thing when you make his day," said Claire.

Morgan's eyes bloomed as large as sunflowers which forced her brows high on her forehead, and she cocked her head in Claire's direction. "Good to know, a little late on the information, but good to know."

"I'm getting more coffee. Stan, Morgan?"

"Sure."

"I'm coming with you, a little uncomfortable," said Morgan, nodding towards Stan.

Stan blew her a kiss. "You love me, and you know it. I'm one of those teddy-bears you stuff with what you want inside." He held his arms up in the air with his palms pushed towards the ceiling and showed all his teeth in a scary grin. "That's all that's inside of me, what you put there!"

"Ignore him, Morgan, he's been like that all morning."

She giggled. "He is like one of those bears."

They entered the office area and Claire poured out three coffees. "Really, Morgan, can't think about it now."

"Are you okay?"

"I've just got a lot on my mind. I think we've gotten nowhere, and Stone will be here to see what we've accomplished. Not much."

Morgan's eyes softened. "Is that all? You appear distracted."

She turned and took Morgan's hands. "You have to promise not to tell Stan."

"Sure, maybe."

"I know it's crazy, but I can't stop thinking about the painting that Gabe did, the one that's locked in the grey chest in the office." Her eyes shifted back and forth.

"Oh, Claire. Leave it alone. We could burn it."

"No. It was the last thing Gabe did, and it has messages in the work. I want to see if it's changed." Her voice was louder than she'd intended.

"Claire, you need to forget about it. It's cursed with that evil woman's energy. You could bring her back." A tear fell down her cheek. "You're scaring me. She could take the man I love. I know I promised not to tell Stan, but this is crazy. No, it's madness."

The tension dropped from her face and released her skin back into a smooth soft position. She hadn't thought of Morgan's feelings in the matter. She was being selfish.

"Yes, of course you're right. I don't know why I said that. I'm so sorry."

Morgan's voice lowered to a whisper. "Claire, she might be putting thoughts into your head to get you to look at the paintings. Did you think of that?"

Claire mumbled. "No."

"Are you sure you can manage the thought of it? We could take the chest to a location you aren't aware of just to protect all of us."

She smiled. "Yes, don't worry. I'm one tough cookie." *Oh god another cliché.*

They both carried the coffees back into the main room. Stan's eyes scanned over one of the files in his hand, he shook his head, looked up and took the drink from her outstretched hand.

"The only thing I found that makes all the murders remotely connected is that damn bull."

She sat down. "Well, then let's start there."

Morgan sighed and sat on a chair next to her with distant eyes and said, "That's too bad, but if it's all we have as a connection I can scan one of those pictures with the bull and see what we pull up. I'll see if Stone will let me go back to his office and we can use the police computer, fingers crossed."

Claire smiled and asked, "Good idea. Have we heard anything more from the engaging Marvin Schwartz?"

Stan lifted his head, and his eyes danced back to life. "No, but I managed to find a woman who will seal the rift. She and I were going over there tomorrow. I'll call Marvin today and let him know, but we don't really need him there."

Claire flinched. "Were you going to tell us?"

"Yes. I just did. I'm sorry this ghost communication bothers me; I'll try to get myself together. One of my clients suggested her, so I met her for coffee. She's impressive. I just hope it works. She goes by the name Madame Frost. Morgan, tomorrow night at 4pm, can I pick you up then? She's meeting us at Marvin's house."

"I wondered if you were going to ask. Of course."

Claire said, "I'm glad that's moving forward, and you found someone. Hope it works. Any news on new customers?" She looked down at one of the boxes. "By the way, I'm coming with you, thanks for asking."

"No, there was nothing new in VM or messenger," said Morgan.

Claire glanced at Stan. He hadn't spoken and his face wasn't lit up like a neon sign. She knew he didn't want her to go, because she might see him in a weakened state if something happened. "Stan, you're staring."

"I'm just surprised that you want to come with us. Okay. Sure."

"That's settled." She smiled at him, and he nodded his head, slowly releasing a slight grin.

Luckily, the doorbell brought their attention somewhere else. It was Charlie.

"Hey, good morning, guys. Can't stay but I wanted to drop off this book. After you told me what happened the other night, I thought this might help. It's a book on portals, found in the back under some old encyclopedias."

Stan asked. "Really, Charlie? Who has encyclopedias anymore?"

"I do, of course, where else would I hide these books? Claire it was great having dinner with you Sunday night. Eleanor had an enjoyable time."

Claire smiled. "Me too. Did she leave town for her next book signing?"

"Yes, unfortunately." A shadow crossed his face, his head dropped momentarily, then he lifted it and smiled.

"You like her, then? I see the sadness in your face when you mentioned she left. You should date her."

"Yes, I do like her, Claire. I might think about it."

"Well, thanks for the book," said Stan.

"No problem. Glad I found it. Gotta run. Have a good one." Charlie turned, waved over his shoulder and was quickly out the door.

Claire was always glad to see Charlie and sad when he left. His energy was magical and brought joy to a room. She wished he would've stayed for a while.

"What's the book?" Claire was anxious to know what interesting book he found lurking in the back of his bookstore; they were usually the best ones.

"Well, black cover, tick, scary fog, tick, and the portal looks like it's in the woods, tick; drum roll please...*How to Close a Portal*, tick and tick."

Both girls laughed.

Morgan stood, sipped her coffee, and slapped Stan on his shoulder. "Sounds like it's got the high-five ratings."

"Looks like it." The Tubular Bells music brought a twist of Stan's head in Claire's direction; he stared at her with his creepy carved pumpkin eyes. "'Wait, they're playing my song,' said the lady in grey, 'come out and play'." He moved his hands into a palm up position and his fingers began seducing the air. "Come to us."

Her eyes narrowed and she grabbed her cell.

"Hello? Oh, I'm sorry to hear that, Detective. We'll see you tomorrow. Okay, bye."

Stan, still on a sarcastic roll said, "I take it that was the detective and he's not coming."

"You must be psychic. Something important came up."

"Did I miss something?" Morgan looked confused.

"Stan hates my choice of music on my cell. He thinks it'll draw out the lady in grey."

Morgan's eyes grew. "Oh. That might be possible. Does it feel like she's trying to tell you something lately, Claire?"

Her words bit into Claire's heart like a short blade. She received Morgan's message loud and clear, but she only mustered two words. "Et too?"

"I told you, Claire. I think you should change it." Stan jumped on the opportunity.

She closed her eyes and spoke slowly. "I will not change my phone. I like it and I don't believe that particular music will summon a woman who was born and died long before the song was written."

Morgan looked at Stan and pointed at Claire, but her concerned expression didn't match her words. "I want to change my vote to common sense."

"Nice. I get it, Stan. We're all concerned, but we must live our life. I'm sorry, I don't know what to say," said Claire.

His bottom lip protruded. "Could you say you'll contact your mother for some of her brownies? That might help."

The girls laughed at his attempt to not agree, and transferred the fact he didn't agree with them into food for his stomach.

"I'll see what I can do."

"Thanks. It hurts less now."

"In fact, I'll call mom now." She picked up her cell and dialed putting her on speaker. "Mom, hi, two things; first can you make Stan some more brownies?"

"Yes, I'd be glad to."

Stan's voice lowered to the point that it thickened with nausea. "Thanks, Hailey. I am happy to hear that, and the pain is gone now."

"What? Are you okay Stan? I'll make two batches. Claire, what's happened to Stan.?"

Stan smirked and gave a thumbs up.

"Mother, no he's not in pain, and oh my god, don't make him two batches. I'm in pain now. He's fine." He grinned and nodded with two thumbs up. "I'll have you know you're creating a monster and once that happens, he'll have to come live with you."

"He could live here if he needs to," said Hailey.

"I know he could live with you; I'm just saying you're creating a...oh, never mind. The second thing is I need to see Nana. Could the three of us do lunch this Friday at Holidays?"

"I don't see why not. How about one."

Good, I'll see you there. Love you and give Nana a kiss." She ended the call.

"Yay! I'm getting brownies. They are the best." He did a little dance around the room.

Morgan laughed and joined him in the dance. "I've had them. Bring me one, please."

"You got it, only because you're such a good dancer."

Claire giggled. "You both need to dance eating all those brownies. Oh, what the hell." She joined them on the dance floor, but not before turning on some rock and roll on her cell.

Two songs in Charlie showed up and threw his coat on a hook. "Don't stop. I'm coming in! Sorry I had to leave earlier. I didn't know we were dancing!" He threw his arms up in the air and turned.

An hour later they closed the shop for the day.

"Charlie please join Stan and I for dinner? We're walking to Warm Vibes down the road."

"Sure."

The three of them headed to dinner and waved to Morgan who hurried home to her family.

Chapter 9

Current: Boston, Massachusetts. Friday; closing the tree portals.

She poured a cup of coffee. "Toast?"

In a subdued tone Stan answered, "Yeah."

Claire handed him a slice to go with his two hard boiled eggs. It was Friday and the detective told her he'd get back to her later on Thursday, he hadn't. She was worried. Probing into any type of murder was not just dangerous, but all consuming, and mentally exhausting. His mysterious darkness nagged at her.

It could be nothing to worry about, it might mean he's not getting much sleep, after all, her obsession over the paintings appeared to be getting the better of her and now was interfering with her sleep. She needed to see them, just for a peek. It wouldn't matter whether she looked or not if the paintings had changed or hadn't changed, she didn't decide that the lady in grey did. Either way it would be a clue into what they might be dealing with in the future.

Maybe, her two friends were right, and the woman in grey was sending her subliminal messages via the music on her phone. She'd change it first chance she got.

Stan momentarily removed his eyes from his plate of food, and they'd changed from sparkling sunny waters to dark pools set amongst dying vegetation.

"Claire? Are you okay? Your eyes are bloodshot, and I've never seen you with bags under them before now."

Wonderful.

"Yes, I'm fine. I didn't sleep well." She quickly poured another cup of coffee and filled up his empty one.

Someone knocked on the door and changed where the conversation was headed. She was glad, if he knew why she'd lost sleep he'd remove the chest and the paintings.

She put the pot back on the coffee maker. "I'm up. I'll get it. Expecting anyone this early?"

"Nope."

She looked through the peephole and tilted her head. "It's Detective Stone."

"What? Really?"

She opened the door, and the detective hurried past her and into the eating area.

"Morning guys. Sorry to bust in on you like this, but it couldn't wait. I have news."

Claire followed him into the kitchen. "I was concerned when you hadn't called me back yesterday. Would you like some coffee, or breakfast?"

"Just coffee, black. Sorry." He slipped off his coat and threw it over an empty chair and sat down.

Stan continued eating, she handed the detective a cup and sat down next to him. "What's the urgency?"

"I followed these murders back through time and I believe it all started with a man named John Sutton born in 1802. I thought I would look up information about supposed solved murders, and I found him. A serial killer. They found thirty women buried around a lake, after a group of neighbors saw him roughly handling a 16-year-old girl, and they took justice into their own hands. Apparently, no one liked or trusted him. He was on their radar after women went missing. So, they tied him to a post on the porch of his own home and burnt the house down. They watched him and his house burn to the ground, like it was some kind of sick theatre production. Some say he never screamed. That took place in 1820. The man was 40 years old."

He stopped talking, took a sip of coffee, nodded, and smirked with a grin that showed a man quite pleased with himself.

Stan said, "I'll bite, how does that fit?"

"The man had a son, Robert Sutton." He looked at both and nodded. "You could've been right all along, Stan, because Robert Sutton also had several sons. Genetics."

"That's true detective, family can play a role in how a person was raised and then there's hereditary personality frailties," said Claire.

Stan grimaced. "That's a subtle way of saying mentally a serial killer from birth."

Claire said, "I suppose so."

Stan's brow creased together forming two deep lines above his nose bridge. "Are you saying you believe it's not a paranormal event, then?"

The detective narrowed his eyes, and held theirs for several minutes, and finally said, "Nope. Not saying that at all. Sometimes the world makes you go insane and it's nothing to do with genetics or how you're brought up. It is what it is, but because the son was there when they murdered his father it must've played a significant role in how he grew up. Drum roll please, guess what people said the child held on to that he wouldn't give up, and clung to it like it was his soul." He stopped talking and smiled.

Stan shrugged his shoulders. "Really, we should guess?"

Fireworks lit up her thoughts and she leaned back in her chair. "No way in hell. The bull."

"Bingo. I think I might like a piece of toast now."

Stan jumped out of his seat. "You've got to be kidding me. Of course, you want a piece of toast, torturing us takes work. Dragging out that story was like selling a novel." He patted the detective on the back. "Good work. Where do we go from here?"

"I didn't realize he had a son. John had never married. It's possible the child was from one of the women he kidnapped. Too bad there wasn't DNA testing then. Robert married and had several boys but sold the land years later to a woman named Mary Skyward. It was just property after that. No one lived on it, and she died 45 years later and left it to her daughter, Rose Cliff."

Stan raised his eyebrows. "Is that the same Rose that sold the land to Todd? Why did you look so far back, detective?"

"Yep, the same Rose. Something nagged at me and made me look further. Rose had a different last name than her mother Mary, because her mother married twice, her first husband Dan Cliff and she shared a daughter, named Rose. Mary's second husband Luke Skyward died young, and Mary's daughter Rose never married."

Her head hurt between her eyes, and her mind raced to catch up. "So, Rose sold the property to Todd Griffin, and he built on the same property where John Sutton murdered all those women and buried them? And women started to disappear again? Am I thinking correctly?"

The detective nodded. "Yep."

Stan said, "Okay, detective then you believe the bull is attached to a piece of land, or it's never been moved from the property to know if the paranormal follows the bull or the property? But we can't prove that Todd Griffin murdered anyone. The only thing we can prove is the bull appears on what is the same property when new owners move in." Stan rubbed his stubbled face. "Unless you believe that the bull is possessed by an entity that murders women."

"I don't know. That's what I have you people for. There's one problem, the son of John wouldn't have been alive in 1895, at least he didn't commit the murders we're looking into, but there could be other murder victims we're not aware of. And then there's the thirty women that disappeared in the John Sutton incidents, at least that's what they thought, we know there could've been more. Let's compare that to the 30 boxes in a different time frame, are we looking at groups of 30?"

Claire wanted to be indifferent to the news, until they had more information. "Detective, are you going to look into locating the sons of Robert, they would've been alive during the murders. The 30 is an interesting thought. So possibly two connections, the bull, and the number 30. We shouldn't overlook anything."

The detective nodded and put more strawberry jam on his toast. Between bites Stone said, "Yes, I'll check into it."

She smiled. "More toast detective?"

"Sure, I didn't eat last night, or this morning."

"Would you like eggs?" She poured him coffee.

"Nah, I'm good."

Stan held out his cup for a refill. "If the killer is possessed by the statue, it could be anyone. It may or may not be John Sutton. If we believe that his son Robert possessed the bull when his father burned, then we start there. I guess we start there anyway, something Claire and I already decided to do, start with the bull. We need to find out everything about the bull that shows up everywhere, we need to find out why."

"Right. What evil would possess a bull statue and why," said the detective and sucked in his cheek.

Claire sat down and joined them. "The paranormal constantly plays with the physical perspective of our reality. We're not trained to keep up. Even though I believe in the paranormal when a shadow moves across the room, I find myself wondering if I really saw it. A man's spirit may not be in the statue, but a curse might've been placed on the bull. An evil curse might make horrible things occur. It's been known to happen."

"Sure." Detective Stone nodded.

Stan filled in the detective on what he'd discovered about the bull being an obsession for Todd.

Detective Stone waited until Stan finished speaking and quickly jumped in after his last word and before Stan had taken another breath. "John's son, Robert had several sons. The bull could just be a toy, or an item people enjoyed having around, but the fact that so many people are obsessed with it means we need to consider it a major player in the murders. Robert changed his last name because his dad was a murderer, to protect him, and his children, I'm sure."

She said, "Stan had mentioned to me earlier that the bull could've been used as a weapon in the murders, which might be significant. It could explain why the spirit of Margaret whispered bull to him. Can we prove how they died?"

Stone said, "The only bodies that were found were the ones on the property of John Sutton, too many years have passed. According to the forensic files they did sustain trauma, but nothing specific. I'm trying to locate Sam Dodgers, he's still alive. He might shed light on the subject, after all he lived on the same property, if I am reading these files correctly. Time changes things and wording was slightly different, as well as laws."

Claire sipped her now cold coffee and said, "Where is this property? I might go there and feel something."

"No can do. For some reason, the files have been smudged by the addresses and other information. I'll have to dig deeper to get it."

She said, "It might not be paranormal. The only thing we have connecting the women are certain men, which highlights their being involved. The bull for now could just be a coincidence, like the number 30. I'll re-check out information on a black bull and see if it's listed as a magical item. One never knows."

"It's possible. I'll try to locate Sam and the sons of Robert Sutton to see if that turns up anything. What he changed his name to was taken off the record books, possibly by a detective at the time protecting the child. Could prove difficult."

"Thanks Stone," said Stan. "If you find out about the sons of Robert or locate Sam, give me a buzz, I would like to join you on the interview if possible. That might be why the address was smudged, as well."

"Sure, I could use your intuitive input. Man, I'm hungry."

Claire smiled. "Would you like an omelet, detective?"

Stone sucked in his jaw and said, "Oh, why not. Thanks."

"No problem," she said while cracking eggs and dropping them in a bowl.

"Great. Stan what's going on for you today just in case I get lucky?"

"Not much. Just the usual dog devours dog world." He laughed so hard; it caused his two partners to join in.

Claire placed the omelet on the table and the detective quickly ate it.

"Delicious." Stone finished his toast, guzzled what was left of his cold coffee and stood up putting on his coat. "Thanks guys. I appreciate your help in this investigation. Have a good one." He grimaced, turned, and showed himself out.

"I'm not sure he's telling us everything. Are you Stan?"

"I know what you mean. A dark shadow creeps closely beside him, and did you notice he sucks in his jaw all the time? Nervous tick, I guess." He stood. "Hey, we should go, it's late."

"Yeah."

***

The sunset threw vibrant colors across the boughs of the trees, as the cold twilight reached out and took hold of any remainder of warmth left in their human bodies and sent it packing.

She shivered. "I feel them."

Stan grabbed her arm. "Claire, what do you feel?"

"I feel the pain of the trees. It hurts my heart. I never knew I was so connected to them."

She wasn't sure if she could endure their agony. A deep breath of chilly air helped. Her eyes watered, she closed them, but the ache in her chest continued. She should've stayed home.

Morgan grabbed her other arm and laid her head on her shoulder warming her slightly.

A door slammed nearby, and Marvin ran at them with his arms flailing wildly around his head. "What's going on?"

Stan looked at him. "I left you a voice mail message that we'd be here this evening."

Marvin relaxed but the hair on his head didn't, neither did his voice. "I didn't get it. What are you doing here, then?"

Claire was leery telling him anything. "We're just checking the trees out. I had to see for myself. You don't need to be here."

She wanted him gone; the pain was too much with him yelling.

His eyes suddenly matched his hair. "Good." He turned to leave. "Who's that woman," he said with a frantic edge to his voice.

The three of them turned at once. There she was, Madame Frost. Her long golden hair glistened in the darkness. She was tall and wore a white knit hat, and a long white wool coat, her boots were black, and she carried a dark bag in one hand and reached out to shake Marvin's with the other. He looked uncomfortable, but her presence demanded they shake hands, and he did.

"You must be Marvin, I'm Madame Frost," she said in a soft fluid British voice.

"Yeah. I'm not needed here today," he said and went inside the house. Seconds later his head peered between an opening of a curtained window and watched them from a safe distance.

Madame Frost had a thing about her, an aura that was confident and alluring. Her skin was pure white, almost ghostly. She smiled at Stan. Oh, my god, her smile pulled you deeper inside her beauty.

Stan stood there staring at her like a schoolboy, mesmerized by her spirit. He was gone. There was only one thing to do.

"Ouch! Claire, why'd you kick me?"

Claire looked at Morgan, the two smiled.
Morgan said, "Oh, I'm sure it had to be done."

Before Madame Frost reached them her perfume, or essence of a cool winter's morning reached them first. Who was this woman? Good grief, even she could fall in love with this bewitching lady.

Frost held out her white gloved hands and took Claire's in hers and when she spoke her voice was like a gentle rain. "You're Claire. So good to meet you." She winked at her then turned to Morgan. "Morgan I'm glad to meet the woman who helped Stan survive the horrible ordeal of the vile demon dogs. You're brave and that will be needed here."

Claire's cheeks heated up. Stan told this woman about what happened with the dogs and wouldn't tell her. She had to pry out what information he did give her. She felt a twinge of anger mixed with jealousy. She wanted to scream at him, but didn't want to make a scene. Besides these new feelings about Stan confused her and left her a little confused.

"Thanks, but it wasn't bravery, but survival," said Morgan.

Madame Frost touched her hand and nodded. "We must start. I feel the trees. There are three portals."

She reached into her pocket and pulled out a small piece of chocolate, ate it slowly, enjoying the moment. She winked at the three of them. "It helps me relax."

Frost then took out a vial from her pocket and a tiny brush. She dipped the brush inside the liquid and wrote symbols on three trees. Claire didn't recognize the symbols. An ancient dog-like pattern. She lit candles in an enclosed apparatus she had in her bag. Setting them in a circle around her and Stan, as he threw salt around them.

She never hesitated and started incanting, rising in tempo until the holes became clearer and a glow circled each opening. Then her words turned into ethereal symbols like the ones on the trees. The shapes floated through the air and reached the hole of one tree. The three of them watched her as she moved the symbols around the hole and stitched it closed. Once the symbols finished the tree had a scorched mark that sealed the opening.

The sealing of one portal awakened something in the other trees.

Loud panting sent chills down Claire's body. Snarling deafened the panting. Growling commenced as demon dogs poked their heads through the last two openings.

Madame Frost went into a trance, as Stan held her close to his side. The symbols moved to the second tree.

A fiendish scream grew in strength and the blackness of its shadow moved quickly forward pushing the dogs out of the way, mixing its hellish sound with the beastly, painful yelp of the dogs.

Something else looked out.

Its degenerate gaze of evil took Claire's breath away, she was drowning. "The demon from the airport!"

Another shout broke past hers raising into a high-pitched horrific scream. "It's Maureen! My god it's Maureen!" Morgan backed up and stepped on Claire's foot.

Her friend continued backing up. Two people seeing different images made Claire realize it was a demon that played with their minds.

"Morgan, stop," she said and grabbed Morgan's arm and shook it, in hopes of getting her snapped out of the illusion. "It's a demoness."

The demoness spat at them and screamed so loud that it rippled through their bones. Claire and Morgan held on to each other.

Then she saw Stan, locked in the trance with Madame Frost, before she could react, the demon was out of the tree flying towards Madame Frost and rammed her, knocking the elegant woman to the ground with Stan. The salt hadn't protected them.

Madame Frost cried out like a bullet just blasted her stomach wide open. The symbols diminished before they were finished sealing the portal closed. Stan lay there in a stupor with a fixed smile of a jack-o-lantern. Her heart broke and her head filled with images of Gabe.

Loud howls filled the air, and one demon dog followed the demonic creature out and disappeared along with the entity in a flash of fire.

Claire stood in shock. Morgan held her hand tightly as their hands shook violently. She squeezed Morgan's hand, then let go.

"Stan." His name was barely audible through her lips. It was Gabe all over again. Her feet wouldn't move. Fear stroked her insides until she had collapsed to her knees.

Morgan bent down and pulled her up. "Claire, we need to move."

A door slammed and Marvin ran across his yard screaming. "They're out, you've let them out! What have you done? I have to move; I have to move. Leave here now. Leave!"

He turned and began running back to his house. Once inside they heard the heavy bang of the door as he closed and bolted it shut.

Claire watched him with tears running down her face. Together the girls faced Stan.

Madame Frost was unconscious, but alive. Stan still grinned.

The locked grimace on the medium's face scared her. She looked at Morgan and gasped for air. She grabbed her chest as the world fell on top of it and began to crush the life from her body.

Morgan took her hand. "Claire help me get Stan up."

"Oh my god, Stan." Her whispered words followed her to the ground, as she fell to her knees again and lifted his head to her lap. She stroked his hair and stared at his face.

The strong hands of Morgan sat him up and pulled his head from her grip. Morgan snapped her fingers in front of his face, nothing.

His head hung like a rag doll. Claire slid her hands behind his neck and lifted it up. "Don't you leave me, Stan!" She screamed and slapped him hard across his cheek.

His eyes rolled. "What the hell?"

The moment was historic, like the first tree planted, anywhere ever, the most glorious sunrise rose next to a sunset, and her heart filled with windows of glorious light. She kissed him without thought, right on the mouth, hard, desperate, and without remorse.

It was incredible, she could hear the music of Tubular Bells, and that made her laugh.

Stan stared at her, but never said a word.

"You were sitting there grinning like an expired carved Halloween pumpkin that never got to witness the great pumpkin. Claire had to slap you. We thought we lost you," said Morgan.

"Oh." That was all he said, but he continued to stare at Claire, making her uncomfortable.

Morgan said, "I called for an ambulance, I can't revive Madame Frost."

Stan moved in slow motion. "What happened?"

"What happened? Your friend called forth a demoness who escaped with two hellhounds and they're loose on Boston streets. That's what happened. We need to get out of here. I hope nothing else comes out, but we can't stop it."

The ambulance quickly responded, and the sirens moved off into the distance as they drove Madame Frost to emergency.

"I hope she's okay," said Claire as she grabbed the spell-caster's belongings.

They walked to the car and watched Marvin watch them from his window.

"Stan, do you want me to drive, you had an incident," said Claire.

"Nope. I'm good."

He was always good according to Stan. They got in the car and Stan drove Morgan home.

"We'll talk tomorrow, Morgan," said Claire.

Morgan nodded. "What are we going to do about the demon?"

"I'm not sure. I'm calling Nana."

Stan seemed distracted and never mentioned the fact that a demon and its allies would cause chaos out there on this brisk and quiet evening.

She didn't want to talk about the kiss, and apparently neither did Stan.

His voice was soft. "We should check on Madame Frost tomorrow. You know what, I'm sorry I made fun of your Tubular Bells music. It's really not that bad. In fact, I think I like it." He looked at her and smiled.

Her heart fluttered and sank to her stomach.

Chapter 10

Current: Boston, Massachusetts. Later Friday Evening; Demons loose

It'd been a long day, and it felt good to be home.

"Night," said Stan as he headed up the stairs.

Hanger in one hand and coat in the other Claire quickly turned and faced him and left her chore undone.

"Woah there mister, not so fast." They needed to talk about everything that had happened at the trees.

He stopped on the third step up and looked over his shoulder. "What?"

She'd been hard on him about his inability to cope with the paranormal lately and worried they were drifting apart. His eyes almost broke her heart. There was exhaustion and vulnerability in them she'd never seen before now. *Be gentle Claire.*

"Hey, I could really use a drink. What about you? Let's have a little Friday night fun. You in?" She hung up her coat.

Her mind searched for other scenarios that might keep him downstairs so they could talk, if he said no. She held her breath.

The sun had set, and the moon had risen for three days inside her soul before he finally spoke. "Okay. Let me hang up my coat, jump in a warm shower and I'll be down. I'm still a little cold."

"That's a great idea. I'm doing the same. Meet you in the middle."

He grinned and continued up the stairs. Finally, a genuine smile. 'Meet you in the middle' was something they always said when the tension was high, and they were off on their own tangents. It always brought them back to the middle ground where they could think more clearly after a good laugh.

She showered, dressed, and headed to the kitchen; he was already pouring them a brandy.

"Nice choice," she said.

He smiled and handed her a glass.

Recently, Stan showed signs of withdrawal. She linked her arm in his and walked him towards the couches in front of the fire he'd obviously started after his shower.

He took a seat, and she sat across from him so she could watch his face. It was the same chair Stan had sat in when he watched Gabe all night, after the woman in grey had possessed him. A slight chill penetrated her body and caused goosebumps to rise on her skin one at a time.

Stan smiled at her and for a moment it released the tension in his face smoothing out the creases. She leaned back in the chair, and breathed deeply before she spoke, it helped.

She concentrated on her tone of voice, so it was light and airy. "I'm sure Madame Frost will be alright; we can visit in the morning. Those things happen dealing with the paranormal. I think she might've forgotten a step, I'm not sure but we can check it out in the portal book if you want."

"Yeah, sounds good, but you can call her Lily, that's what she told me to call her, because she felt the Madame was too formal. I think she had it right, but wasn't quick enough to close them."

She forced a grin. "Okay, Lily it is." She looked directly into his eyes, and her mouth tightened. "Stan, I did nothing to help her. I could've, but I stood there watching like a bystander. That wasn't smart. At the time I didn't want to interfere with her job, but that's not an excuse. I should've done something."

"Like what?" His glare challenged her, and it bit her in the heart.

"I could've asked her if there was something I could do, but I didn't. Stan, you saved her life, whether you realize it or not. You got in the circle and held on to her, and that gave her strength. You know that. In any paranormal situation success is based on the power of unity. I would've never forgiven myself if something happened to you when I just stood there watching. It scared me, I thought you were gone."

He sipped his brandy, his eyes smoldered, then his lips tilted slightly into a wicked grin. "So that was a welcome back from the dead, now I won't have to live with a guilty kiss?"

He caught her off guard. Stuttering sounds came out as incoherent balderdash.

He laughed. "Relax. It was just a kiss. You'll never get rid of me that easily." His eyes glazed over, and he stared past her shoulder into the other room.

She was afraid to look. Maureen could be there; anything could be there. She slowly turned her head and saw nothing more than items in the room. "Stan? What's wrong?"

His eyes shifted to hers and his voice broke into tiny little fragments of glass that shattered in midair before they fell to the ground. "Claire, we let them out. We let out the dogs and then we let out a demon. How the hell are we supposed to put them back in the portal, much less find them? And for the record, unity doesn't always work. It didn't help Gabe. And you're wrong. I brought her into this, and she should've done one portal at a time, sewed it shut and then moved on."

She took his hands and ignored the comment about Gabe. "I don't know how to put them back, or close the portal, but I know someone that might."

Stan jerked his head towards the door. "Is that someone banging on the door? Who could that be at this hour?"

"It could be anyone, it's only 8 o'clock. I know it seems later."

She opened the door, Morgan, and Derry stood there grinning.

Morgan held up her hand and walked in. "Don't say a word. Derry and I agreed the demons are a priority. We need a solution. Cheyenne is staying the night. So, what do we need to do?" She went straight in and sat on the couch. "Hey, Stan how are you doing? Pour me one of those."

He grinned. "Sure."

Derry shrugged at Claire and followed his wife into the room.

She knew that Morgan had seen paranormal occurrences before the demon dogs, but the horrific events were hard to get used to.

Claire asked, "Morgan are you alright?"

"Sure. Just having a drink with my friend, Stan." Her mouth drooped and her eyes closed. "Of course, I'm not alright. We let out demons. How do we find them and put them back?"

Claire hadn't answered but grabbed her cell. "Mom, hey, I left Nana a message about an hour ago, not sure if she got it, but we have a situation. I know we already switched today's lunch to tomorrow, but instead would you and Nana come over now? Yes, I'm okay, I just need to talk. Thanks. See you in a few."

Stan stood up. "I'm getting the portal book. It's clear no one will sleep until we figure this out."

The moment he left the room it felt like someone turned on a heater, he took his cold energy with him. She sipped her drink and waited.

When he returned, he appeared mentally better, clearer in his eyes, and in his mission. His voice got stronger. "Here's the book. I know we can figure this out." He looked at the three of them and his sideways grin returned. "We're putting those demons back in hell where they belong."

She shook her head and smiled. "That we will. You guys look through the book, I'm making coffee for mom, and nana, I imagine Logan will come with them."

"Sure, but just saying, I think your mom and nana might want something stronger than coffee."

He might be right, but maybe it was more for her, and not the guests, because the smell of coffee always revived her and brought back good memories. It was a comfort smell she hadn't realized she needed until that moment.

The rich aroma was the first thing that filled her senses when she'd been awakened by the sound of clanking dishes when she was a little girl. In fact, she hadn't remembered a morning without the smell of coffee starting her day. It was a confirmation she was alive. She lifted her chin, and energy rushed in and flooded her body.

"I'm making it anyway."

"I found something," said Stan.

Morgan looked over his shoulder. "Where?"

"Right there." He pointed to a page in the portal book and looked up at Morgan. "It would appear we have a closure, and Claire was right she did forget something in the spell. Putting a block on the other one while she closed another. Sorry, Claire, I didn't know. I brought her there."

"No worries. Let's go into the other room."

They headed into the kitchen area and sat around the large glass table that reflected the golden lights of the home. She busied herself with setting out some cut up apples, cheese, slices of French bread, sliced cucumbers, and hummus.

Stan poured everyone another drink.

She sat the food on the table. "Do you see how to draw creatures back to the portal they escaped from?"

"You won't find that information in that book for a novice," said Nana looking over Morgan. "Door was unlocked so we walked in. I assume by your comments you've let something escape, if that's the case I'll need something stronger than coffee."

Claire looked at Stan, and both grinned. "I have your favorite Amarula Cream; over ice?"

"Yep. And now we need to get serious." Nana pulled out a chair and sat down.

Claire said, "Hi mother."

Hailey hugged her daughter. "Hi, I'm glad you called us. I'll just have a cup of coffee, thanks."

"Me too, unless I'm going to be needed in demonic combat then pour me a cup of what she's having," said Logan as he pointed at Nana, but his piercing blue eyes narrowed and dulled. He hugged her and sat down next to her nana.

His weariness for the supernatural was understandable. He would help if needed, because he was that type of person, but it would be against his better judgement. He wouldn't leave the people he loved alone on the battlefield.

By the time coffee was served Stan had informed them of what happened earlier that night when the demons escaped.

"I'm going to need a complete description of the dogs and the demon that came out, but I should be able to round them up. We'll need to do it now, before they cause trouble. I want to know what your friend said in her spell, every word if possible."

"Stan, you write it down for her. Do I need to get you anything to take with us for the spell?"

"No," said Nana holding out her glass for a refill.

Morgan frowned. "Are we doing it here?"

"Heavens no child, we need to get back over to the portals. Let me finish this drink and you can pour me another, then we'll have to go." She had a twinkle in her eye like a young girl, then quickly downed her second drink and handed the glass to her granddaughter.

Claire hugged her. "I don't know what I would do without you."

"I thought of that too. You need to continue coming by for lessons. We haven't started back at your lessons since your trip. There is so much to learn, and I don't want to leave you flailing about like a fish out of water. We need scheduled days, my butterfly."

"I wanted to have lunch to show you another book, but that will have to wait," she said and poured her another glass of liquor."

Her nana downed that drink too. "I'm still working on the other book I confiscated from you. Interesting, and one we'll need to discuss in length, but not today."

Claire said, "I'll get my coat, so we can get going."

Hailey frowned, held her mother's hands and kissed her cheek, then turned to her daughter, and did the same. "I'll drive back home. This isn't for me, but be safe and come back to me. Claire, make sure your Nana gets back home okay, will you?"

"Yes, we will."

"I'm going with them."

Hailey faced the man she loved, closed her eyes, as her chest rose and slowly deflated followed with a slight breath of air that escaped into the energy of the room. It brought sadness.

"Of course, you are," said Hailey in a quiet tone. She kissed him. "I'll see you at home then. You be safe." She left through the front door without saying another word.

Nana looked at Dan. "She'll accept it, but never understand. Let's go. Stan, you drive. I got your message so came prepared." Nana hurried to the door, threw on her coat, and picked up a bag she'd left there when she'd arrived.

No one argued.

Claire looked out into the cold night as snow started to fall. She'd climbed in the back with Nana and felt her stern presence, her face calm, expressionless.

Stan's eyes were wild looking and fixed on the road in front of him, and she noticed his clenched jaw. He blamed himself and she knew he would never let that go. Afterall, he brought Madame Frost to the trees.

The priest sat across from Stan, and his expression was as unreadable as her nana.

Derry and Morgan followed them in their car.

Sometimes she wished she were normal, and didn't have these feelings. Nana was strong, and if the dear lady ever wished that she herself were normal, she had never expressed it, at least not to her.

She looked out the window and watched the dark spirits as they raced beside them. They followed the car to the trees. She wondered what they wanted, and why this activity sparked their interest. The wind howled, as though warning the demons to run and hide. She thought of Susan, Gabe's grandmother.

Chapter 11

Boston, Massachusetts. June 1975, the murder of Sally Dodgers

I loved her face, not the shape of it, but the tenderness hidden behind the depths of her deep blue eyes. No, 'trapped' would be a better word, because her soul wouldn't allow the gentle spirit to escape. What would be left if it had? A robot, an empty shell, or a lost soul searching aimlessly for what she'd already owned. She held her feelings close to her heart, and it drove me wild.

I wanted to taste them, to devour them, and lavish them all over my body. My excitement could hardly be contained. I licked my lips in anticipation.

"You have a wicked grin," Sally said. Her voice was soft, teasing, and seductive, as her eyes danced in the candlelight and peered out from under nicely trimmed eyebrows. Her blonde hair fell lightly over one eye. She lifted her manicured hands and slid her hair behind her ear.

It annoyed me.

I moved in behind her chair and pulled the hair out and allowed it the freedom of movement. I leaned in close to her ear and gently wrapped my fingers around her neck. It was so small. I licked her ear and whispered some words that sounded harsh and brittle. It wasn't a language that I knew.

It got a reaction.

Her eyes rolled up into her eye sockets, her hand dropped a slice of bread onto her lap, and a delicate whimper escaped into the room from her tiny painted mouth.

My head reeled; he was coming. I despised him. Dinner was over.

The wind whistled like the sound of a train and forced its way in through the slightly opened window. The tiny flames of the dinner candles were quickly extinguished. A fuse popped and darkness flooded the room.

"You can't have her. I want her." I raised my voice loud enough to cover the sound of the train. Then I lifted her out of the chair and held her close to my chest.

She flinched from my voice, but I knew she was still weakened from the words I'd whispered in her ear, that the devil planted in my mouth. Her arms flailed, and she resisted my hand against her neck. I lifted her face from my chest and held it firmly towards mine. I kissed her lips.

Her eyes shone with fear.

"Don't move, I have a flashlight."

My head was pounding and the heaviness in the room weighed me down, as I struggled and moved towards a drawer that kept my flashlights close in case of emergencies. Her body was part of me as I shifted her weight with mine towards the light.

I stopped often and touched her soft face and caressed her hair, a reassurance that she would be fine. He had no right to claim her as his own.

Her eyes searched for answers in mine. I had none. I didn't understand the reason I did what I did, so for that reason, and that reason only, I offered no answers.

I knew my kitchen well, even in the dark, but it was harder than I thought because she fought against each step we took. The quiet was corpse like as we moved together towards freedom until she whispered.

"Do you feel the heaviness in the room?"

My eyes popped, as my eyebrows lifted. Who did she think she was to feel the weight of his presence? This was my game, not his, but it didn't matter who controlled the game, did it?

My eyes narrowed and I pulled her so close I felt her heartbeat against my chest. My voice rose like a plane taking off at an airport. "Of course, I feel it. Do you think I'm an idiot? I am the reason he is here. I am the reason he brings the heaviness, the fear, and the power. Without me, he wouldn't have a puppet." My head tilted to the side and a grin cracked my face. "This isn't just me. Who is it then? He talks through me, John, the demon. It's us; freeing you from your weak and insignificant self. You can thank us later."

The moon shone on her face, that beautiful face. Her eyes searched for a way out, and I knew her mind wished she'd never come to dinner.

The evil grabbed my foot and slithered up my body. His breath seeped into my eyes, into my nose, and into my open mouth.

"*Kill her.*"

"No." I was surprised I thought he owned all of me. My head hurt with him inside.

"*What?*"

He didn't like my answer and pushed against the inside of my head with a battering ram and tried to take down the wall of my resolve.

"*She's making fun of you, looking for a way to escape you. She wants you to be trapped like her in a world filled with deception.*"

"You're tricking me."

I moved closer to the flashlight drawer. She moved easier, with me, in fact. I think she liked me and was on my side. I smiled.

But the demon didn't like to be managed, and he hit me again with the battering ram and blasted my resolve out the window where it moved quickly away, so far away I couldn't feel it anymore.

I wanted to scream but didn't. Instead, I laughed, a villainous chuckle like the world was all mine. I was the Frankenstein monster, and lifted my head, and locked my eyes on my dinner guest.

The candles re-lit.

At that moment she was mine and collapsed against me, but her eyes begged me to leave her soul intact.

"Oh, I will. I will trap your kindness inside your soul forever, where no one will find it and take it for their own."

I relaxed my grip; she had accepted her fate. She fooled me and broke free.

He was right, wasn't he? She deceived me, tricked me, and ran towards the door. She opened it and turned towards me. I caught and held her eyes, the kindness was replaced with repulsion and fear.

"See, someone is already stealing your joy from your soul. We can't have that, can we?" My voice held an edge to it that sounded like I mocked her. I didn't, I was sincere. "Sorry."

She ran out the door.

"*Go after her.*"

My resolve found its way back to me. "Quit pushing me. I don't like you very much." My head reared back as I searched the room for the devil that haunted me. "We've met before. I thought you were gone."

Its voice quivered with seductive tones, like honey that slowly dripped on bread. *"You missed me--I can tell, otherwise you wouldn't have brought her here for us to play with. Run after her."*

I listened and moved to the door, but I wasn't done voicing my opinion. "I brought her for me, not you. I would never miss you. I'm tired of you bossing me around."

Once in the doorway I saw her beautiful self still moving towards the woods. She was slow and kept looking back, which slowed her down more. Why do they always keep turning around? Just run.

I eventually caught up to her and grabbed her by her arm.

Her hand curled into a fist, she swung around and hit me hard across the face. "Ouch." It stung me and caused me to lose my grip. I might have a black eye.

I wasn't angry at her but at that stupid voice that wouldn't let me be. "Look what you caused by pushing me all the time. Quit distracting me."

The evil poured from my eyes, nose, and mouth. It raced towards my doomed guest.

It engulfed her. She stumbled and fell face down in the dirt.

The demon shadow made hand motions for me to move closer, I did, and it entered me.

To my surprise I welcomed it back.

She was crying. I hated that; it made me sad. I hated his song even more.

"Sing it."

His voice demanded it and forced it out of me. I lifted her up off the ground and brushed the dirt from her face.

I sang: "Stay by my side bluebell, stay by my side forever, in eternity we touch, in eternity we breathe."

She held her tears and tried one more time to reach me. "Please let me go. Save me. Give me more time to live."

"Oh, my darling Sally." I squeezed her close to me, smelled her hair, and kissed her sweet lips. "Time was never in front of you, behind you, or next to you. It just doesn't matter." I brushed her clothes off and pulled leaves out of her hair. I kissed her again on the mouth, then the cheek. She didn't understand, but she wouldn't get away again. "I am saving you. As for time, it's in each second and each second is so grand it holds you in place. That's how we'll save you."

I picked her up and carried her back inside the house. She wept and I kissed her one last time.

Chapter 12

Current: Boston, Massachusetts– Nana at the portal.

She was small in stature, but her presence loomed over the woods and easily matched the tallest tree. The glow around her would have blinded the five of them that assisted, except for the fact that they stood in the middle of it, feeding off the energy it manifested.

The cold and wind moved around them beating at the light, unable to penetrate, unable to freeze those that worked to return the evil to its den.

All of them had instructions from Nana, no one came without a job to do, she made sure of it. Before they started Nana sealed the other two portals, but intended to open the only one Frost had closed. She worried it hadn't been done properly.

"Now," Nana said, her words soft but firm.

Claire moved closer to her and started incanting, a gentle spell to guard the circle, unlike the words that spewed from her Nana's lips. A language she herself had never heard and didn't understand, at that moment she knew she had a lot to learn. Stan stood behind them with a lantern just in case the aura dimmed. He held a bag of salt that had already been laid around them, but if something broke the circle, he had it covered. The excommunicated priest stood next to them with his bible and holy beads, speaking words in Latin. He was still a holy man, priest or not, the church couldn't remove the spirit of who the man was, what drove his soul...it was God. Derry and Morgan held hands and held Logan's incense burner filled with the intoxicating smell of frankincense and recited their own mantra.

Nana held her hands up into the air and her voice rose to the heavens. Lightning flashed and cracked against the dark cloudy sky, a firework display without color.

When Nana finished summoning the beast, it was up to her to open the portal. The spell to protect the circle was simple, Stan knew it and took over. Nana continued chanting pulling the beasts and demon. Claire's voice grew louder and blocked out the noises that twisted her thoughts and scrambled them into the chaos that might prevent her from remembering her true intentions. She succeeded.

A rip echoed through the trees as a large gaping wound exposed the hellish inferno. Something wailed in the distance but quickly moved closer to the group and bared down on them with uninhibited screaming. The noise hurt her ears. A mist grew in the darkness, and the gaping mouth of the demoness swiftly circled them. Her presence brought tears to her eyes, while her screams caused

Morgan, and Derry to hold their ears as they dropped to their knees. Claire continued with Stan to protect their circle.

The demoness answered the call as an unwilling participant. Her hair was silver and stringy, and her growling grimace exposed upper fangs that made her look like a vampire, she tried to break the circle, spitting, and clawing at the ground as she crawled around the base of the bright light. Her extended nails tried to tear a seam that would give her the power to kill them where they stood, but when she touched it, her head reared up, blood oozed from her mouth and her eyes rolled up in her lids.

Nana sped up the spell forcing the demoness to the tree opening slinging her muscular body against it. The demon grabbed onto the tree, ripping the bark to stay on the outside, but it lost and flew headfirst into the tree, cursing and slobbering.

When Nana finished putting the creature back where it belonged, she leaned on Dan Logan's shoulder trying to remain standing.

The nod from her grandmother told her it was her turn again. She pulled everything she had from the energy around her to close the tree portal. It was too much; she was quickly out of breath and couldn't go on. The demoness was grinning, saw her weakness, and tried to maneuver herself to get back out, but then Stan was on his feet and placed his hand on her shoulder, his strength combined with hers was all she needed to complete the closure.

She let herself fall into Stan. His reassuring bear-like hug made her feel safe; a long breath of fresh air filled her lungs that she quickly exhaled into the now dark woods. The light was out.

All she heard was their own breathing.

"Curses." Nana stood up straight. "We didn't get the hell hounds."

She nodded and smiled. Nana was stronger than when they fought for Gabe. She'd been in the home too long and not able to practice her magic. It made a difference today.

Logan said, "Maybe, Stan and I can pull them in?"

"No."

The woman had nothing else to say. They gathered everything up and went back to their cars.

Nana said, "Morgan, you, and Derry go home. There's nothing left to do tonight."

Morgan's eyes narrowed, and looked intently into the eyes of Nana, it wouldn't help her, no one could get past Nana's glare. The stare lasted about a minute before Derry grabbed Morgan's arm and pulled her in the direction of their car.

"Thanks, everyone. Call us in the morning, please," said Derry while opening the door for his wife and helping her in, and before she could protest, he shut the door, waved, and quickly walked around to the driver's side and got in. The vehicle was soon out of sight.

"Stan, don't you find it strange that Marvin didn't come out or watch us from his window?"

"I was just thinking the same thing."

***

It was a sunny Saturday morning, typically they didn't work, but she had a feeling today wouldn't be a normal day off.

There were voices in the kitchen. She yawned, checked her phone, no messages, but it was already 8:30. She went to her bathroom, brushed her teeth, showered, and entered the breakfast area by 9:00.

Stan handed her a coffee, two hard-boiled eggs, sliced tomatoes, cucumbers, and two strawberries on a small plate. She smiled and nodded, but she was slightly upset that she hadn't been notified that they had company.

Claire said, "So, good morning. I'm not surprised to see you two here this early."

Morgan sipped a cup of coffee. "I couldn't sleep all night. I know it's our day off, but we need to fix this."

Derry sucked in his lower lip and nodded. "Sorry, Claire. Good morning."

Stan stood by the sink with a grin that almost reached his ears. Oh, he loved this. She'd always pushed everyone else to move forward, pursue the spirits with gusto, never letting up, and now her fierce motivation that thrust them into overdrive just came back and bit her in the butt.

"When did you two get here?"

"Stan, let us in around 7:00. I'm surprised you didn't hear us banging on the door," said Morgan.

"Nope, sound asleep. Stan should've woken me up."

He topped up her coffee, she glared at him, and he just grinned. "Now why would I wake up a sleeping angel?"

She sighed and looked at Morgan, then Derry. "We were going to the hospital this morning to check on Lily, but we can discuss this when we get back."

Morgan opened her mouth, but Claire's phone cut her off. The blasted tubular bells were chiming; she might have to change it now. Stan must've heard it too, that night when they kissed. It had to be the reason why he decided to like the bells. She was annoyed and her voice sounded annoyed when she answered her phone.

"Hello. Oh, no-okay. Are you all alright? That's horrible. What room number? Why not? We were going to visit Lily anyway. Okay Stone, take care.

"Well, Stan it looks like you won't be going with the detective to speak to possible criminals anytime soon. He's in the hospital for at least a few days, and then he's supposed to take it easy for a week or so. He thought he had a stroke, but he didn't, just exhaustion."

"That's not good," said Morgan. "We'd like to come with you to the hospital if that's okay?"

"Sure, if you want to visit Lily. The detective doesn't want to see anyone. He sounded darker than normal. I hope he's okay." Her brows creased, soon she would have a permanent wrinkle there. Her world was more complicated since the days of her and Gabe. More spirits, more people, less time for herself, less freedom of thought, all of which added stress to her life, but made it interesting and a by the seat of one's pants life.

Morgan said, "Well, it's up to him if he wants visitors. Since I was up late, I checked information about the black bull. Interestingly enough the symbolic associations were death, fighting, male fertility, resurrection, sacrifice, and strength. Other beliefs regarding the meaning of the bull were based on it being a good thing, I guess you could interpret it however you choose. I'm not sure if that helps."

Stan's overextended grin faded. "Well, you gave us more to think about. I'm still not convinced the bull is evil, or that it's possessed, but we have to keep an open mind. The spirit that implanted the word into my mind might've put it there because her killer owned one, not that it was the reason for her death."

Stan was hiding again. He didn't believe that for a moment. He was scared because he believed the bull was evil or possessed with darkness that reached through centuries committing heinous crimes. She knew him too well, but it was okay because that's what kept him focused and able to work around unspeakable and hard-to-explain events in the universe.

Detective Stone worried her, she sensed something following him, but couldn't decipher exactly what that was; darkness without thought, essence, or a clearly defined purpose.

Chapter 13

The darkness of Detective Brandon Stone

The streetlights reflected the shadows of large monsters, and the rain caused their skin to glisten with the sleekness of a reptile. They hadn't moved even as the rain poured down on them and covered their wrinkles in tiny puddles. They watched the night, and they watched him.

"Brandon, what are you doing in the dark?" She hadn't turned on the light but sat down next to him.

"Nothing mom, just watching the rain."

He could've told her about the creatures that lurked around the streets at night, but it wouldn't matter, she would never see what he did; the monsters wouldn't allow it.

"You're worried about your dad, aren't you?" She rubbed his shoulder.

His eyes grew wide, and he looked into the gentle eyes of his mother. "Why does he always have to be late? He misses everything." Her smile caused him to lower his head. He was only eight, but old enough to understand it was hard on her, as well. "Sorry, mom. I worry about him. He has a dangerous job, and after Detective Lenard was shot and killed..." He looked out the window because the tears were coming, and he didn't want to be a sissy, he cleared his voice. "I miss him."

She leaned over and hugged him. "Me too but watching the night won't bring him home. Let's get you something to eat."

"Sure."

The house was quiet as they made their way down the stairs and into the small kitchen. It was humble, clean, and decorated for Christmas. Every year his mother placed a fake poinsettia that was opened in full bloom on top of a wooden cabinet. A cookie jar that had belonged to his grandmother smiled out at him from behind the bright red flower. He knew nothing was inside of the closed lid, and he grinned every time he saw it; it reminded him of the pancake syrup lady.

He sat down at the small metal table that had a green Formica flooring over the top with a silver metal edging wrapping the circular shape. Jingles jumped on top of the table purred and moved back and forth against his arm while his mother lifted the steaming lid of beef stew.

He named the crazy cat Jingles because they'd found him last year hiding on their porch two days before Christmas, he wanted to believe Santa had dropped him off as an early gift. The kitten had been almost frozen, and it took three days of tender loving care to bring him back to life. Jingles did as he pleased, to the disapproval of his mother, but he found the cat independent and admired that quality, a quality he would embrace for himself later on in his own life.

The softness of Jingle's long black hair had gotten the young boy in trouble, as he daydreamed and rubbed his fingers through the cat's thick coat and forgot about his mother's rules.

"Get that cat off the table! How many times have I told you to keep him on the floor? Do you want hair in your food?"

"No." He'd said no, but he didn't really care if he had a hair or two, he probably wouldn't notice anyway.

He placed Jingles on the floor so his mother could put the hot soup in front of him. He was glad they were on a holiday break it always meant he could stay up later. She gave him a slice of homemade bread with melted butter. He dipped it into his soup and filled it up with gravy.

"Do you want to help me decorate the tree after dinner?" His mother smiled at him as she placed her soup across from him and sat down.

"Sure." He didn't sound too excited, but he was.

He took her hands in his, her voice was soft as she said grace before they ate.

"Mom, why don't we ever wait for dad to get home to decorate the tree? I don't remember him ever helping us." Maybe he should be used to his father's absence, but he never would be and wanted him here.

She smiled. "Eat your soup, son. You and I are magnificent decorators, and your father enjoys the show after he gets home, long after you're in bed. He sits in front of the fire and sips on a warm tea and nibbles on some cookies while admiring the lights. We all have our jobs."

"Yes, momma, I suppose."

He picked up his spoon and gathered a bean, a piece of potato, and one small bite of beef and wondered what his job was in the family. He supposed the jobs he had were ones he didn't like; clean his room, homework, help his mother, don't have feelings, and basically do what he was told whenever he was told it.

They finished dinner and he helped his mother clean up. He noticed she didn't leave a bowl of soup out for his dad. It was more common these days since he'd moved into homicide. Life had been better when he was a street cop.

Mother's face lit up when she brought out the ornaments. He grabbed the colored bulbs, and she took one end and began putting on the lights. He just stood there as she wrapped them around the tree, occasionally she asked him to grab the lights and hand them to her from the other side. He could only help when the lights moved down the tree within his reach.

His mind wandered while he placed bulbs on the tree.

When his dad was a street cop, they went to street fairs and played ball at the park. Once he'd taken him to the movies, while mom worked at the hospital. She was a nurse, and her schedule varied week to week, there were times when she had to go in when there was an emergency, and that was because they were three blocks away. She could get there quicker than others and could walk. She never complained about anything, not his dad being late, or the walks to work. She'd told him that she was proud of the job his dad did and that they both needed to support him, because it was hard work. The walking she said kept her in shape, and she enjoyed helping others. He smiled at her as she handed him an ornament, at least she was home tonight.

His father just started his new position in August and Brandon watched his dad become quieter, more secluded, darker, and in a few short months his dad formed a permanent crease between his eyes. It was the monsters that changed him, the ones that hid in the deepest shadows of the world where evil trampled over beautiful living things and played in the sacrifice of others. It was the blood, the cutting out the happiness that stole the light from the world and gave the monsters the power to grow until they washed over a city like a tidal wave from a tsunami. Some nights he felt like he was drowning in it and his dad was lost in the waves of evil.

His reaction was his own fault. He shouldn't have gone into his dad's study last month when he was working late again. Some nights he didn't come home. One such night his mother was sleeping, and he thought something, or someone was in his room. He'd turned on his light and went to get a drink of water, but on his way back to bed the door of his dad's study begged to be opened, and his curiosity had gotten the better of him. But after what he saw, he knew it was the monsters that had beckoned him into the study. They wanted to be admired for their work, and their ability to hide in the shadows of broad daylight scared him more than the shadows they played in at night.

The blood, the lifeless bodies were torn apart without care, the crime scenes overflowed with the evil that marked their territory, leaving their signature hidden within the picture for someone to find it.

That night the world changed for him. He returned regularly after that first evening because the horror of what he saw wouldn't let him rest. The blood consumed his thoughts, he didn't know why he couldn't look away, but his mind raced to find the clues needed to piece together the crime.

He didn't like playing ball with the neighborhood boys, once in a while he would ride bikes with his friends, but his interest was in the murders, and even riding bikes had him looking for clues to a crime that might have been committed, but that no one knew about, not even the cops. His obsession belonged to him and no one else, it was connected to a place inside his thoughts. His purpose. It was a mystery for him to figure out, and a way to be closer to his dad.

"Penny for your thoughts," said his mother.

They finished the tree, and his mother handed him a cup of cocoa with marshmallows that floated on top. It reminded him of icebergs. She turned out all the lights and then lit the tree. Her grin lit up her face and she sat next to him on the couch. The fire was already blazing away, the colors of the flames held him for a moment, then he shifted his gaze to the four stockings that hung from the mantel. He used one of his dad's old white knee-hi socks and painted Jingles name down the front in red and then he painted what he thought looked like holly in green and sewed two red buttons on the top of the leaves to make it look real. He was proud of that. Jingles seemed to like it.

The lights twinkled on the tree, but instead of making him smile, it reminded him of the monsters that stalked the city streets at night as streetlights and car reflections moved along the buildings in search of a victim.

His parents wouldn't be pleased if they knew what he'd done, but if he helped solve the crimes just maybe his dad could be home more often. He finished his chocolate.

"Goodnight mom."

"Oh, you're going to bed already? You've been terribly quiet tonight. Are you coming down with a cold?"

"Yes, I'm going to bed. I might be."

He said yes, but he was only going to his room to think, or maybe to dream about the murderers and their victims. The nightmares came more frequently and sometimes he would awaken in a cold sweat, but he never screamed, not ever. That would show weakness and if he screamed, they would come and they would twist his body into one of those giant pretzels the vendors sold on the streets in one of those small wooden framed carts.

The victims died because they screamed instead of fighting. He trained himself to fight. The Drunken Monkey video showed him how to fight. He found it in his dad's office one night when his mom was called into work. With the house locked and him being alone, he'd watched the video and practiced their moves, after his homework was done.

He should've stayed longer with his mom, but he had his own job to do. He brushed his teeth and went into his room, sat on his bed, and watched the street through his window. The rain turned to wet snow.

He thought he saw something move. It was hard to see clearly, the buildings collaborated with the criminals to conceal their movements.

The monsters would never get him. He knew about them, how they thought, and how they signed their work, but most important he wasn't a screamer, he would fight.

He looked under his pillow and glanced at the notebook he kept information in, things he saw about the murders that looked important, and grabbed the knife that he'd placed there from his mother's kitchen and moved it gently between his fingers. It was sharp and shiny. The edge of it took his mind to a dark place and for a moment he thought he saw blood on the knife, he closed his eyes, and looked again. It was still there, a tiny spot where he rubbed his finger along the edge too closely.

He needed to be prepared, but didn't want to use it...at least for now.

Chapter 14

Two weeks after Detective Stone's hospital stay: the Sally Dodger interviews.

Stan was glad to be out again and working on something other than the paranormal, even if it was with the gloomy Detective Stone. He'd been getting headaches by the end of each day after spending too many hours looking over books and the internet researching information connected to portals, the Rose book, and anything related to Claire's past run-in with the demon at the airport. She may not be worried about it, but he was. Nana was looking into it, but she never shared anything she might've found, so he needed to gather his own intel.

Claire wasn't herself these days and seemed preoccupied, and he wasn't sure where her mind was vacationing when he was talking to her about their business, or anything related to it. She would just smile and stare past him, and on more than one occasion she looked over his shoulder with wild eyes that had freaked him out. Every time she did that he'd quickly jerked his head around and wondered if a spirit lurked behind him ready to suck his soul.

The drive was long and gave him too much time to drag a rake across his raw fears.

"I hope you know where you're going, Detective?"

Brandon glanced his way. "Of course, I do. We're going to talk with Meg Fangel, sister of Sally Dodger. I need to speak with her myself and get a feel for what she has to say."

"Sure, I get it, but I hope you're not lost. We've been driving a while; it must be dinner time."

He turned down an unplowed side street and pulled into a driveway of a small ranch home. "Nope, we're here."

His sense of humor was wasted on the detective.

Both men got out of the car. Stan grinned. "I hope she knows we're coming and bringing a fierce wind of memories that she might have buried."

"Yes, she does." He gave Stan a sideways grimace and walked to the door without waiting for him.

The door opened and a tall lean woman with shiny silver hair that hung to her shoulders motioned for them to come in.

They stood in a small living room with simple furniture and hardwood floors. Two cats were curled up together in an oversized basket, looked up, and quickly became bored.

When Meg spoke, her voice was soft and abrupt. "Please sit. I don't know how I can help you, but the memories are like yesterday for me. I'm sure you can understand why?"

The detective sat and apologized for bringing up such a tragic incident in her life. Meg nodded and sat across from them.

The house was warm, but the woman had a heavy knit sweater on with a shirt peeking out below the sweater's hem. She wore jeans and had a red housecoat with snow people on it over the top of her clothes. A spirit frozen since her sister's disappearance now wrapped itself in warmth to bring her solace.

Her dark eyes narrowed. "Gentlemen, I loved my sister and loved her husband Sam, but after what my sister told me when she moved into their new house after leaving New York, I didn't trust him. He was dark and preoccupied in a sneaky kind of way. Sally had finished her nursing degree and was able to move back here and be with her husband. I wish she'd stayed in New York."

Stan asked, "Was she afraid of her husband?"

"No, not at first. She'd been back about a week before getting hired at a local hospital on the night shift. That was in 1970, I believe. They lived happily as far as I could tell for the next five years, then she earned the right to work day shift and that's when it all changed." She played with her hair and pulled it around her ear, twisting it over and over.

"What changed?"

Her head slowly turned towards the detective. "Everything. My sister came over the second night home after her new day shift started and she was scared out of her mind. She stayed with me for several nights until Sam called and wanted to talk over dinner. I begged her not to go home, but she insisted she would be fine. I never saw her again." Meg's eyes bore into the detective like a frightened deer in the headlights of an oncoming car that couldn't do anything about it. Fate.

"Did she say what scared her?" Stan asked the question but wasn't sure he wanted to hear the answer.

Her eyes shifted to Stan's and her pain ripped into his heart. "Yes, Stan, of course. Sam had gone mad, threatening her life and called her horrible names, talked to himself, and accused her of all sorts of things. She said he was a man possessed. As I said, I begged her to stay, but she wouldn't. She thought she could help him, after all, she loved him. I saw the fear in her eyes, and after she left my house, I wept."

"I know you didn't see her again, but did you hear from her again?"

Meg shook her head and looked down at her lap. "No. I called and called the house, no one answered. I called the hospital and found out she hadn't been in for almost a week. That wasn't like my sister, not at all. I finally drove over there with a police officer; I think his name was Stone. Sam told us she walked out on him, and he hadn't heard from her, but never reported her missing, because he didn't think she was missing. Can you believe that evil SOB? He didn't think she was missing."

Brandon leaned his head to the side. "Did they question him in further detail?"

Brandon didn't tell the lady that the detective had been his father.

"Of course, they did. They grilled him, but there were no leads and nothing to go on, and worst they couldn't find Sally. Nine other women were reported missing during the same time frame as Sally. How is that possible, Detective?"

"I don't know, Meg. That's why we're still working on the cases. Do you know anything about the other women? Having that many disappear might be why they had a hard time zeroing in on your sister's husband. One wife goes missing, it makes it easier to suspect the husband. Do you happen to know their addresses?"

"No, I don't know a thing about the other women. I wasn't sure it was true, just neighborhood gossip, or that creep Sam started the rumors to throw the hounds of the hunt. Well, you can chat with the guy who built the house, I think it was James More, he owned a small building company that bought the land. Also, that criminal who murdered my sister lives in Wisconsin while she rots alone in some forgotten world of the dead. Sorry, the house is not in a city per say. The address has changed I'm sure over the years. I've blocked out that house, and could care less what the address is, whether it still exists or not."

She was bitter and the years hadn't erased the anger.

"If you can't remember anything else we'll show ourselves out," said Stan.

Stone stood and walked to the door. "Thank you for your time."

They'd almost closed the door when she grabbed it and said, "I almost forgot. Sally said there was evil in her husband, and he was obsessed with a black bull of some sort. I couldn't get her to explain to me what that meant, but it bothered her and when she talked about it, she wouldn't look me in the eyes. I hope that's helpful."

"Thanks. It might help." Stan placed his hand on hers offering what comfort he could, and both men nodded.

Their silence made the walk to the car longer than it was, they got in and simultaneously shut their doors. The sound had that soft and barely audible thud he liked. But today it drifted somewhere in between the snow that fell quietly to the ground and the dead-air that circled the men's head like a funeral wreath. It suffocated him.

The detective wasn't a chatty man and for that he was grateful.

It was a long drive until the car finally pulled up in front of Nudges and Nuances.

"You coming in detective?" He said it, but secretly hoped he wouldn't.

"Yep," stated the detective.

"Wonderful," said Stan with a little too much edge.

"What's wrong Stan. You don't want me to come in?"

"Of course, I do. I'm just in a mood today. Let's go see what trouble Claire has gotten into."

***

The shop was warm, and Claire sat looking over several books with Morgan huddled close by.

"Hey," said Claire without looking up.

Morgan looked up and said, "You two look cold. Coffee?"

"Sure, thanks Morgan," said Stan, "but I can get it."

"I'm with him," said the detective and followed him to the back room.

They returned with hot coffee and sat across from the girls.

"How'd it go?" Morgan seemed more interested in their findings than Claire.

The detective sat back and stared out the window, his voice flat like a tire that just deflated and had nothing left to give it forward motion. "Sally mentioned a bull to her sister."

"What?" That got attention. Claire lifted her head, and her eyes bulged from their sockets. Slowly she sat her coffee down on the table by the books, her hands were shaky.

"You okay, Claire?" Stan didn't want her to be upset, but at the same time the devil in him was glad something brought her out of the fog she'd been in for a week. That was the Claire he knew.

Her hair fell over one eye when she turned towards him. "Yes, just a little shook up. We saw it in pictures, but why would Sally mention a bull to her sister? Not to mention Margaret Trend, I assume it was her that mentioned it to you."

"It was a ghost, Claire. Apparently, Sally mentioned that her husband was obsessed with the bull and talked to himself. It was concerning enough to let her sister know how scared she felt."

Claire shuddered. "I bet a spirit possessed the bull. Why would a spirit want to? I didn't find anything on such an item in any lore, having said that it doesn't mean it couldn't happen. We're limited by our own knowledge."

Morgan raised her brows and picked up one of the books strewn about on the table. "Interesting enough in here it describes how objects can be manipulated to contain a soul." She flipped through the book and held open a page. "This explains how sorcerers, priests, devil worshipers or any such persons wanting to cage a demon, or a demonic human spirit should go about doing it."

Brandon said, "Seems hokey."

His partner in crime's head turned slowly towards the poor detective, and Claire said, "Bite your tongue detective. After everything you've experienced, anything's possible. Think of the collected items by the renowned paranormal investigator Lorraine Warren and her husband Ed."

"Yeah, you're right. It's not that I don't believe in demons and spirits, but the action of sending something inside an object, well, you know, I never bought it. Do you think it's possible that a person could create a spirit using an object? What if a person dies and wills their spirit inside an object so they can continue tormenting people, could that be our bull?"

"Oh, detective, now you're cooking," said Stan shaking his head. "Of course, that could be our bull. If not, why are we on this job? You thought it was paranormal, well now we know it must be. There are stranger things in the world than possessed objects, Detective." He overemphasized the word detective; it was what he did.

Claire smiled at him. "Okay, boys. We need to see if we can find that bull. Have all the boxes been gone through?"

"Yes, unless there are other boxes related to these events, we aren't aware of yet, anything is possible," said the detective.

"Well, you need to go through any that you might find with a name connected to what we already know," said Claire.

The detective nodded. "We just found out about Sam living in Wisconsin. When we got coffee I rang and confirmed our flight out. Stan and I leave tomorrow."

Claire looked at him, he wanted to smile, but instead his face contorted into puckered lips and his eyes narrowed into slits. He didn't want to make this trip with the fun and talkative detective.

Claire shook her head once, pursed her lips, and rolled her eyes which gave him a rating that pushed him so far off the chart he fell into a hole and with the toss of her head she buried him alive.

He coughed a little and tried to force out the substance called humiliation and cleverly produced a twinkle in his dark eyes. "I can't wait to go. I hope we get more answers."

Claire frowned and tilted her head contemplating if he was sincere, he laughed.

It forced a smile out of her and soon everyone was laughing. The joy of being a jerk was all about the technical ability one has to manipulate the laugh into a chorus of forgetfulness, soon no one cares nor remembers what you did to annoy them. He was brilliant.

The ring of his phone further saved his life.

"Hey, Stan here. Oh, how are you doing?" It was Lily.

After a while he hung up the phone and smiled.

"Who was that?" Claire had the curiosity of the cat, and he enjoyed playing with that.

"Who do you think it was?"

"Stan, knock it off. Who was it?"

He laughed. "You can't stand not knowing. It was Lily. She was released from the hospital and is doing fine. She wants to meet for coffee. I got the feeling she wants to finish what she started."

"There's nothing for her to do. Nana is taking care of things. She should leave it alone," said Claire.

"Yeah, I suppose you're right."

Another phone rang. "Busy day for phones," said the detective. He answered, got up and moved to the front of the store and stood facing the windows.

"I need more coffee," said Claire. "Anyone else?"

"No, I'm fine, "said Morgan.

"Do you mind?" He held his cup out.

"Nope. Got you covered, Stan."

The detective put his phone in his pocket and came back towards the group. "I had my assistant check on something for me. It seemed Meg forgot to tell us who Sam sold the house to before he ran to Wisconsin. A woman named Mabel Star. She sold the house, but I have her new address.

Chapter 15

The ghost of Sally Dodgers

Stan loved flying, but not today. Detective Stone sat next to him, and the detective's hands fidgeted with the jacket that laid across his lap. He started to count how many times Stone buttoned and unbuttoned the front of the dark coat he was noted for wearing. Thank God he hadn't worn his bloody tie. That would've been inappropriate.

He smiled and looked out at the clouds. Stone wouldn't care whether the tie was appropriate or not, that was the part of the dark and quiet guy he liked, and why he tolerated him. The detective was his own man and never driven by anyone's agenda but his own. He could relate.

Claire seemed lighter the past few days, but he hadn't liked leaving her and made sure Morgan had her back.

He should've moved that damn chest that Claire was so interested in opening. When Morgan confided in him that Claire wanted to see if the picture had changed, he'd freaked out. Morgan had paced and talked to herself about keeping her mouth shut the whole time he ranted and raved. He'd finally settled down and spoke rationally about the situation with Morgan. They were both worried and knew something should be done. He didn't think anything would help except to get the chest removed from temptation, but they were in such a hurry to leave, and Claire was always around so he never had the chance to eliminate the threat.

When they landed, he would call Morgan and see if she and Derry could get it moved out of there. He would suggest a storage locker. That would be a great idea for items that shouldn't be touched by unknowing hands. If they got a hold of the bull, it should be included in the list of dangerous items, if it couldn't be destroyed it needed a place where it would no longer do harm.

That made him think in a different direction. He and Claire wouldn't be around forever to keep things locked away. They needed to see about hiring younger people to have as apprentices, just in case. They could pick and choose in whom they would confide. It was crucial to keep this business going with proper and skilled hunters of the paranormal.

The detective gripped his chair as the plane began to descend.

Stan raised his eyebrows. "You okay?"

"Yep. Just never liked flying. I take a Benadryl an hour before I get on. Helps me relax and with allergies I might encounter on the plane."

"Good idea, I suppose."

After the smooth landing and a quick departure from the airport, they hurried into a waiting uber and were quickly transported to Fairfield Hills Apartments. The units were all on ground level with their own private entrances and each unit had attached to it a small and well-groomed yard that welcomed them to the front door.

"We won't be long, can you wait?" The detective handed the driver some cash.

"Sure, for about a half-hour then I leave." The man's broken English sounded like he'd moved here a while ago from India, but still carried enough charm of the language to detect his heritage.

"Fair enough," said Stone.

Both men hurried up the walk and knocked on the door. It took a few minutes for someone to answer.

A tall woman opened the door. She had dark hair and wore a casual set of scrubs that covered her slightly round figure. "Yes?"

"I'm Detective Stone and this is Stan Bradley we're here to speak with Sam Dodgers. I called yesterday to let you know we'd be here."

"He isn't well, but I suppose you could come in, but only for a minute or two."

"Sorry to hear that. We won't be long."

"Good luck getting anything out of him that makes sense," she said and pointed to a man who sat in a rocking chair. He had a bald head, and his eyes stared off into space behind a pair of thick-rimmed glasses.

Stone moved close and sat on the table in front of Sam. He didn't look like a killer, but what did a killer really look like? He thought a killer would be wild-eyed, a forced calm exterior with nervous hand movements, not looking a person in the eye, laughing, and pretending like they didn't know anything about anything. That was his point of view, possibly not Stone's. He thought of Stone on the plane with the nervous hand movements.

He decided to let Stone do the interview while he looked around the house for bull statues.

The kitchen was small. The nurse stood by a small counter and poured herself a cup of coffee. He smiled, she didn't.
There were very few distractions in the tidy home, no pictures, no statues, no trinkets, no books, in fact, if it weren't for a TV, chairs, tables, and coffee pots he would assume no one lived here.

He moved on into the bedroom, checked the drawers of one dresser, because only one dresser existed, opened the closet, not much there either. He looked under the bed, in between the mattress, and under the pillow being careful to put it back the way he'd found it. He moved to the bathroom, sparkling clean, a few towels and shaving items, toothpaste, soap, only the essentials.

A loud cry prompted him to move quickly into the living room where he'd left the detective.

"Get away from me. I can't take it anymore. Go away Sally, quit haunting me!"

Sam swatted the air, closed his eyes, and sobbed into his hands. "She never leaves me alone. I don't know where she went, but she must be dead to haunt me so long."

The detective pushed. "What did you do with her, Sam? Where's the black bull?"

He screamed and his nurse came running. "I don't know what you mean. She never leaves me alone. I never owned a bull, I hate bulls. Sally, get out of my head you evil bitch."

"I think you better leave now. I told you he was sick."

"More likely he's got the sickness brought on by guilt," said the detective.

The woman creased her brow. "What guilt are you talking about?"

The detective jerked his head towards the woman. "Guilt of a serial killer."

The woman's eyes grew, she gasped, and her hands grabbed her throat.

Stan swallowed hard. "Can I ask where you stay?"

She quickly recovered and answered. "Next door. Why do you ask?"

It was clear she didn't like being questioned.

Stan questioned her further. "Have you ever seen a ghost?" He felt the presence of Sally Dodgers and it gave him chills.

"No, of course not. I'm not insane."

He smiled. "No, and I wasn't implying that you are, but we've experienced them and we're not crazy."

Stone's eyes narrowed into a glare that focused on him. "Look, we just need some answers. Do you know who he might have sold the house to when he moved? Any paperwork. I'm not sure how long he's been in your care. What was the address?"

She moved towards the door but answered his question. "Yes, a woman named Mabel Star, and you might want to tell her girlfriend to stay away from us. She comes up here at least once a year trying to tell us he needs to give her the money back. Seems they sold it right after they bought it and lost a lot of money. Sam's insane, and I don't have that kind of money. It takes every dime he has to keep this place up and pay me for my time. Goodbye."

"Thanks," said Stone.

The uber just started to move but saw them as they came out of the house and stopped.

They hurried to get in.

The detective grunted. "Can you take us back to the airport?"

"Sure."

Stan said, "Well, detective you might be losing your mind. We already know the address and the name of the woman who bought the house, according to your assistant."

"Yeah, but I just wanted to make sure we had the right information. That things match up."

"Fair enough. Well, Stone what did you make of that place? I checked the rooms and found no bulls. In fact, it appeared no one lived there except for the necessities of food, furniture, and appliances. You were a little harsh on the nurse with the killer thing, and before you say anything, I shouldn't have mentioned ghosts, but I felt her...I felt Sally Dodger."

"I thought you might. Why would she pester him if he weren't guilty? I would bet my badge on him being a serial killer."

He tried his hardest not to laugh. The darkness that loomed over the detective made him wonder if he could be a serial killer. The detective was calling the kettle black. Took a serial killer to know one. Claire would smack him if she heard his thoughts, she disliked his use of cliches, but he rather enjoyed them. He grinned, yep would keep using those.

He rolled his tongue in his cheek. "I wonder why those girls think they should be financially compensated. Buying a home is a risk."

Stone shook his head. "Who knows, but maybe they were frightened away."

"Yeah. Can't wait to have a chat with those ladies."

Their flight wasn't scheduled to leave for several hours, so they went to an airport shop, had lunch and coffee.

Trying to have a conversation without being awkward wasn't easy with Stone.

Stan tried anyway. "Long trip and not much to go on except a name."

Stone looked up from his sandwich. "It's enough. The smallest information can lead to the truth. We know Dodger doesn't own the bull, got another lead, and I realized he was a serial killer. He may not realize it, but he is. That makes me think the bull is in control. Sounds crazy, but he even tried to forget it, or he was pushed over the edge so far that his memory is gone."

Stan grinned. "Yeah, you're right. When are you going to visit the gals? Do you want me there?"

"I'll need a day to locate them, and yes, you should come."

"Good. I'd like to ask why they left in such a hurry."

"Me too," said the detective under his breath.

Chapter 16

July 10, 1925- the death of Margaret Trend

I was frightened of him, I loved him, and it was love that compelled me to keep coming back. I didn't want to lose him, not like that.

"You're shaking. Do I scare you?" His words were spoken with a sinister edge that hurt my ears.

Chills started at the back of my neck and gradually moved down my back. I didn't want to look at him, but I did. His eyes were dark and cold and sent frozen shards into my brain. I shook more. "No, I'm just cold."

The moment the words left my mouth, I regretted it.

"You're not cold. It's summer and 89 degrees." His eyes narrowed. "I think you're afraid of me."

His fingers were laced with evil and slowly weaved their way through each strand of my hair depositing fear on every scalp follicle that I owned, and darkness raced toward my mind until my veins were ice, and I couldn't move. I stood still and watched his eyes bore into my heart until it bled.

"I love you." I didn't think those words, but they quietly streamed through the air fluttering about like they might mean something to him...and he would hear me saving us both.

His nostrils flared like the bull on his mantle. I hated it. It changed him or seemed to.

"I know, you do. That will make this easier. You are not liked by 'him,' and he doesn't want you to love me."

I never figured out who 'him' was, but Todd talked to 'him' like he was a real person.

At the beginning of his mental breakdown, that's what I called it, he'd argue about who was in control of his actions, and not with me. I was just a bystander. Eventually his anger grabbed hold of him like a noose around his neck until he screamed at someone he saw that I didn't. On more than one occasion Todd would shout, 'leave me alone,' and held his ears against an unknown terror.

Then it changed; the laughter, the violent outbursts were now directed at me, and there were nights I wasn't allowed to stay over because he had a headache. I returned late one night and saw a woman sat at the table. It broke my heart. I left immediately and stayed the night at my friend's house but couldn't tell her the truth. I was too ashamed.

In my own unstable state, I foolishly returned the next evening after fighting with myself and my friend, who relentlessly tried to convince me to stay away from the madman, after I'd broken down and told her the whole crazy story, bull and all.

He stood staring at me with his eyes glazed over as I questioned him about the woman who he'd apparently had dinner with last night. He denied it and his expression of a lost and confused boy had me almost ready to question my own sanity, if not for the dirty dishes, and the leftover dinner still on the table from last night, and the candles that I loved were burnt down to the wick.

I suggested therapy for both of us, which made him angry.

He believed that the other person that lived inside his mind hated me.

Then I noticed blood on the table and floor.

Now, I faced uncertainty and wished to God I hadn't stopped by to reason with him. I wanted to scream, it wasn't an option, because the knife he held in his hand might find its way to my throat. I couldn't trust it. I didn't want to die today.

"Who doesn't like me?" I choked out the words. A question I had asked over and over again and received no answer. Today would be no different.

"Don't pretend you don't know 'him.' I hate when you play dumb."

He grabbed my arm and slung me down on the chair. Panic welled up inside my chest. I felt the tip of cool steel on my neck. My body succumbed to uncontrollable spasms; it caused the blade to cut into my throat slightly. The warmth of the blood itched as it trickled down my neck. I closed my eyes to think. My heart took over my mind and tried to convince me it was a dream, and I was supposed to awaken to coffee and sunlight streaming through my bedroom window.

"Now look at what you did. You made me cut you. You wanted it. 'He' said you would."

I opened my eyes, stared into his eyes, and searched for the man I once knew. "Todd, I love you, you don't have to do this. Come away with me. Let's go back to the city." If I could get him away from here, I knew he would be okay, we would be okay.

I was as crazy as him if I believed that I could get through to him, it never worked in the past.

His laughter made me close my eyes again. I couldn't bear to see someone else inside his body and mind. They weren't his eyes. I took myself to the beach where a warm summer breeze lifted my spirit, ever so delicately. I needed those thoughts to control my rapid breathing.

He was going to kill me. My eyes burned as tears formed. I fought like hell and pushed them back. I had to stay focused. I desperately used what warmth I could conjure up from the beach and released my body from the frozen and immobile state it was in.

His arrogance made him think he had control over the situation, and he liked it. I might have a chance of survival if he believed he was in control, all the while I schemed to break free and run.

He was faster than me. That wouldn't work. I would have to kill him first. Could I do that? Could I kill another human being, much less one I loved? My eyes fell upon the cold, uneaten dinner, and the pool of blood on the tablecloth was the diversion I needed to help me center my emotions. Yes, I would kill him because my life depended on it.

He was a murderer, the blood indicated he'd slain the woman he'd been with last night. My heart hurt for her, and I calmed my racing heart. I played his game and waited for the moment.

Now, I wanted to laugh. I felt in control or was the overwhelming desire to laugh brought on by fear and hysteria.

The top of my laced dress ripped under his hands, as he kissed my neck. I felt sick. Yes, I could kill him because he was no longer himself, he was a demon and a murderer.

Once I put it into my head that I needed to kill the demon, that freed me.

I wasn't a killer, so I beat my head into the proverbial wall and tried to reason one last time. I told myself it was to get him relaxed.

"Todd, I came back to talk with you about moving into my place. It's in town and closer to everything. What do you think, Todd?" I used his name; it might bring him out and send the demon back where it came from, at least for now. I would repeat it over and over to get him to release me.

The pressure of the knife against my neck released.

My heart thumped against my chest like a church bell chime that might've given me away. I tried to control my hands as they shook and grabbed the knife from his relaxed grip. It surprised him.

I jumped out of the chair, he laughed and came towards me, the bull on the mantel fell to the floor. Startled, I faltered for a moment, he reached for me.

The knife attached itself to my mind becoming an extension of my nervous system; it reached out and came down on the arm of the demon. The cutting of meat was easy, but it hit bone and was thrown from my hand.

I watched as the knife slid across the floor further from my reach.

His scream got into my head and lodged there like a squatter. My eyes found his eyes and for a moment it was Todd, the love of my life. His chestnut brown eyes went hazy, and then he was gone. Blood poured from his arm, as he lifted it and knocked me into the counter and out of his reach. I grabbed a knife from the countertop and ran for the door.

I made it to the door, but looked back one last time. He wrapped a towel around his cut and kept moving.

The sun was dropping in the west throwing shadows in the woods, the woods I'd use as my sanctuary. I ran down the stairs and towards the abundant forest. I didn't hear the door behind me open and close. He might be slowed down by the wound. I ran up the slight hill towards the deep wooded land.

The wind blew my hair, and I felt free.

A memory of a little girl running down a hill that was covered in dandelions spoke to me from my past. I held three of the delicate flowers that had turned to seed, and I watched as the breeze helped them escape into the sky where they would find a home and share the seeds of their family next summer. I had believed the faster I ran the larger the family would be.

Thunder in the distance startled me and I felt the cold of the blade that still stung the sensitive part of my neck, and it reminded me of the dire situation I had put myself in by returning to save my relationship. It couldn't be saved, in the back of my mind, somewhere in the commonsense area I'd already known that. Hope? Did hope rule over common sense? Hope was just a wish, a manifestation of an idea that helped me survive, but I had given it too much importance, and now there was none. Hope was just a word for the weak.

As I ran the color of the wild blue indigo flowers that flourished to the side of me couldn't be saved in the distance by the crushing color of the red lucifer crocosmia.

I thought about that and veered into the woods, brambles cut me and tore my nylons. The blood dripped down my legs; there was nothing I could do about my now ruined green tea dress; fashion didn't matter when I was running for my life.

I was no different than the evil spirit that sought control of my fiancé. I too wanted Todd to be controlled by my wishes and leave the home he'd loved, but my desire was to protect him, not destroy him.

There was a large tree in front of me, an oak. I went to the other side and peered around. I didn't see him, but the woods were dark.

I tried to keep our relationship together, and had learned too late that I didn't let it go soon enough. Desperation was a form of madness, and I had succumbed. I slowed my breathing and listened for any movement. Nothing.

Keep moving.

My low-heeled shoes were a blessing and made it easier to maneuver the deep forest that was covered in large layers of moss.

My legs stung from the cuts as the poison seeped into my pores. I stepped away from the security of the magnificent tree. The smell of the woods intoxicated me. Mushrooms, and sweet earth followed me as I shifted back and forth through tall brush and old trees. The trees lumbered overhead like a canopy to protect me from the coming storm, and the starless night had provided a darkened blanket I might be able to stay hidden under until I reached the road.

What would I do then?

There was a lake here somewhere. I'd only seen it twice during the day and had no idea of its location in the dark. I didn't smell water, so I must be headed in the right direction. The lake would mean I'd gone too far into the woods and away from the road.

Tears fell to my cheeks.

'No Margaret, don't you cry, be strong,' the words of my mother sounded an alarm. She was running beside me, guiding me to the road. She'd died four years ago but her voice was clear.

Tears blinded me, made me fall, led to self-pity, and spurred on failure. I wiped them away with the back of my hand and focused on the freedom of the open road, and then moved slowly forward crawling along the ground.

I planned to follow the road while hiding in the trees that ran alongside it. Todd would come after me, he wouldn't let me go, not tonight. My hands tightly gripped the handle of the knife until they ached, and my fingers no longer seemed attached. A noise caused me to turn, then pain took me into a void.

***

The hot sun burned my face. I opened my eyes, shielding them from the bright light with my right hand over my brow like a tiny umbrella.

I hurt all over and had no idea why I had awakened outside in the heat of what appeared to be early evening. I stared at the sky and watched the sun as it battled with the moon and refused to set.

I sat up and opened my tightly clenched hand. The engagement ring for Margaret screamed at me, 'murderer.' The diamond was lusterless, and covered in blood. I shivered. *What happened? Where was Margaret?*

"Margaret!" My scream fell across the land on deaf ears.

I was weakened and bled badly. Confusion pumped into each of my tiny brain cells and left me whimpering like a lost puppy.

"Margaret." Only the blades of grass covered in blood heard the whisper.

I wasn't far from the house. I crawled to the porch and pulled myself up the three stairs that lead to the landing in front of my door. I used the railing and lifted my bruised body into a standing position. I tried to remember why a tea towel was tied around my arm.

There was no one out there. I wobbled inside and used the wall as a balancing guide until I reached the sink for a drink of water. My tongue swelled inside a mouth filled with dirt. The cool liquid engaged a sense of relief. Margaret had been there for dinner, and the unfinished food looked unpleasant on the plates. She must've been here last night, judging by the condition of the food.

I couldn't remember her being here. I raised my hands and allowed my head to fall into their bloody warmth. A loud moan escaped my mouth. "Why can't I remember?"

Exhaustion drove me to the couch where I collapsed, and drifted off into a deep sleep.

It was dark when a knock on the door awakened me from nightmares too hellish to believe.

I was in pain and still bled slightly. A few wounds had congealed.

Barely able to move I forced my body into motion. It could be Margaret.

Two police officers stood at the door.

I didn't want to talk, but I opened it anyway. "Can I help you officers?"

"Todd Griffin?"

"Yes."

The officer that spoke my name was an older man with a thick and shaggy grey moustache, who looked me up and down like I was his movie date, and he disapproved of my attire. The younger one gulped and averted his eyes from the bloody mess that stood in front of them.

"I'm told that Margaret Trend frequented your home and that you are engaged to be married."

"Yes, that's true." My voice shook.

"We'd like to come in."

Something broke inside my head and I backed into the room.

"Is she dead? No. No. That can't be. I loved her." My words of anguish sounded fake, like I was a bad actor in a horrible play, and I couldn't escape because the curtain wouldn't close.

I backed up to the couch. The room began to spin.

I heard someone talking, but their words quickly faded away into blackness.

***

I felt like I had a bad hangover. I eased my eyes open, and they revealed a clean hospital room. A nurse messed with an IV next to me that was hooked up to my arm.

She turned. "Oh, good you're awake. I'll be right back."

The last I'd remembered was two policemen wanting to talk to me about Margaret, and my reaction was insane. Dead? Why had I believed Margaret was dead?

The nurse returned with a glass of water and helped me into an upright position. "Drink it slowly. You were dehydrated and cut up badly. Are you hungry?"

Her round face and large dark eyes with a tiny mouth almost made me laugh. She reminded me of a marionette. She looked young. Her black hair was up in a hair net.

"No. I'm not."

She wasn't going to take no for an answer. "You should eat something. I'll bring you a cup of soup that should be easy enough on your stomach."

She sat the glass of water on the tray and abruptly left the room.

Margaret might be dead. How could I live without her in my life? My head pounded above my eyes, I closed them and allowed my thoughts to drift to happier times with Margaret. It was true I'd been a complete idiot the past six months and didn't deserve her as a wife.

I drifted into sleep, a dark and violent slumber; one you had if you were a hit man.

"Mr. Griffin?"

The soft whisper of a man's voice jarred me out of a violent dream where I was about to stab a woman in the throat, to the peaceful environment of the hospital room. I was thankful.

It was the older policeman that came to my home.

"I hate to bother you, but I need to talk with you about Margaret. You were pretty cut up and lost a lot of blood and when you passed out, we got you to the hospital." He looked down at a notepad. "Frankly, Mr. Griffin, I was surprised by your reaction. Shouting that she was dead. That doesn't look good for you. Do you mind telling me how you got so cut up and why you had what looked like a bloody engagement ring on the couch? I need you to identify this ring. Did this belong to Margaret?" He held up a bag that had Margaret's ring in it. My head thumped and reached my ears like a siren that wouldn't shut up. I started to hyperventilate. My eyes focused on the bloody ring.

"Margaret." Her name was barely a whisper of smoke that moved about the room and formed an image of her spirit that stood before me, accusing eyes, and a bloody knife in her hands.

The older officer twitched his moustache and leaned in over my head. "What's that you say, Mr. Griffin?"

I stared back and he withdrew from my side, frowned, and nodded to his partner who'd just entered the room.

"I think Mr. Griffin needs rest and has confirmed that the bloody ring did belong to his fiancé Margaret. We'll be back sir. And I'll want to know why dinner was left uneaten with blood on the table and floor. Looks bad Mr. Griffin."

I couldn't let them leave. A story filled my head, and I rambled on about Margaret and I being attacked by intruders. I wasn't sure if it was real.

They didn't go far and stood outside my door. I heard them talking.

"So, what do you think about his story, sir?"

The gruff voice of the head investigator was loud and clear. "I think his story about being attacked is dreamed up in his own delusional head. I tell you Jensen, those are killer eyes inside the head of a psychotic schizophrenic."

"Sir, let's get some lunch and come back by then he should be able to speak to us."

"Yes, but I doubt it, Jensen, I doubt it entirely."

***

I was glad to be home, the last two days of being questioned by the police had taken a toll on my well-being. They didn't understand I'd lost the love of my life.

The shadows quickly filled the cold walls as darkness closed in.

I made a quick supper and went to bed.

The house was quiet. My dreams weren't. Margaret haunted them. Her ghostly figure appeared to me over and over again. She held a knife and screamed. "Leave me alone. I love you."

The dream was confusing. A contradiction in her statement. Then she disappeared. I searched like a wild man, desperate to find her, and again she appeared. Then I heard the voice of 'him' as he spoke into my mind. "Kill her."

I awakened in a cold sweat, and I remembered. There was no one else, just me. My God, I killed Margaret. My head spun out of control as I stood up and moved into the kitchen.

All the deaths I had committed rushed into my heart and stabbed at it with the knife I'd used to murder those women.

"Guilty." Their voices shouted as their lifeless bodies bled and floated towards me holding knives out to take my life.

I am guilty. I went to the barn, got some oil, and returned to the house where I poured it all over. Then on me. I had no remorse for taking my life. The pain would be unbearable. Deserved.

"Guilty," I said.

Spirits surrounded me and their evil grins beckoned me to come to their side.

I heard the pounding of hoofs; the bull was running. It was 'him.'

"Coward."

His one word slapped me across the face, but the pounding of hoofs drove me forward. I lit the match and dropped it. I was past redemption.

"Yes, I am a coward, and beyond a shadow of a doubt guilty."

The fire tore at my flesh and ripped it open exposing blood, tissue, and bone.

It was hell.

Chapter 17

Current: The Paintings Beckon

Claire was finally alone at Nudges and her excitement and fear almost caused her to go home and not be tempted. Her body shook and all her fingers were riddled with pins and needles and made it difficult to open the door that led to Gabe's study.

Ever since Stan left with the detective the thought of opening the chest haunted her and drove her to near madness. It hadn't been a moment here and there, no, it was an inferno that grew inside her soul until common sense collapsed under the flames and the organized information locked behind neatly painted doors within her mind blew open. It made her vulnerable.

She opened the door and stepped into the quiet office that once belonged to Gabe.

The light behind her flooded the room. The chest was gone.

"What the hell." Her voice rang loud enough to wake the dead.

The flames from her soul's inferno billowed inside the skin on her face and warmed her cheeks.

She flipped on the light and scrutinized the room. No chest. She breathed deeply to avoid suffocation from the deception of her long-time friend, Stan.

She'd stepped closer to the persuasion of evil and would've released the damnation of the lady in grey's proverbial pandora's box.

Stan knew her recent behavior towards him had been more than a mood swing, or maybe Morgan told him, and if she had it was understandable.

She dropped her head, looked at the floor, and controlled the anger that threatened to ruin her relationship with Stan.

She moved towards Gabe's chair and sat down behind his desk. Every morning he'd sat there with his coffee in hand and quickly swung his chair in a circle that nearly tipped out the warm liquid onto his pants.

Her fingertips gently slid along the smooth leather arms of his chair, something she'd done at least a hundred times, or more, since his death. She felt his energy that was left behind where he'd touched the chair, and it moved through her fingertips and up her arms. Tears streamed down her face, a waterfall of emotions that were suppressed inside her heart since Stan had brought her back from self-sabotage where she'd been lost in guilt for not being able to save Gabe.

"Claire."

No, it couldn't be. She looked up through blurred eyes.

"Gabe?"

"Yes, my darling. Don't cry. I came to warn you not to open the chest. It's evil, she's evil. I love you and need you to move on."

His eyes were still grey skies on a rainy day. She ached for his touch. "I can't move on."

Gabe's smile faded and his hands went to his heart, one on top of the other. His eyes dropped and narrowed, as he nodded in acknowledgment.

She pushed the chair back and rushed to him, but before she reached him, he faded back to the world of the dead.

"I'm sorry, but I can't ignore it." She spoke the words softly in the empty room.

Her treatment of Stan brought shame into her heart. The darkness of the paranormal world consumed her soul. The witch had reached beyond the grave and enticed her to play the game she'd started centuries ago and wanted her to open the chest.

Claire enjoyed games and hadn't liked losing to Maureen during their first encounter, and the loss was a grave one.

"Lady in grey, I feel your disappointment, well hear this, I'm coming for you demon witch and when I do the ball will be in my court, and you will lose. But we'll do it when I'm ready."

The temperature in the room dropped 30 degrees or more.

"Got you, demon."

***

Nana stared into her eyes as she sat in front of her at one of their favorite restaurants. Those eyes entered Claire's mind, but when she spoke there was no clue that nana already knew without asking a question what the answer was going to be.

"So, butterfly, what's going on in that beautiful mind of yours."

The waitress came by with coffee and took their orders.

"You're kidding, right? I know you already know."

"If it wasn't 8:30 in the morning I'd order champagne," said Nana, as she tilted her head and sipped coffee.

Nana was a game player, much like her. Claire asked, "And what would we be celebrating, you lovely lady? And don't think for a minute that I didn't notice you shift the topic."

Nana grinned like a dealer that knew the player had just lost to the house. "Oh, nothing important, but I found the demon dogs and they're tucked away back where they belong, and did I mention your little book, I think I have a link to it."

She gulped and swallowed her coffee and avoided a projectile eruption. "What? That's amazing. I should've known you were up to your hands in magic when I hadn't heard back from you."

Nana ignored the comment and said, "Where's Stan? I thought my favorite guy would come with you."

We landed right back to Nana's original thought. She looked down and quickly answered. "He's with the detective in an interview about the crimes we're helping him solve. They flew to Wisconsin and should be back this evening."

Their food came.

Nana sat an egg on a piece of toast, sprinkled on pepper, and folded it over.

"Breakfast, my favorite meal of the day. Tell me butterfly what's going on with you and my favorite guy?"

She was amazed by Nana's ability to complete a mundane task, not bat an eye, and moved on to asking that awkward question that left Claire's cheeks warm and her body squirming.

She put down her coffee and for a moment watched Nana as she sipped coffee, continued eating, and looked up and smiled.

"It's complicated."

Nana raised an eyebrow and stopped eating.

"Really?"

It wasn't a question but a 'don't dance with me butterfly, just answer the question.'

Claire looked into her eyes. She had the clarity of a forty-year-old and the spirit of a teenager. "Okay, I've been unfair and mean to him the past month. He never said a word, but took the chest and moved it where I couldn't find it. That's all."

Her dark eyes lit up and she winked in verification of being right and slightly nodded her head. Her coffee cup lifted to her mouth, and she glanced at her granddaughter over the rim. "So, Claire you wanted to check on the paintings. Your curiosity might cost you another life, could you live with that outcome."

Nana's ability to spank her without a touch blew her mind. "No, I couldn't live with that outcome."

"Then be thankful you have Stan. He is a true friend who looks out for you. Let the past go and move on, butterfly. You don't want to lose Stan."

It was true, and if she continued to treat Stan the way she had, he would be forced to leave for his sanity.

She picked up a spoon and played with her black coffee stirring it until she had a vortex inside of her cup and wished she could jump in. "He told me the same thing." A tear formed in the corner of her eye.

"Who told you the same thing?"

She stopped stirring. "Gabe did. He came to me at the studio and told me to leave it alone. I was blunt and said no. He knew better than to argue with me and left." She looked up.

Nana sat back in the booth, almost curled up like she was ready to plant herself there until she smacked some sense into her granddaughter, or at least convinced her to let it go. But she never said a word.

The waitress came by smiled and poured out more coffee.

"Thank you," said Nana, leaned over, and grabbed her coffee.

Claire said, "I see your point about Stan. I'll try to get a handle on it."

"You need to come and see me more often. We still have work to do, and now more than ever. The Phoenix book is a problem and a mystery," Nana said.

"How so?" She grabbed her cup, sat back, and got comfortable.

"I've never seen anything like it. There're three different types of old-world scripts, and I don't understand two of them. The one I might be able to figure out appears to be written in a strange poetic form that masks the truth of what it is, using metaphors that made my head hurt trying to figure it out."

"Wow, that's interesting. Don't you find it a little frightening? You usually have no problem deciphering books."

Her playful eyes showed their age. "Yes, I do find it slightly intimidating. I might need help."

"Okay, I can come over and help you figure it out. When do you want me there?"

Nana lifted her face and locked her eyes on hers until they grew into orbs like mini crystal balls, but nothing was revealed-the blackness forbade it. "Oh, no butterfly. I mean someone of my caliber. You can't help, but I know who can."

"You're scaring me. Why would you need another witch-like yourself?"

A shadow fell across Nana's face. "In the middle of the book is a binding spell. I'm locked out."

They never said much after that, and after nana left, she took out her phone and made a call.

"Hello."

"Hi, Morgan. First, I'm not angry, but where is the chest? I'm sure Stan pulled you into his drama."

"I can't say. We are concerned for you, Claire. Your obsession is unhealthy."

Claire said, "Can't say because you don't want to or can't say because you have no idea where it's at?"

"I'm sorry, Claire I don't want to discuss it with you, right now. Talk to Stan about it when he gets back. I just walked into the store. I canceled the incoming calls to the office phone as you said and redirected the number to my cell, yours, and Stan's. No new messages. Gotta run possible customer just walked in."

The disconnect of the cell sounded more permanent than normal. She laid her phone on the table and knew she had to let it go, with the books they had in their possession and the demon from the airport, too much was at risk to get Maureen back in the picture. Her curiosity burned with desire, but her common sense was hopefully taking control.

If she couldn't help with The Phoenix book, she needed to continue studying the golden rose of 22 petals book.

"Penny for your thoughts."

She knew that voice. looked up and found her friend stood by the booth. "Charlie. It's great to see you."

"Mind if I sit?"

"No, I was about to leave, but now that you're here I think I'll stay for a while. This weekend? Dinner with Connie Downs?"

"Yeah, sure, but not at my house," Charlie said.

"Why not?"

"Your home is more inviting, plus I wanted to speak with you about something important that might require your expertise. Strange paranormal events are happening around my home. Not sure what's going on."

Charlie averted his eyes and stared off into space, reached his arm up in the air, and got the waitress's attention.

"What can I get you?" The waitress responded quickly.

Charlie said, "Two eggs and toast will do me fine. Any toast with seeds will work."

She was polite and turned her attention to Claire. "And you?"

"Oh, I don't want another breakfast, but maybe a coffee refill?"

The three of them chuckled at her comment.

The waitress poured her another cup. "Can I get you some ice water?"

Claire grinned. "Two, please. That would be wonderful."

Charlie nodded.

She looked at her friend. His eyes peered at her and twinkled with mischievous mystery. He was adorable.

"Well, tell me then, what's going on over at your home?"

"I couldn't sleep last night. I walked out on the porch to get some fresh air and there they were, dancing orbs flitting about through the trees. Loads of them. I thought that was right up your ally, my friend."

"Wow, that's cool. All these years I've never known where you lived. We've met out or at my house. I guess it's about time I came by your place. Can't make it until Monday if that works. You making dinner?"

His laugh was infectious. "Yes, I guess I'll have to, won't I? You won't come unless I offer a perk. I am a great cook, not to brag. The house is nothing too exciting, but it's home. How about we shoot for 8pm Monday night, my place, and what time this weekend at your place?"

"Saturday evening at seven? That day and time worked for Connie. I thought being at our house might not make it seem so date-like and you could just get to know each other. I think you'll hit it off."

"Oh, I'm sure we will. You do have a knack for setting people up." He chuckled and the waitress brought his eggs over easy on toast. He glanced at his breakfast and said, "Simple breakfast for a simple man."

The water was a thankful sight. Her over-reaction to recent events left her parched.

She drank it heartily and then said, "Charlie, you are not a simple man."

"No, I suppose not. Dinner at my house Monday at eight then."

"Sounds great. I look forward to dancing with the orbs."

Without warning her stomach did a backflip that left her queasy.

He nodded. "Dancing with the orbs. Interesting. And you, my friend are not a simple woman."

She tried to smile, but something inside of her drank it and spat out a frown accompanied by a deep crease between her eyes, so deep her eyes blurred.

"No, I am not." Her voice was dark and the sound of it unrecognizable.

Charlie looked at her with widened eyes, but quickly they softened into a look of concern. "Claire, are you alright?" He touched her hand with his and tilted his head.

The feeling cleared and her embarrassment disappeared. Her smile came back. "Sorry, Charlie I had a moment. You know how that goes with those of us who feel outside of our world."

He nodded his head and laughed. "I do indeed." He took a mouthful of eggs. "These are delicious and garlicky."

"Good. I do love garlic, myself. I put the powder on everything, except fruit. Stan should be back tonight."

"That's good. I saw Nana outside on my way in. She looks good but preoccupied. I said hello and she walked right past me without a glance."

"Yes, she worries about some of the crazy things her granddaughter does or wants to do. That's enough to enhance her preoccupation."

He looked up and his left eyebrow rose. "You? I don't believe for a minute that she would worry about anything you're not handling properly. Has she had any luck with the book of the Phoenix?"

"Oh, my friend, she does have occasion to worry about my interests. I feel that book is playing on her mind, as well. More than one magical language in that book, and part of it is sealed. She needs more help with it than I can offer. I'm intrigued and would love to help with it, but I think until she gets it figured out, I would only be a nuisance, if you know what I mean?"

"I think I do. If anyone has a skill and a challenge to that skill is in front of them, they certainly don't need the distractions of a novice questioning everything that they do." Charlie handled the wording with delicate precision.

Claire said, "Yes, I do understand her feelings on keeping me in the background on that one, but I was glad she filled me in."

He pushed his plate back. "That's me done. I've got a busy day, and you were kind enough to hang out with me and keep me company. I appreciate it, Claire. Until Saturday unless I run into you sooner."

He stood, smiled, paid his bill, left a tip, and quietly left the building.

She watched him and wondered who Charlie Burns was. Hell, sometimes she wondered who she was, the woman known as Claire O'Leary, a woman with a long line of witches in her gene pool, from Ireland to Scotland, and a fire that couldn't be put out, even when it got out of control.

Chapter 18

Dinner, the bull, and orbs

Dinner had gone without a hitch. Unless you wanted to count the fact that Stan arrived an hour late, so dinner was cold. Connie was nervous meeting a new man, as a dinner date, and knocked the bottle of Monti Bussia Barolo onto the floor and shattered it. Charlie accidentally dribbled white sauce down the front of his nice blue shirt and onto his jeans, and she over-baked the homemade bread drying out the inside.

Connie was getting ready to leave and it was only 9:30.

She tried to convince her to stay. "Connie, really, it's no problem about the wine. Those things can happen. You didn't have dessert yet."

The dessert was supposed to have been a cheesecake from a bakery down the road that had the most incredible delicacies, but Stan forgot to stop and pick it up. The only thing she had to offer was some leftover oatmeal and date energy cookies she'd baked two days ago.

Connie hugged her and smiled. "It's okay, Claire. I'm rather tired tonight."

Charlie grabbed his coat. "Wait for me Connie, I'll walk you to your car. Maybe, we could go for lunch sometime."

"Thanks," said Connie and slid her arm into his outstretched one.

Claire said goodbye and shut the door.

She went into the kitchen where Stan was already cleaning up the dinner from hell.

He grunted. "Sorry, I forgot dessert and was running late."

"Well, no worries. It fit perfectly into the theme of the evening, drastically done dinners, with no leftovers."

He lifted his head, sucked in the left side of his lip, and his eyes grew underneath raised brows.

The two of them burst into laughter. Tears ran down her cheeks and her side ached.

"We blew the lid off of that dinner. We should host our own TikTok gig, 'The Aftermath.' He barely spat out the words before his voice choked and his laughter threatened to cough out a lung.

They hadn't laughed that hard in a long time. It felt good.

"Coffee?" She smiled at him, and when he touched her arm her body twitched, and her stomach sank. *Oh, no Claire, stop it. No desire, just friends, just friends.*

"That'd be nice. You buying?" His question was lit up with a smile that reached into her heart until it almost burst from the joy of it.

"Haha, very funny. I'm capable of brewing a pot of coffee." She looked at him again and quickly looked away. *What was she, a schoolgirl?*

His eyes grew. "Hey, what's wrong? Why are you looking at me with those strange-looking eyes?"

"Why sir, whatever do you mean?" She faced the sink.

"I'm not sure what I mean. It's like you're studying me for some weird paranormal sacrifice that involves a ritual of some sort."

She turned and laughed. "If it was, you'd be the last to know."

His hands flew over his head hiding his face behind the symbol of a cross his fingers managed to create. "I thought so. Begone evil witch of the paranormal world."

She grinned and changed the subject. "I'm going to Charlie's on Monday for dinner, it seems he has orbs in the woods. I guess it's the first time he's seen them."

"Damn. I'll be with the detective at a gal's house named Amy Day. It would appear that she knows about the bull. Stone can go on his own if you want, I can cancel and come with you. The orbs seem more interesting."

"Here's your coffee, and no. You weren't invited, my friend. Only evil witches of the paranormal world were sent an invite. If I need you, we'll go back, but it sounds interesting."

His brows creased together. "Anything I should know about? You and Charlie an item?"

"No, of course not. It's just orbs and dinner. I'd rather have you with the detective, you know tapping the paranormal part of the investigation. Why would you say that? You jealous?"

His face reddened and he looked at his cup. "Heck, no. I just wondered that's all. I get I should be there helping Stone, but orbs, how cool is that?"

He ignored her question, again evading his feelings. She often wondered if he had feelings for her, but it could ruin everything. Clearly, they had feelings for each other but knew better than to cross the friend zone into the dating zone. She didn't pursue it.

"Yeah, it's rather cool," she said.

"I suppose you're right; I need to be with Stone. Sometimes I think he's the murderer, oh not years ago but now. He's rather dark."

Her head jerked towards him, and she shook it. "No. I grant you he is dark, but he wouldn't commit murder."

"Maybe so, but there's something about him I just can't put my finger on. You felt it too. I'll keep a close eye on him. Interesting. A murdering detective, but it wouldn't be the first time that's happened."

"Oh, Stan I like Detective Stone, and I feel he wants to solve this murder more than anything. Why else would he invite us in? To blame it on the paranormal? I don't think so, it is paranormal."

"Okay, I'll drop it, but I'm still watching him.

***

Monday arrived quickly; the weekend was a blur.

She thought of Stan and Stone going to the house of Amy to possibly find out more information on the bull. She walked into their shop, as the reassuring tinkle of the bell sounded. The smile on her face was for Gabe, he wanted the bell and found it in Spain when on holiday. There was a cross made of iron inside the iron bell that made a lovely sound; the sound more delicate than it looked.

"Good afternoon," said Morgan.

"Good afternoon to you. Thanks for covering for me this morning. I had some errands to deal with. Has Charlie been in?"

"Not yet. What's up?"

"We're going to dinner at his place. It seems he has orbs in his woods. Would you like to join me?"

Morgan turned in her direction and poked out her bottom lip. "I would love to, but the twins are playing their instruments in a concert at school tonight. Usually, they have it on a Friday, but apparently their teacher is leaving on Friday for another position on the west coast. Today was the only day it fit into her schedule."

"I tried to get in earlier, but traffic was bad, and Charlie will be here in a couple of hours to pick me up. I suppose I'll go over some of the smaller files and call clients to see if all is still okay. I'll be in the back if you need me."

"Sure, there's nothing else to report. I was straightening up the place, but if it's okay with you I'd like to head out early."

Claire turned and smiled. "Of course, you deserve it. Enjoy the night out with the boys. And I'm sorry that you had to tell Stan about the chest. You had every right to. You might've saved me."

"No worries, we're good. I'll leave now then. You do the same, Claire, and enjoy your evening. I can't wait to hear about the orbs. Exciting business."

"Yes, it is. Exciting business," she said, as Morgan grabbed her coat, waved her way, and left, out into the cold afternoon air.

She headed to the back and welcomed Gabe's old desk and sat in his chair, sliding her fingers down the arm in a slow loving manner, taking in his energy.

After ten phone calls and two cups of coffee the front doorbell chimed.

"Claire, hey, it's Charlie. Are you back there?"

"Yes, almost done. Come on in." She glanced at the clock over the doorway, 5PM.

He walked in the small office and said, "That can wait we have a very important date, and I got out something special for dinner."

"Yes, I'm excited. I've never seen your place, and the orbs will be amazing. Let me lock up and we can go. At least it's dark early, that's good for the orbs. I hope they put in an appearance."

"With you there, I'm sure they will."

They headed out and got into his jeep.

"I've always wanted a jeep, especially for the winter's around here, "Claire said.

"Yes, it comes in handy. Look at this traffic. I'm out in the country, so it might take us an hour or so, I hope that'll work with your schedule."

"Sure, no worries. Stan is out with Stone on an interview, visiting a couple of gals that happen to live in the country, as well. I'll message him when we get to your place, and he can stop over later and pick me up when they're done."

"Sounds good."

She made small talk on their drive, asking about his date on Friday and what he thought. He smiled and never said much about her, just that she seemed really nice, and it might be difficult to be in a relationship with her, because she clearly wasn't over her husband.

That might present a problem with her husband still in the picture, so to speak. She completely understood Charlie's thoughts on the topic, you never could tell how a spirit might react to his wife with another man...dead or not.

She'd always enjoyed the darkness of the countryside, where you could almost count the stars in the vast sky.

Charlie turned off onto a dark country drive that was lit only by a couple of small reflector signs.

"Here we are, home sweet home. I haven't brought someone here in years. I think I've wrapped myself up in work and travel, and eating dinner out most of the time. I hope the stove still works." His chuckle was like the sound of glass being tapped with a fork. It made her laugh.

"Well, even if it doesn't, we always have cereal, right? You do have cereal, Charlie/"

His smile wrinkled his skin on the corner of his eyes and for some reason it comforted her. Maybe, because her dad's face had also done the same thing. She still missed him.

He pulled up to a small cabin with a nice front porch, land and woods surrounded the place like a home placed at the end of a tunnel.

She sent a message to Stan on his cell to give him the location and told him to hurry over for the fun, and if he was lucky, he might get some dinner.

"Well, Claire, let's check out the woods first. Maybe they'll come for you. Remember, I told you they don't always appear, and I just recently noticed them. I'm not sure if they've always been there or just now decided to show up."

"Sure." She'd worn a warmer coat, hat and gloves knowing she might be outside on this frigid evening.

"It's beautiful out tonight, even if it's cold," he said.

"I think I feel something, something dark." She shivered.

"Well, I'm glad you can feel something, I can't even feel my toes."

She smiled at his sense of humor, much like Stans.

They walked for a while, moving in the direction of where he'd seen the orbs and interestingly enough, that wasn't where she felt the darkness lurking.

They chatted quietly for about an hour when Charlie decided he needed to start dinner or they'd never eat, and the cold made him hungry.

She nodded in agreement, but decided she'd stay out for a while and wait until dinner was ready.

"Okay, have it your way. I'll let you know and get a fire going to boot."

"Thanks, Charlie."

He squeezed her hand and left her alone in the dark woods lit only by the stars and a sliver of a moon that peeked over one of the highest trees she could see. She really liked Charlie. He was kind and had a giving nature.

She sat on an old tree stump and focused on the energy that surrounded the woods. After a while, the darkness that lurked close by finally softened into a paler shade of grey and brought with it a sort of magical feel.

The snow under her boots sparkled and she couldn't resist picking it up. When she was a child, she'd thought the snow was crushed diamonds full of a quiet and secret magic. Glancing at it now, she really did feel the same way about snow and magic. Her eyes closed as her hand folded around the snow in her palm...something brushed her cheek.

Her eyes flew open, and she fell backwards onto the soft ground as orbs circled her and moved about the trees and gently touched her head, feet, arms, and legs with what she'd describe as gentle nudges, or hugs.

They were clear in color, but they shimmered with white delicate sparkles and moved quickly about. She could see through them, and if she could hold one in her hand it would fit nicely, like a softball. The orbs made no sound. Their energy was in the movement.

"What are you?" She asked them aloud, but knew they couldn't answer her, but she felt something from them...sadness and fear.

She tried counting them, but they moved so much she couldn't tell. She got to 25 and started over.

They were trying to tell her something, but she had no experience with orbs, certainly they must have been people, and these were their spirits, maybe trapped here, or maybe just being what they are. Some believed orbs were fairy folk.

She needed to find Charlie. Dinner could wait.

The orbs followed her all the way to the edge of the woods, but went no further. Instead, they became a frenzy of electrical activity and moved so fast, she could no longer make out their shapes.

She made it to the top of the porch and turned. Their mass of soft light lit up the woods.

She opened the door and went in.

Charlie had a nice fire going, and it was cozy. Dinner smelled amazing. She shook her coat off outside and hung it on a rack by the door.

"Charlie, I saw the orbs." She could barely contain her excitement.

His voice rang loud and clear from a short distance away. "I'll be out in a minute, just changing."

"The fire's lovely and dinner smells great."

He had a small and cozy home. The table was set with nice china, and she moved about with anxious anticipation over what she'd seen in the woods. He would be a great one to help with this encounter, although she hoped Stan would get here soon and not take too long on their interview.

She sat by the fire to warm herself and looked about admiring all the books he had on display, some of them were filled with history, magic, and scientific studies that covered various topics, from the paranormal to the big bang theory.

One caught her eye, and she knew she had to read it. She stood and took a closer look. The words were ones she didn't know, ancient in origin. The cover was bright red and had splotches of black all over it. *Interesting.*

She nearly jumped out of her skin when Charlie turned on some music.

"Charlie, that's not the best music for dinner, and if you don't mind me saying a little loud." She wasn't sure if he heard her, there was no answer.

She shrugged, stood on her tiptoes, and pulled the book from the shelf, and with a start she grabbed the object behind it and fell over backwards onto the floor. Charlie stood over her, grinning, and reached out his hand to help her up.

"Charlie, what the hell is this?"

"Oh, that? I wondered where it got to."

Chapter 19

The beginning-1802-1820, John Sutton and the bull

I was eight years old when my mother died at the hands of my father.

He was violent and drank heavily.

It was a warm July 4th, and the sun was just setting over the trees on the west side of our farm. I always sat on the porch and marveled at the beauty, and often wondered where the sun disappeared to, so the moon could shine instead. The fireflies lit up the trees as the darkness fell over me. Where did they hide in the daytime? Their lights were a magical wonder, my mother's words. I sighed and placed my hands behind my head. The screen door opened, and my mother joined me.

She smiled as her dark hair fell over her eyes, until she pulled it back in place. Her raven eyes twinkled in the moonlight, she took my hands, and we danced on the porch, as she hummed a song that would stay with me forever. It was a song she said she made up, and insisted it wasn't particularly good, but I loved it as much as her.

A man walked along the road towards us, or should I say staggered. We knew who it was, and my mother's demeanor changed with the sight of him, and so did mine. I despised him and wished he would never come back. We were happy until he returned.

My father reached the porch, and my mother headed inside.

"Where you going woman? Don't you want to play with me in your magical woods?" His voice was harsh and condescending as he grabbed her arm and turned her around to face his monstrous face.

"Not tonight, Dale. Your dinner is done. I'll heat it up for you." She turned and he let go of her arm, but followed her in.

The night was over, and I followed my father into the house, in case she needed me.

He started screaming about the food and grabbed her and wanted her to go into the woods with him, she managed to jerk away from his grip, but that angered him more.

"Don't you want me?" He held her by both arms close to his boozy breath.

"Not when you're like this Dale. Let's get some food in you first."

"I'm sick of your food. I will have you." He pulled her closer to him, and she screamed.

I watched helplessly as his large sausage fingers closed around her throat draining the lifeforce from her small frail body. My screams echoed hers until she stopped...but, I screamed even after my father left, and continued until my Aunt May grabbed my hands and pulled me close to her, almost close enough to suffocate me. I didn't care.

***

My Aunt May was my mother's older sister and lived with her husband Alfred in a small apartment in the city, but with my father now imprisoned and my mother dead the court allowed Aunt May to have ownership of the house until I was 18 and then I would become a new farmland owner.

My aunt was nothing like her sister. She was harsh, cold, and had no romance in her soul whatsoever. Although I was lucky that my aunt and uncle were on their way to our house the day my father murdered my mother. there was no telling how long I would have screamed. I imagined until my voice gave out.

Alfred didn't do much to liven up the place, but he did take good care of the land and buildings on it. He turned the farm into a profitable business, and if it wasn't for helping him out in the early mornings I might've run away. He taught me how to run the business and took me into town where we sold our crops. It was hard work, but the job gave me something to wake up to.

He'd brought in many farm animals, as well, and I became attached to a grumpy chicken whom I named Gerdie, and a pig that inherited the name Oink, for obvious reasons, and I can't forget Marvel, a beautiful black mare that let me ride her bareback and into the woods she'd go. We were a family of sorts.

I detested being on the land where my mother was murdered. On a good day, her face smiled on my heart and her song played in my ears until I felt her close. On a bad day I heard her scream and watched her slump to the floor where my dad left her as he walked past me and out the door. I never saw him again. I avoided the spot where she lay with no breath in her body and her limbs weakened to nothingness.

No one helped me. I was left to understand her death and get over the sadness on my own, I never did.

She'd left me a gift, a black bull. It was the last thing she'd given me. She'd found it when she was a little girl and kept it because it was shiny. Later she'd learned it represented strength, stamina, and confidence, and some religions believed it was a representation of heaven. She wanted me to feel safe with it and if she wasn't around, I should remember to be strong every time I looked at the bull. I held onto it all the time and when I was busy on the farm, I kept it safe in my pocket.

Aunt May taught me school every day after chores and breakfast. I didn't mind learning new things. She was a tough teacher and would smack my hands with a stick if I daydreamed for one minute. At night I would lie in bed and hold my fingers and hands from the pain and blisters. One night Alfred came to my room and put a salve on them and bandaged them. He wrapped them over and over until I could barely move my fingers, but he winked at me and said, "All done. There's enough bandages to prevent her from hurting you, or you from being able to take class anyways."

The next morning, I worked through chores with the help of my uncle and could barely eat breakfast with my hands wrapped. Aunt May gave Uncle Alfred a mean look like a bulldog ready to pounce, but cancelled classes, except I still had to listen to her lecture me on history, for the next week. She managed to give me several exams by allowing me to answer her questions aloud. Alfred was the best.

***

We followed a set routine for the next ten years. I never played with other children but grew fond of Albert.

One morning I went to see why Uncle Alfred hadn't come to breakfast, and there he was dead as my mother had been, but without a forced trauma that made their corpses look quite different.

I went back to breakfast and finished eating. Aunt May had just come in from gathering eggs. That was the one chore she enjoyed each morning.

"Well, did you get that lazy man up, boy?"

I hated it when she called me boy. My dad called me boy. I had a name. "He's not getting up." That's all I had to say about it.

"What are you saying?' She moved towards Alfred's room. "Alfred?"

I put my hands over my ears, but I could still hear her screams and sobs that pulsated through my blood, touching every part of my body. I think I was about to burst from the inside out. I didn't think about that, instead I stared at my hands, the ones Alfred had saved.

Aunt May came out of the room sobbing and sent Mike, a live-in-farm hand to notify the clergyman.

It seemed hours before a coroner showed up to take Alfred away. I would never see him again. I hoped he was somewhere safe with my mother. There must be a place that holds beautiful souls inside a magic box where they can live amongst gentle rains, flowers, fruit trees, vegetable gardens, and magical animals that help them harvest for a daily feast. They might not need food but could still grow gardens for the pure joy of it. Maybe, there could be sunny days all the time.

I watched them take Alfred away and went out to do the chores. Aunt May went to her own room, leaving the eggs on the table and never came out of her room for five days. I think she finally got hungry.

I turned 18 when she was in her room and made a nice dinner and cake to celebrate. I had potatoes and chicken. The next day a man came with a decree that said I owned the land. That was when I sent Mike away. He could be quite bothersome. I suppose I could let my aunt stay here so long as she didn't call me boy, or boss me around anymore.

I wasn't sure if she had it in her, her will had left her, and I was basically alone, but that didn't bother me at all. I liked being alone.

***

Three years later Aunt May passed on while walking down the apple orchard. I wasn't sure if she would see my mother and Uncle Alfred. She was a nasty woman. Maybe, there was a special place for nasty people like her to go where they could enjoy tormenting other souls through eternity.

I sat at her wake and wondered about the people there. Sat in the front row of the pew were three churchgoers; I recognized from frequent visits to our home. They tapped me on my head, hugged me, and shook their heads, like the sadness of her passing would affect poor me. It didn't. I didn't like her at all. I only let her stay there because she'd tried to teach me what she could, so I owed her that much, didn't I?

Time seemed to stop, and the loneliness crept into my soul like 'The Black Death.' I tried to date, and brought a girl my age, named Jane, to the house, but she didn't like the bull my mother gave me, and made fun of it. I didn't like that and had to kill her. I buried her in the woods, and no one knew where she'd gone. They didn't suspect me, the whole town felt sorry for me.

I didn't like killing, but it needed done, for my mother. Maybe, I had an illness like my father, but I didn't think so, because I didn't drink alcohol.

I had a different kind of sickness and started talking to the bull about how I felt, and there were times when it answered me, or I imagined it was my mother talking to me. I wanted to live in the bull, I was sure that's where my mother had gone, so I gathered dark magic books and started my practice of demonic witchcraft. I became quite an expert.

I needed to send beautiful souls inside the bull to tell my mother how much I missed her, so I started looking for women that were kind, but had no large family. I sacrificed them to the bull. All except one. I never knew her name, to avoid attachment, but kept her for a while. She gave me a son; I named him Robert. After he was two, I sacrificed her too. She was causing too much trouble. I didn't kill her in front of my son. I wouldn't want those memories to haunt him like they did me. The souls would be able to keep mother and Alfred company.

They were all buried in the woods together, so they could help each other reach the magic portal. I placed the bull in the woods so they would find it at night when their spirits were alive. I killed so many that I lost count.

One night the bull warned me that the town folk were coming for me. I had nowhere to go. I set up a ritual in the front yard with the bull at the center of it, but they came too soon. It was a mob, and they had a rope. I couldn't hide behind pity any longer. I couldn't fight off thirty strong men who grabbed me and tied me to the front porch post, but not before I handed the bull to my four-year-old son. He held onto it for dear life.

I sang her song, "In eternity we touch, in eternity we breathe, but now, we break the rules."

They threw chemicals on me and then a torch. Some screamed and spat a name at me, like I was irredeemable. "Demon go to hell and burn." I went up like a dead pine tree. I felt no pain. I didn't know why. I proceeded to transfer my soul to the bull, and watched my body burn, and then I watched the only life I knew, and the only home I had ever known go up to the heavens in thick dark smoke.

I was still awake though, inside a dark place, inside the bull. Mother wasn't there and neither were the women I killed. I was disappointed. The bull was the magical portal, or so I'd thought. I was wrong.

A tall man took the bull from my son's tiny hands and buried me in the woods. He never cried, even as they ripped his father from his hands and led him away.

It took years before someone dug me out of the earth and when I awakened, I wanted revenge, and I wanted to play.

My name is John.

Chapter 20

White lies beyond the dead.

"I just got a text from Claire giving me her location. We can join her later. There are orbs after all."

Detective Stone took his eyes off the road for a moment to glance in his direction. "Sure, we can. Is she over at Charlie's? I think I remember something about her saying he saw orbs."

"Yeah," he said, and looked out the window into the night. Spirits were moving through the woods to the right of him. He wasn't too happy that they were appearing more frequently. He'd opened a door. "Man, I love the country, but the roads are so dark. A little scary."

"You, okay? I didn't know a guy of your type would fear a dark road; you deal with darker things than that."

"Yes, you're right. Did you ever murder anyone, Detective?" *Yes, he blurted it out.*

Stone shuddered and kept his eyes on the road. "I have killed people, but not murdered. I would like to believe there's a difference."

Stan nodded. "I believe there is."

"That's a strange question, Stan."

"I suppose so, but I had to ask." The darkness he'd felt around the detective required that he had to ask, not that it mattered, people lie.

"Well, it looks like we're almost there. Are you ready for this, Stan?"

"I guess I am. Nothing shocks me anymore. I hope we don't cause them much anguish, the gal I spoke to on the phone was named Amy. Nice lady, but I think she'd been through a lot. Her partner is Mabel, and according to Amy, Mabel will not be able to help us much. I'm not sure why, but I'm sure we'll find out."

The detective nodded as they pulled onto a driveway that was lit up all the way to the front door of a small cottage that appeared to have every light on inside. Stan wasn't sure if it was lit up for them or to keep away unwelcome guests.

Trees had been cut away from the cottage and the remnants of a small garden lie to the left of it, with a small greenhouse next to it. Even the greenhouse and garden had solar lights around them, and smaller ones that ran along a stone path to the front door of the house. It was daylight in this dark wooded lot. He couldn't explain why, but somehow that made him feel slightly better. The spirits weren't as noticeable in the light, although it didn't mean they weren't there.

He shook his head as a shiver ran down his body.

They parked the car and shut their doors as the door of the cottage opened and made the night even brighter if that was possible.

A small dark-complected lady with bouncy black curls beckoned them to join her inside.

A fire blazed away and brought warmth to the room. The walls were painted a bright green, with a flowered patterned couch that matched the wall colors and the yellow shades of the only two windows in the immediate space. There were a variety of children's books and artwork sitting upon a wall of shelves. Mabel Garner authored them. A thin woman with red hair sat on a red leather chair with bright pink slippers on her feet that were thrown over an ottoman. A grey blanket that matched one side of her head of hair was thrown over her. She stared straight ahead.

Amy reached out to take their coats and he noticed she had tattoos on her fingers, 'love, and soul.'

"Thank you," said the detective.

"Thanks for coming. I always hoped someone would listen to me about what happened, it's been years, but the memory is still fresh."

She spoke quietly, hung up their coats, and walked like a zombie just going through the motions.

"Amy let me introduce us first, so you know who we are before we start asking questions. I'm Stan. I spoke on the phone with you and I'm glad you're willing to talk with us. I hope it's not too painful for you." He pointed at the detective. "That's Stone, Detective Stone."

Stone nodded and shook her hand. "Interesting tattoos."

She didn't say anything about his comment. "That's Mabel." She pointed to the girl with red and grey hair in the chair. "She hasn't spoken since the incident with the bull, and those books you noticed were written and created by Mabel, all the artwork, as well. That's stopped since then, as you can see."

The detective's eyes lit up. "So, you saw the bull?"

An elderly woman entered the room bringing a tray of cups and raisin cake cut into small pieces. She sat them down on a glass table in front of the couch. Her clothes were simple sweater and jeans, and she had beautiful dark skin that glistened in the light.

Amy said, "That's my mother, Jackie."

Jackie smiled and said, "No need for introductions. I'm glad someone is finally taking care of this madness. My daughter and her partner had to move from that evil haunted house and got no compensation for it. They lost all their money." She pointed at Mabel. "Just look at her now, and no one to help them. It left her that way and I just wanted to scream. It was the first time my Amy found happiness. She had light, but not anymore. The house drained the light right out of her."

Amy said, "Mother, enough. I still have light. No need to go on about it to these men who are trying to help."

Her mother waved her hand at Amy, brushing her off. "You don't have light child. Anyway, would you like coffee or tea?"

"Coffee would be great," said Stone.

"Me too. Black for both of us," said Stan.

Jackie turned and smiled. "You men seem to understand black is the best." She left the room chuckling all the way out.

"Don't pay any attention to her. She likes to rile people up. My daddy was white, so clearly, she loves hers with a little cream." She winked.

Both men grinned.

Stan liked Amy.

Her mother returned with coffee and poured out a round for each of them.

"Nice bold coffee," Stan said.

Jackie nodded and said, "Yep, if you're going to drink coffee you need to taste it. None of that watered down sickly mud water."

She had a fire in her, and he knew Jackie would get along with Claire's nana.

The detective shoved a piece of cake in his mouth and washed it down with a swig of coffee. "Okay, Amy please tell me everything that happened, including what happened to Mabel."

"I'm not sure what happened to Mabel, and the doctors have no clue either, but it happened the day we moved into the cabin, and it wasn't a stroke either."

"Did she just quit talking? What happened prior to that?"

She stared into his eyes. "Stan, she'd gone out to get our luggage, and I was heating up our dinner, when I heard the door close as she entered the cabin. My back was to her, but she said my name with a quiver of fear in her voice that forced me to turn her way. The sound she made still hearts my heart. Her face had gone ashen in color, and she'd asked me if I heard the window break. I hadn't and told her so. She'd stared at the window with wide eyes, chewed her lip and backed away from it until she reached the hearth. I watched as she slid down to sit on it. You see there was stone built up to where you could easily sit in front of the fire opening."

"So, she heard a window break, but nothing was broken?'

"No, Detective, nothing was broken."

Stan asked, "Amy, if there was no broken glass where would she get that impression? And what made her come in the house scared?"

"I can't account for the broken glass sound. Mabel wasn't one to make up things or get spooked. However, when we got there, she thought she saw someone inside through the front door window. It bothered her enough to pick up a stick and check the house out before we could relax."

"Interesting. And did you leave the bull?" The detective went right to the bull.

"Of course, we left the bull. It wasn't mine, and honestly it gave me the creeps, and don't ask me why, but it did." Amy's curls bounced as she shook her head and repeated what she'd said to make sure they believed that the bull was to blame. "I don't know why, but it gave me the creeps The bull was cursed."

Stan said, "We do have an interest in the bull, Amy. You told me over the phone it was in the cabin. Where and when did you find it?"

"Well, it was after Mabel backed up and sat on the hearth. I sat down next to her, but had to pick up this shiny black bull that was next to her before I could sit. I held it in my hands for a moment and remarked that it was a strange thing left there. Mabel looked at it for a second, but seemed uninterested, so I placed it on the mantel, and that's where I left it. So, whoever purchased the house after us would have it, unless they tossed it or sold it. But I think it was a cursed object. I know I said that already, but it was. We barely got any money for the place; it wasn't enough to pay off our mortgage."

Detective Stone spoke up. "Sorry, that happened. Why would you think that the bull was cursed and not the house? Why didn't it effect you?"

"Some people aren't effected by the paranormal, I think. But, look at her, her hair is all grey on one side of her head and it happened that same night the instant she glanced at the bull. Cursed it was."

Both men looked at each other.

"Mabel wasn't able to tell you what scared her outside then?"

Mabel started quivering and tried to speak the moment the words left Stan's mouth.

Amy ran to her side.

"Eee." That's all Mabel said, but her eyes shifted to Amy.

Tears rolled down Amy's face. "It's okay Mabel. You can tell me." She took Mabel's hands in her own and gently rubbed them.

"Eeevil...orrrrrrrr."

Stan felt fear and his body shook, but he said the one word that terrified him to his core. "Orbs?"

Mabel screamed.

Amy threw her arms around her and hugged her tightly. "She hasn't said a word since that day."

After a few minutes, her scream turned to fast panting. She looked at him and gathered her thoughts to speak, although her words were broken. "Stan, I heard you. There is evil in that house, and victims. The orbs are afraid of the evil."

He and the detective jumped out of their chairs at the same time.

Amy was overjoyed with Mabel coming back to her and hollered for her mother to come and see. Jackie came into the room in time to see him grab Amy and pull her up to face him.

"Amy, the address what's the address of the house with the orbs." He felt faint his knees weakened, and his hands shook. She wasn't fast enough. He shook her. "Tell me the address," he screamed so loud Amy's mother pushed him away and caused Amy to fall onto Mabel.

Mabel said, "I remember it."

He held his phone up to her so she could see the address Claire had messaged him before they arrived, Mabel nodded.

"My God! We need our coats. Detective we need our coats."

Jackie was already throwing them at the two men. They both grabbed them and ran out the door. It was cold, they didn't care.

When Stan got outside, he whimpered like a dog that was scared and freezing. "Claire."

***

Claire's head made uncontrollable tiny movements left and right...left and right and tried to wrap her mind around the object she held in her hand.

She looked at Charlie. It wasn't Charlie. His nostrils flared, his mouth lifted to one side, and his eyes...fear thumped against her heart...they didn't belong to Charlie, there was no pupil-the white was a sickly green color, and they narrowed so much his brows came together in the middle of his forehead at the bridge of his nose. Her hands shook and her fingers tingled. The bull in her hands glowed a soft red. She didn't want to let it go and held on for dear life as she backed towards the closed door.

"Oh, Claire. I'm so glad you came for dinner. Please sit down." He took one step towards her.

She bolted for it and found herself on the porch with no coat as the cold breath of the night air bit into her exposed skin. She ran down the porch and followed the orbs into the woods, as they circled her their pain ripped through her body and burned her guts until she puked all over the frozen ground.

She heard the door of the cabin open and close.

"Silly girl. You can't hide from me. You'll be joining the orbs soon; you can help them inside their world."

She lifted her head and wiped the vomit from her mouth with the back of her sleeve. "Charlie, this isn't you. You're stronger than him. Beat him, Charlie. Fight back."

His laughter entered her ears, and it felt like trickles of blood ran from them.

The orbs weaved around the trees and were so fast that their shapes blurred into one mass of white. She didn't want to die here.

Charlie walked slowly down the steps and moved in her direction. He was going to kill her, that much she knew.

She had to stand her ground and waited until he was standing in front of her before she spoke. "Charlie, we're friends and this bull," she held it up into the air, and raised her voice, "is a killer, an evil entity, he is not you."

His eyes lifted and he shook his head, as if to clear his consciousness that was lost in a fog and bring it back to his control.

It bought her a moment to think. She saw the necklace around her neck glowing. It matched the intensity of the bull. Her fear had blinded her to the pain that her fingers felt as she held the demon. Until now when she realized the burnt flesh of her fingers stung with pain.

She couldn't think the orbs were screaming in her mind.

"Shut up. I can't think." Her voice released the entity to resume control over Charlie.

He made a lunge for her and took her down to the ground by her ankles. Her scream filled the woods, but only the orbs and trees would cry with her and hear her screams until she was dead.

"No," she said in a weak voice that was filled with sadness and despair. She thought of Stan, her mother, nana, and how sad it would be if her friend killed her in this horrible way, and with all her knowledge she might have to let go...of life.

He was laughing and slid up her body as he plastered it to the ground. She was on her stomach and couldn't stop him, and his weight was crushing her insides. The snow froze the delicate skin of her face, and a tree branch cut into her cheek.

She almost let herself drift off, until a nudge tickled her mind. She took her necklace and placed it against the bull that she still held in her hands...an explosion rang in her ears, red light filled the entire woods, as far as she could see. One by one the orbs grew and the electrical sparkles that belonged to their spirits shattered the sides of the orbs releasing them to find their way home.

She was dying, and Charlie grew heavier until his weight felt as though it doubled, she couldn't breathe. Her ears only heard the quietness of death, she threw up, and her body trembled violently ready to erupt, her head spun, and the beautiful darkness took her to Gabe. His hand reached out for hers, but she couldn't reach him...*Gabe.*

Chapter 21

Releasing the dead, and back from the dead

He and the detective saw the red light in the woods when they arrived and decided to follow what didn't belong. He saw her before the detective, his heart leaped from his chest, he was suffocating.

"No, no, no. Claire, Claire. Come back to me." His screams bounced off the trees.

Her body, and Charlie's glowed red. It took both him and the detective several minutes to pull Charlie from her limp body. Claire and Charlie were attached by some paranormal experiment that left them cocooned to each other. The red glow dissipated when they removed Charlie from her body. Stan turned her over. Her burnt and bloody fingers still held her necklace, like a lifeline to the living world. She wasn't breathing.

"She's not breathing, my God, she's not breathing." His voice a horrific whisper.

The detective pulled him away from her and started CPR.

He watched the detective like it was a movie, a viewer not a participant. He became detached and turned his attention on the electrical energy that swarmed the woods like thousands of fireflies.

It was eternity, he moved beside her and took her hand. "No...."

***

"Stan, you're screaming in your sleep again."

He opened his eyes and Stone stood over him. He quickly looked at the unconscious Claire lying like a corpse in the hospital bed. He still held her hand and hadn't released it in days, unless he had to for the nurses and doctors.

"Yeah, still the same nightmare. Have Nana and Hailey been in yet this morning?"

The detective handed him a coffee and an egg sandwich. "Thought you could use this, made the sandwich myself. No, they haven't been in yet. I think Hailey said around noon."

"Sure, I think that Nana is working some kind of magic, you know how she is. I still don't understand why she removed Claire's necklace; I thought it was supposed to protect her."

"Can't say, Stan, but there must be a reason. I'm almost ready to close the case files. Different men murdered all those women, but all relating to one man, at least that's what we believe, since the name of the bull was John. I did some research on him and it all fits. He had a rough life, and the police are still digging up bodies in the woods. They will match most of the bodies to our victims. At least, that's a form of closure. The land belonged to his family, and they already found the remains of a young girl missing during his lifetime. He left things on them, items, clothes, names, as a way of letting us know who he killed."

Stan said, "Killers usually have a place for those things, but seeing as it was really an entity that couldn't store things, it was best left with the victims, I guess." He took a deep breath. "Stone, I haven't thanked you for bringing her around and being there. The crazy thing is, I thought you were the killer. I'm sorry for that too. Claire never believed it though."

Detective Stone chuckled. "No worries, I do have a dark side, my friend."

Stone called him friend, yes, they were friends. They'd been through a lot. He still worried for Claire and wanted her to come out of the coma. He missed her smile and their bantering. He'd let her down.

"Great sandwich. I appreciate it." He finished it and drank some coffee. "How's Charlie? It's not his fault, you know."

"Yes, I know. I authored a report making them both victims of a serial killer that disappeared. Their cases may collect dust and remain on the cold case file list. Charlie is still in the psychiatric ward. His mind appears fried, for now, and they're not sure if he'll ever be normal. I know Claire won't want to hear that."

"She won't. We both liked Charlie a lot. I guess that's one reason he quit bringing women home, he might've sensed something was off. Really sad."

The detective pursed his lips and grunted. "Yes, it is. Well, I'm going out to the crime scene and help anyway I can. No sign of the bull. Not sure what happened to it. I guess we'll never understand the importance of the bull."

"I'm still confused where the bull went. Claire had it when we arrived, but in the commotion we forgot to pick it up. It still should've been there when we went back to look for it. Sure, Stone, I know you need to stay on the crime scene. Keep me informed. Let's have dinner tonight around 8pm and catch up."

The detective headed out the door. "Sure thing. But let's go across the street to the Padre Restaurant, I'm tired of hospital dinners. Your being here every second isn't going to bring her around any sooner."

That made Stan smile. "You're right. You've got a deal. But, you only had dinner here last night."

Stone said, "Yeah, but I was in the hospital a few days prior."

Stan nodded. He didn't want to be gone when she came around. He needed to see how her state of mind was. He closed his eyes and drifted back to sleep.

He awakened at the sound of Nana's voice.

"Good afternoon, sleepy head," said Hailey.

He jumped up and hugged her and then Nana.

"Good grief, don't I get one of those?"

His head jerked around to find Claire sitting up smiling.

"You bet you do." Tears flowed down his cheeks, and he almost tripped over a chair trying to get to her as quickly as he could without running. He held her, hugged her, and kissed her on the forehead and then the lips. He couldn't stop kissing her, he wanted to stay like this forever, break a record or two.

Nana said, "Enough of that lover boy."

They all smiled.

Claire said, "Nana told me the energy of the two powers colliding might've destroyed the bull and the spirit of John with it. That's why she removed my necklace. She had to take it and be sure he wasn't inside my charm. That wouldn't be good." She grabbed it as it dangled again from her neck. "That's one powerful weapon."

Stan nodded. "The detective will be interested to know that the bull was possessed by John's spirit, and possibly destroyed. I guess he already knew the spirit of John was in the bull but now it's confirmed by Nana. I suppose we'll never know how that happened."

Nana said, "Well, he probably used some ancient black magic to enter the bull before he burned to death. Claire don't ask about the books. I'm still working on them and I'm always getting interrupted."

"I wasn't going to ask Nana; you'll finish with them in time for me to heal. I must say, for now, I'm not interested in those ancient books. I need to recover." She faced him. "How's Charlie?" Claire's eyes were bloodshot and the concern in them drove into his soul.

"He's not well. They think his mind is gone and they're not sure if he'll come back anytime soon." His voice cracked.

Claire smiled and looked to Nana. "Well, we'll have to see about that, right Nana?"

"You bet. Like I said not enough time to work on those books of yours I took."

"Stan, we're going to lunch. Would you like to join us?" Hailey took his hand and smiled. "You need a break, now that Claire's awake."

He didn't want to leave her, ever. He mumbled. "I had a sandwich."

"Stan it's okay, go and enjoy lunch. They told me you slept here and didn't leave my side, and my friend, that's been days, so I think you might need a shower or two."

He looked at his wrinkled clothes and nodded in agreement.

He had to do it and blurted it out. "Claire, marry me." Just like that, he'd lost his mind. He looked into her eyes and thought he saw a light red glow, but before he could say anything that might cause them to have him committed, Nana grabbed his arm and the three of them headed out the door.

"Stan, are you mad? Get a hold of yourself. You need good sleep and food. See you later butterfly."

"Sure," said Claire.

***

She'd brushed off the question Stan asked her; besides, she wasn't sure he'd said it or that she'd heard him right. There was a larger concern. The room was quiet. She closed her eyes and opened them again, but nothing changed. Claire's world was painted red.

About the Author

Cheryle L. Linturn is an author/artist and graduate of Connecticut School of Broadcasting/Branch, Illinois. She's won various Editor's choice awards for her poetry, including publication in several anthologies. Her poetry has taken 1st place, 2nd place, and 3rd place in diverse types of competitions. Loving poetry has given her a unique perspective to authoring novels.

Being passionate with any form of writing, the author has written lyrics that have made it to publishers and won three ribbons for her songwriting skills. She's written screenplays, and children's books.

Her curiosity with things that go bump in the night led her to design and construct haunted houses for schools and several businesses. This interest in the dark and haunted things moved her towards writing a series about paranormal experiences she's had in her life.

Feeling things from an empathic point of view allows her to be open to supernatural experiences, leading to the fictitious series, Paranormal Soul.

Cheryle doesn't believe in writer's block. "There are too many variables that always surround us drawing out our creative side. A story created from a pencil, a cloud, a glass of water, a smell, a sound, can explode into a super nova across the universe of words. We can build a story from every tiny incident in our own lives."

The author has published one children's book, ghostwritten a fantasy trilogy, a sci-fi trilogy, and an adventure trilogy, and has written two of her own poetry books, and "Vanishing Blue," the first book in the Paranormal Soul series.

Cheryle is surrounded by nature in rural Indiana and will continue to check the woods for shadows and chilling encounters, while noticing smells that end up where they don't belong.

Other books by Cheryle L. Linturn

Vanishing Blue/ Paranormal Soul Series

Houdini's Adventures in France (children's book)

Winter's Chill (dark poetry book)

Whispers (light and dark poetry book)

Dracaena (fantasy book on Kindle Vella)

Books to release in 2025.

Purple Dreams Paranormal Soul Series book 3 (about otherworldly languages)

And We Had Tea (poetry book

Author notes:

If you have any paranormal experiences you would love to share in my novels please contact me, and your name will be referenced in my book.
Http://www.authorcllinturn.com/ or email:
cllinturn@authorcllinturn.com, or find me on Facebook, LinkedIn, or Instagram.

Notes:

On the next few pages, I would like to share with you some of the incidents in White Lies Beyond that were created based on experiences that I've had over the years of my life.

My hope is to tap into more experiences of the paranormal, but sometimes I feel I hold back, maybe, I am slightly fearful. But, I've accepted all of the supernatural events with curiosity and a desire to know more about them. As in the story, some will be left unanswered, because they have to be, I can't put an answer to some things that might be more complicated than what I'm capable of grasping, and I wouldn't want to do the occurrence an injustice.

You are welcome to go to my webpage www.https://authorcllinturn.com or on Facebook, or email me at cllinturn@authorcllinturn.com I would love to hear your stories, and with your approval use them in my series, giving your name as a credit, unless you wouldn't want it used.

Thank you for reading and I hope you enjoy the journey.

About the roses.

When my dad was ready to move on to his next adventure, he had an incredible view from his hospital bed, a view of intuition. One that belonged to a vase of roses that sat on a table across the room. It was a gift from a florist; one he'd used to buy a rose for the birthdays of each of the residents at the home he moved into after my mother passed.

The reason he did it was obvious if you knew my mother's name was Rosie, not to mention she loved roses and had vines filled with red ones that climbed up our house for years. He bought them to honor her memory.

Well, the last day my father and I were together in the hospital room I commented on the beautiful roses, and he shared the story. I offered to bring him a rose to smell, because they were amazing. He told me no, in a firm voice that if you knew him you'd back down and not question him. The stern response might've been from years in the service as a young man during WWII.

He said just remember the story, Cheryle. He wanted me to understand why he bought the roses. I thought it was nice the florist gave him such beautiful ones in appreciation of his purchase over the years..

After my dad passed we were driving back home on a cold and rainy day on a four-lane highway with forests to one side and highway on the other going the opposite direction, in other words a lot of road and woods.

There was no traffic, and the windows were rolled up because of the rain and cold. We were alone. That is until the smell of roses filled the car. I asked my husband if he smelled something. But he was already sniffing the air and said, "It smells like roses, like we just walked into a florist."

A feeling of warmth flooded over me, and I said, "Hi dad."

It lasted for at least 8 minutes or more, and nothing around us, absolutely no other vehicle. Dad had mentioned to me to remember the roses and now I knew why. It was his gift to me and a message to let me know he was okay.

I called it intuition earlier, but was it? Maybe he knew he was going to give me that gift and wanted me to understand that it was him reaching out to me beyond our mortal existence to say goodbye. I think he emphasized the roses in the hospital room so when the gift arrived I'd know it came from him.

After that I knew we could shop in this world for gifts we wanted to send over from the other dimension to reach those we loved when we passed over. How cool..

Now, I ask for particular gifts from passing loved ones, and yes they've arrived, sometimes years later, but they arrived, nevertheless. So, I ask you to be aware, listen to the life your loved ones live, and understand their connection to you, and what is important to them, so you'll know when the gift arrives and what it is you're looking for.

Cheryle C Linturn

About dogs in trees,

Children, oh, yes they see things we no longer see, or things we no longer acknowledge the existence of, and that's this incident.

As small as it seemed at the time, I never forgot my grandson telling me there were dog faces in the trees in the backyard of my daughter's Arizona home.

He was adamant about it, and of course, I couldn't see it, I was talking to him on the phone in Illinois.

But his sincerity was, yes, believable.

It wasn't my first rodeo with children hearing, seeing, and feeling things most of us would dismiss as a vivid imagination. I wrote that thought into White Lies Beyond as well, because it's fact.

I don't know what he saw, but he was old enough to know what a dog was, so.... I went with it.

As a child and now an adult that hears, sees, and feels things others may not understand helps me understand the importance of being believed. Honestly, I don't need to be believed, but it sure is more exciting telling the story with a fellow believer.

I took the dogs to a whole other level, a demon influence. The names in this story were changed from possible 'doggy in tree' to 'hell hounds in tree' to protect all innocent pups out there who might be peeking through trees at their loved ones. Just saying.

Cheryle C Linturn

About the fish in the pond,

This might blow your mind, but this paranormal event did happen.

We had a pond in our backyard that was teeming with fish. There were Koi, goldfish (a giant one named Tonka), and blue gill.

In the beginning I named them all, and we could see them glide through the water. The pond was only about 30' in diameter. We had a small waterfall, built out of rock formations that also enclosed the outside perimeter of the pond.

I loved watching them, and quit naming them after we noticed schools of fish swimming together. It was incredible. The pond had a liner and when they had babies they would stir up the dirt on the bottom as they circled the babies to protect them from the other fish.

One of the blue gill I called Mango used to jump out of the water to grab a piece of food out of my hand as I held it over the surface.

Then one day, I went out to have a chat, and there was nothing. Nothing, no energy, no color, that's right...no fish.

My husband and I stood there staring in silence. I said, "I don't feel their energy." I can do that. It felt final, dead.

My husband put on his wading boots and got in, as I watched and waited. He thought maybe some were under the rocks, but it felt empty of life. He agitated the water using a net and feeling under the rocks hoping to cause them to show their magnificent colors. Nothing.

For two days we kept looking, confused about what happened to them. There were no dead bodies along the rocky edge.

I just kept thinking there's no life out there.

On the third day, there they were. All of them swimming around like nothing happened. We had a fenced yard, and a quiet neighborhood, and both of us knew no one could collect all of those fish in one go and return them three days later. It was madness.

I left that incident as unexplainable in my book, as a cold-case file, if you will, because it was then and still is unsolved.

Cheryle C Linturn

www.ingramcontent.com/pod-product-compliance
Lightning Source LLC
Chambersburg PA
CBHW072105170626
46813CB00004B/1460